# LAPVONA

ALSO BY OTTESSA MOSHFEGH

*Death in Her Hands*
*My Year of Rest and Relaxation*
*Homesick for Another World*
*Eileen*
*McGlue*

# LAPVONA

## OTTESSA MOSHFEGH

PENGUIN PRESS

NEW YORK

2022

*

PENGUIN PRESS

An imprint of Penguin Random House LLC
penguinrandomhouse.com

Library of Congress Cataloging-in-Publication Data

Names: Moshfegh, Ottessa, author.
Title: Lapvona / Ottessa Moshfegh.
Description: New York : Penguin Press, 2022.
Identifiers: LCCN 2021061028 (print) | LCCN 2021061029 (ebook) |
ISBN 9780593300268 (hardcover) | ISBN 9780593300275 (ebook)
Subjects: LCGFT: Novels.
Classification: LCC PS3613.O77936 L37 2022 (print) |
LCC PS3613.O77936 (ebook) |
DDC 813/.6—dc23/eng/20211217
LC record available at https://lccn.loc.gov/2021061028
LC ebook record available at https://lccn.loc.gov/2021061029

ISBN 9780593492956 (international edition)

Printed in the United States of America
1st Printing

Designed by Amanda Dewey

*FOR*
WALTER

*I feel stupid when I pray.*

—"Anyone," Demi Lovato

# LAPVONA

# SPRING

The bandits came again on Easter. This time they slaugh-tered two men, three women, and two small children. Some smelting tools were stolen from the blacksmith, but no gold or silver, as there was none. One of the bandits was injured by an ax wielded by the slain children's mother—she smashed his left foot. Then he was restrained by neighbors and dragged to the village square, where he was beaten and put in the pillory. Villagers pelted him with mud and animal excrement until nightfall. Grigor, the dead children's grandfather, was too bereft to sleep, so he got up in the night, went to the square, cut off the bandit's ear with a garden knife, and flung it in a lemon tree laden with blossoms. 'For the birds to eat!' he yelled at the bleed-ing man and sobbed as he slunk away. Nobody could say what specific acts of horror this one pilloried bandit had committed. The rest of the bandits got away and took with them six geese, four goats, six wheels of cheese, and a cask of honey, in addition to the iron tools.

No lambs were stolen, as the lamb herder, Jude, lived in a pasture several miles from the center of the village, and he had his lambs penned and sleeping soundly that night as usual. The pasture was at the foot of a hill, on top of which sat the large stone manor where Villiam, Lapvona's lord and governor, resided. His guards were in position to defend him should any menacing individual ever climb the hill. Between the echoing screams from the village, Jude thought he could hear the gut strings of the guards' bows tighten from where he lay awake by the fire that night. It was not by chance that Jude and his son, Marek, lived in the pasture below the manor. Villiam and Jude shared a blood relation, their great-grandfather. Jude thought of Villiam as his cousin, though the two men had never met.

On Monday, Marek, age thirteen, walked to the village to assist the men in digging a trench to bury the dead. He wanted to be helpful, but cowered when the bodies were laid out on the thick grass of the cemetery and the men took up their shovels. The heads of the dead were covered only in thin cloths. Marek imagined that their faces were still alive. He could see their eyelashes grazing the fabric as a soft wind blew. He saw the outlines of their lips and thought they were moving, speaking to him, warning him to get away. The children's bodies looked like wooden dolls, stiff and adorable. Marek crossed himself and retreated back to the road. The men of the village dug the trench easily without him anyway. Nobody cared that Marek had come and gone. He was like a stray dog that wandered in and out of the village from time to time, and everyone knew he was a bastard.

Marek was a small boy and had grown crookedly, his spine twisted in the middle so that the right side of his rib cage protruded from his torso, which caused his arm to find its only comfort resting, half bent, across his belly. His left arm hung loose from its socket. His legs were bowed. His head was also misshapen, although he hid his skull under a tattered knit hat and bright red hair that had never once been brushed or cut. His father—whose long, uncut hair was brown—admonished vanity as a cardinal sin. There were no mirrors in their humble home in the pasture, not that they had any earnings to afford one. Jude was the oldest bachelor in Lapvona. Other men took their young cousins as their wives if they needed one—women often died in childbirth—or traded a few sheep or pigs to a village in the north for a tall girl to marry.

Jude could never bear to see his reflection, not even in the clear, icy stream that ran through the valley or in the lake where he went to bathe a few times a year. He also believed that Marek ought not see himself. He was glad to have a son and not a daughter, whose lack of beauty would be much more injurious. Marek was ugly. And fragile. Not at all like Jude, whose bones and muscles were like polished bluffs beaten by an ocean, soft and luminous despite his skin being grimy and often covered in lamb shit. Jude never let on that Marek's face had an unseemly disproportion; the boy's forehead was high and veiny, his nose bulbous and skewed, his cheeks flat and pale, his lips thin, his chin a stub giving way to a neck that was wrinkled and soft, like a drape of skin over his throat, which was flabby at the apple. 'Beauty is the Devil's shade,' Jude said.

On his way home from the cemetery, Marek passed the pillory where the wounded bandit moaned and cried in a language nobody knew. Marek stopped to say a prayer for the bandit's soul. 'God, forgive him,' he said aloud, but the bandit kept crying. Marek got closer. Nobody was around. Perhaps the stench of excrement had cleared people away in the warm sun of spring. Or perhaps they were all busy watching over the burial of the dead. Marek looked into the bandit's eyes. They were green, like his own. But they were cruel eyes, Marek thought. If he got closer, he thought, he might see the Devil in them. Upon his approach, the bandit cried out again, as if Marek of all people could save him. Even if the boy were strong enough to lift the stocks and help the bandit run away into the woods, he wouldn't. God was watching.

'God forgive you,' Marek said to the bandit.

He got closer still, then deigned to lay a hand on the bandit's arm. Marek could see that his foot was broken, limp, a bone sticking out through the flesh, the skin wrinkled and yellow. His breathing was quick and raspy. Flies swarmed, unbothered by the bandit's repeated cries of jibberish. Marek closed his eyes and prayed until the bandit stopped wailing. He opened them in time for the bandit to spit in his face. He knew not to flinch, as that would show disgust, and God would judge him. Instead, he bent down and kissed the bandit's head, then licked his lips to taste the salt of the man's sweat and the rancid oils caked into his reddish hair. The bandit winced and stuck out his tongue. Marek curtsied and turned and walked away, feeling that the bandit's cries now were not in anguish or petulance, but in rapture of salvation, even if they sounded exactly the same.

Marek left the square and walked calmly now, a feeling of goodness tingling in his left arm, which he took to mean that he had earned a bit of grace while the rest of the village had reviled the bandit and suffered now in darkness, laying down the dead, who were, unlike the rest of them, at peace.

Outside the village, Marek passed a few of Villiam's guards patrolling the road. He smiled and waved to them. They paid no mind to the boy. The guards were all descended from northerners, so they were tall and strong. Northerners were known to be single-minded and cold. They were physically superior to native Lapvonians, and if they had any interest, they could have sacked the village themselves and stomped into Villiam's manor and killed him with a swift elbow to the heart. But they'd been sufficiently tamed and trained after generations of indenture, and now they did the bidding of Villiam as though he owned them.

He did own them, in fact, and all the servants at his manor, and the entire village and the woods and the farmsteads spread throughout the fiefdom. Villiam owned Jude's pasture and the small cottage he shared with Marek. The pasture was bounded by woods, which were Villiam's also.

As Marek now turned into these woods on his way home, he decided he wouldn't tell his father that he had kissed the bandit. Jude didn't understand forgiveness. He was incapable of forgiveness because he was so addled by his own grief and grudges. This bad blood was what kept Jude's heart pumping. The first grief had been for the deaths of his parents when he was a teenager— they drowned in the lake during a storm. They'd been fishing for krap and their little raft had broken in the wind. So rare was a wind so strong that it seemed to Jude that the tragedy had been aimed at him specifically, an evil air cast up from hell to take from him the only family he knew and loved. The second grief was the loss of Agata, his lady, Marek's mother. She had died in childbirth, Jude liked to recount, bled to death on the floor by the fire. You could still see the stain of her blood thirteen years later. 'There, the red still shows,' Jude said, and pointed to the spot by the hearth where the dirt seemed worn down harder than the rest. Marek could never see the blood. 'You're blind to color, just like your mother,' Jude said. 'That's why.'

'But I see my hair is red,' Marek protested.

A punch in the jaw left Marek's tongue flayed by his own teeth. Blood spilt from his mouth on the very spot on the hearth where his mother had supposedly died. Jude pointed again.

'You see it now? Where she left me to raise a child alone?'

Not that Marek got much raising. Jude never held him or rocked him. Immediately following his lady's departure, he'd handed the boy over to the care of Ina during the day while he tended to his lambs. Ina was the wet nurse then, and something of a legend in the village, a woman without a man or child of her own, whose breasts had fed half the population. Some called her a witch because she was blind and yet she was industrious. And she had an intuition about medicines. She traded mushrooms and nettles for eggs and bread, and some people said the mushrooms gave them visions of hell and others said they gave them visions of heaven, but they always cured their malaise—nobody could doubt her knowledge of medicinal plants. They distrusted Ina because of her wisdom, while they still made use of it. She lived down the valley in a dark patch of woods south of Jude's pasture.

Ina was older than anyone could say, and by now her milk had dried up. Marek loved Ina. At thirteen, he still visited her once a week. She was the only person to caress him and give him a kind word now and then. He brought her flowers from the pasture and lamb's milk and chestnuts when they were in season, bread and cheese when there was some extra.

'Did you dig?' Jude asked when Marek got home. He dunked a cup into their keg of water and handed it to the boy.

'They didn't need me,' Marek answered. 'And I was afraid of the dead. I was afraid they were still alive.'

'Those were good people who got killed,' Jude said. 'Only the evil ones get trapped in their dead bodies. That's their eternal penance; the ones who go to hell rot. The ones who go to heaven disappear. Not a trace of flesh is left. Be good and you'll leave nothing behind. Be bad and you'll live forever in your rotting body in the ground.'

'Why were the good dead people still flesh then? Why hadn't they gone to heaven yet?'

'They've got to go into the ground first. Bury them and they disappear.'

'How do you know?' Marek asked.

'I'm your father,' Jude said. 'I know everything.'

They boiled lamb's milk and covered the pot with a cloth to keep the flies away while it cooled. Marek picked the bugs off some potatoes and plunged them and a few whole apples in the fire. They were old apples from the fall harvest. Jude had eaten only lamb's milk, bread, apples and potatoes, and wild grasses his entire life. Like the rest of Lapvona, he didn't eat meat. Nor did he drink mead, only milk and water. Marek ate what Jude ate, always saving a few bites for God: he knew that sacrifice was the best way to please Him.

'Does your head hurt?' Marek asked his father. Jude was rubbing his temples with his knuckles. He often had headaches. His gums often bled.

'Be quiet,' said Jude. 'A storm is coming, that's all.'

'Will it rain tonight?'

'It will rain on Wednesday. Just in time for the hanging.'

It did rain on Wednesday. As father and son walked to the village square, warm spring rain shook the lemon blossoms and haunted the air under Jude's hood with a smell that brought his brighter childhood memories to mind, which he felt shame for remembering on such a day. Jude had not yet set eyes on the bandit.

'Did bandits really kill my grandparents?' Marek asked.

'My parents drowned. You know that.'

'My mother's parents—did the bandits kill them, really?'

'I've told you a hundred times,' Jude said. He told Marek that his mother had been a victim of an attack on her native village when she was twelve, a year younger than Marek was now. 'First they slashed your grandfather's throat, and then they raped your grandmother. Then they slashed her throat, too. They tied your uncles up with rope and threw them in a well to drown. They were just little boys.'

'What did they do to my mother?'

'They cut out her tongue so she couldn't talk, but she ran away,' Jude told him. 'She was lucky to escape. I found her in the woods, nearly dead. Poor Agata. Why do you like this story so much?'

'Because I love my mother.'

'She was a strong girl, but she carried death with her. Death is like that. Like a beggar that follows you down the road. And kills you.'

'Was my mother very beautiful?'

'What a stupid question,' Jude said. Of course, he had invented the girl's name and history. With no tongue, she couldn't possibly have communicated any of this to Jude—she could barely even understand the language of Lapvona when she first arrived. But Jude thought the story made him sound like a hero. 'She was the only one left alive. Imagine the guilt that comes with that charge. Who cares about beauty?'

'I'll feel guilty when you die,' Marek told Jude.

'Good boy,' Jude said.

The crowd had collected in the square, and as Jude and Marek arrived the bandit was being removed from the pillory. They joined a huddle of villagers and watched as Villiam's guards tied the bandit's hands behind his back and dragged him, his legs bouncing, along the cobblestones. They hefted him up the steps and onto the small platform of the gallows. The villagers spoke quietly amongst themselves, a few women sniffling, a few men shuffling violently, thirsty for blood. Grigor, the old man, stood stoically in front of the gallows and prayed that the souls of his two dead grandchildren find peace. The families of the other slain villagers shouted curses at the bandit. Their anger was righteous. Father Barnabas, their priest, had told them so. 'Chastise an evil-doer and God will know you're good.' Marek covered his ears. He didn't like to hear foul language. He was delicate in this way. Even Jude's rough words hurt him in the heart: 'Damn him,' Jude said.

The noose dangled in the warm wind, and Villiam's guards grabbed it and looped it around the bandit's neck. They brought a stool for the man to stand on, but he couldn't stand. He was too broken. His head was left uncovered, as was custom for murderers. Men who were hanged for lesser crimes—lone marauders who raped or thieved—got sacks over their heads. Marek looked at the bandit. The blood from his severed ear had painted his face such that only small bits of glinting white from his eyeballs showed as he lifted his gaze out toward the crowd, unashamed. After a few pathetic slips, Villiam's guards finally lifted him onto the stool and held his legs. The bandit didn't struggle or curse. He said only, 'God forgive you,' the same words Marek had said to him a few days earlier. And then the guards pulled the stool away and he was swinging. He swung and swayed and his legs seemed to buck and pull. His body tensed and held itself, his legs stiff and straight. And then he stilled.

'Is he dead yet?' Marek asked.

'My God, are you blind?' Jude looked at Marek and saw that the boy had covered his eyes with his hat. Jude pulled it off his face. 'Have a look.'

Marek opened his eyes just in time to see one of Villiam's men gutting the bandit with a sword, the bowels spilling out and smacking on the gallows floor. The sound echoed over the hush of the crowd. Marek turned and hid his face in the sleeve of his father's wool sweater, which was full of dried grasses and briars and smelled of the lambs. He gagged and bent and spat at the ground. Something was wrong with his stomach. Jude took him by the arm and led him away from the crowd.

'What's wrong with you?'

'I don't know.'

'Do you feel sorry for the bandit?'

'Yes.'

'Why would you?'

'Maybe he was somebody's father.'

'You think he wouldn't kill his own kin?'

'I don't know.'

'Those bandits don't care for kin. They're the Devil's children. Forget him. He'll rot now. He'll feed the worms. Shall we pick some flowers on the way home?'

'Yes.'

The flowers were still shy and wistful, their buds just breaking into bloom as it was early spring yet. There were bloodred poppies growing alongside the road, and Jude picked some as Villiam's guards passed, marching in tandem toward the village. Jude pretended they didn't exist. He didn't like northerners. He thought they carried an element of evil. Their light hair never seemed dirty, and their skin never showed any signs of wear. He didn't trust men so clean. They only understood the surfaces of things, which was why they appeared so perfect. They took

Jude's depth and pain as weakness, he thought. They didn't respect his thoughtfulness. They saw him and his son as farm animals, no better than the lambs they raised. And they seemed
not to care about the villagers' safety. Not once during an attack
by bandits had the guards defended the village. They retreated
up the mountain to the manor and took aim. That was all. They
were cowards, Jude thought. What he didn't know, of course,
was that the bandits worked for Villiam. He paid them to ran-
sack the village any time there was a rumor of dissent among the
farmers. Father Barnabas conveyed such rumors to the lord.
That was his primary function as the village priest: to listen to
the confessions of the people down below and report any sagging
dispositions or laziness to the man above. Terror and grief were
good for morale, Villiam believed.

To get to Agata's grave, Jude and Marek passed into the
woods. There were horse chestnuts on the ground. Swine were
let to pannage there, and as Marek and Jude walked along they
could hear some snorts and squeals. Past those woods was an
orchard of apple trees, too old to bear fruit. The silver bark was
thick as armor and laced high with the scars from years and
years of villagers etching their names with Xs. Past the orchard,
the grass was thin, the dirt pale and rocky, but as it had just
rained, the ground gave in a pleasant way under Jude's bare feet
and Marek's thin-soled shoes. Marek picked a handful of cham-
omile and cornflowers growing near a trail of runoff, then followed an ostrich fern off the path toward a patch of iris. He
picked an iris in bloom and some young sprigs of freesia. Then

they turned toward a grove of black poplars, where, under the largest tree, was Agata's grave.

Marek was solemn as they walked, his stomach churning and his mind still darkened by the scene in the village square. Of course he had seen bandits hanged and disemboweled before, but there was something special about this man. He hadn't looked scared as Villiam's men dragged him to the gallows. Maybe he knew where he was going. Like Jesus on the Cross.

'That bandit,' Marek said. 'Do you think he had a mother?'

'Everybody's got a mother,' Jude replied.

'Is that bandit's mother sorry he's dead?'

'They aren't like us. They have no hearts.'

'Do you think he had a son of his own?'

'A bastard, surely, if he did. Who cares?'

'Did my mother love me?'

'She died for you,' Jude said. 'That should be enough.'

'Will I see her in heaven?'

'Of course you will. As long as you get there.'

'What about you?'

'Don't worry about me, Marek,' Jude said.

But Marek did worry that his father wouldn't get into heaven. The man had an unkind hand. And when he prayed, Marek had the sense that there was anger steaming off his father's shoulders, the cruelty inside him escaping like a vapor. Not that the man was impious. But Jude's piety was a kind of violent urge and not the love and peace it ought to be, Marek thought. Jude whipped himself every Friday and had taught Marek to do the same. But Marek thought Jude whipped himself a bit too passionately. He'd get sweaty, grunting, moving the whip across one shoulder, then the other, wincing and breathing so hard that spit drooled from his mouth, and then he sucked it in and spat it out violently, as though it pleased him, as though the pain felt good. This frightened Marek because he, too, enjoyed the pain, and he was ashamed of that. Since he was little, a scraped knee or a whipped back, anything to make his body hurt, felt like the hand of God upon him. He knew that wasn't right. So he kept it private, which made his father's shameless display of pain and pleasure seem all the more perverse. All Marek really wanted at this age was to go to heaven, where God and his mother would love him.

'But what if something goes wrong?' he asked Jude. 'What if you don't make it to heaven?"

'If God wills it, I will.'

Agata's grave was marked with a plain, rounded rock from the stream. Jude had hammered a violent chip into the rock as though he really was broken by the girl's death. Jude was illiterate, like everyone else in Lapvona, but he said that the chip in the rock had a meaningful shape.

It was Marek's custom to lie down on his mother's grave, placing his body crosswise as though he were a babe in her dead arms through the dirt. He had always felt that the ground below him was charged with a sense of belonging. He would lie there and gaze up at the swaying branches of the poplar tree and listen for a birdsong. A bee-eater or an oriole might tweet a few happy notes. Marek would take this as his mother singing down to him from heaven. Now, standing by the grave, he heard a magpie song. It was angry and harsh, raspy chatter like an old lady scolding him from her window.

'Why don't you lie down today?' Jude asked, placing the flowers by the chipped stone.

'Not today. The birds are singing too sad a song.'

Jude didn't believe in birdsong. He didn't trust birds. They weren't of the land, and he was a man of the land. He loved his lambs because they were like him. They were drawn to the comfort of the pasture, following the edge of the sundrawn shadows to stay cool and warm according to the breeze. Jude was like that. He was a slave to the day as it rose and fell, and he felt this was his righteous duty—lamb herding was his God-given occupation. He ignored the church bells. He didn't need to track his time. Nature did it for him. He was born in that pasture and felt he would die in it, too. Why had he not buried Agata in the pasture? Marek had asked a few times. Jude would never entertain such a question.

'Let's go then,' Jude said, already turning back toward the woods.

The path they'd worn from Agata's grave through the woods to the pasture was narrow because Jude and Marek never walked side by side. Jude always walked in front. Marek knew his father's body from behind as well as he knew his hands or his face. Jude's feet landed straight on the ground. Marek's step was outward turning, like a duck's, and if he didn't concentrate, the line he'd walk would veer to the right, such was the turning of his body against nature. Jude's ankles were fine, the joint bolted and smooth, and the thin of his leg below the calf as narrow as a wrist. Marek's ankles were swollen and freckled, often scraped by briars and bleeding and itchy. His skin was thin and delicate. Ina rubbed salve on his feet from time to time to keep the skin from peeling or rotting and falling off, she said. 'You're like a snake,' she told him. Jude's calves were round and taut and tan, and the backs of his knees had lines from the tendons as fine as gut strings. His pants covered the rest of his legs, and were patched at the seat and between the thighs. His buttocks were high and strong. Marek knew his father's body was beautiful. But he didn't revere it. He simply respected Jude's physique as a part of nature, the way he found a vulture beautiful, or a cow. He knew that he didn't resemble his father. You couldn't compare a plover to a chicken. They were different kinds of animals. No one who saw the two together would ever guess they were of blood relation.

Jude's hips were narrow, his back was long, his shoulders strong and hunched despite their broadness, penitent. He walked with his head bowed. He took this posture having spent so many years looking down at his lambs. Sometimes Marek regarded him with admiration, a man of the harsh world who had given him a roof over his head, had mannered him in his ways, father to son. And other times Marek regarded him as a man living in the shadow of sin. He pretended to sleep while Jude molested himself every new moon under the sour woolen blanket by the fire in winter, or under the open window in spring. Summers and warm autumn nights they slept in the pasture under the stars with the lambs to make sure the wolves would stay away, Jude said. But Marek knew it was because Jude liked to feel the warm air on his skin as he slept, as though God were touching him in the breeze. Each night that Jude molested himself, he produced a baritone groan of such horror, such pain, only the Devil could be behind it, Marek thought. After the groan, Jude's body stiffened, then rocked, and it seemed to Marek that he was undergoing a spiritual ablution, as though to eject some evil from his body. Marek never let on that he knew this about his father, but he did know it. And it was yet another impediment, he believed, to the man's passage to heaven.

The sky seemed to darken now as they entered the woods. The air was chilled between the trees, no warm wind blew, but the ripeness of the earth smelled sweet and musty still. Jude preferred spring to winter. He loved the color and romance of spring. He loved the sun. Sitting and watching his lambs in an afternoon, not a shadow in sight, Jude could feel God's lips on his cheek every time he turned to face the light. That was God for him—the kiss of sun. God's hand on his bare skin was the one certainty that rose up through the abstractness of truth and thought, everything, and gave Jude a sense of belonging on Earth. He loved the grass between his toes and the soft touch of a lamb against his leg as it passed. He loved the young eyes of his babes smiling at him, their first spring, such wonder and light. He loved the ply of their joints as they moved and sniffed and chewed the sweet grass, the perk of their ears at the first songs of the titmice and chickadees on their way north. Jude's flock were polled and pure white. They were the gentlest lambs, and they stayed babes for a season longer than sheep of other origins. Even their milk teeth were rounder and flatter than others. But they were hair sheep. Not fur. They were only good for meat. So of his lambs each year, Jude kept only a few for breeding and the rest were sold for slaughter. This was the sacrifice he made, as his father had done, and his father before him. After the sale of his flock each spring, Jude tried and failed to hold his tears until he was safe and alone in his pasture with the remaining lambs—most of them would go to market next year, of course.

The lambs kept for husbandry were in mourning, too. Jude couldn't look them in the eyes. He felt guilty for having sent their brothers and sisters to be murdered. Instead of begging them for forgiveness, he treated the remaining creatures cruelly, pretending to forget them when they came in from pasture, then yelling for them to hurry up, as though they were unwanted, left over from a time he wanted to forget. But he depended on those young sheep to keep the flock of new babes on the home range. He didn't have fences out there in the pasture. He had no dog, either. He understood the rhythms of grazing and thirst, and how the lambs preferred to sleep in the shade of the cottage during the day, but under the open sky at night. The babes Jude had now were only six weeks old. He'd watched the ewes' bellies grow since the fall. As the field went dormant in winter, he had fed them hay by hand, almost apologetically. 'I'm sorry this isn't fresh grass and forbs.' He helped to birth the babes in the lean-to, forbidding Marek to speak. 'They don't like the sound of your voice,' he said, and it was true. The ewes would bleat and snort and grunt if Marek came around. Jude understood that the sheep knew that Marek was a baby in his own way, that he would steal their milk for himself if he could, that he would suck the motherhood from them because he was so starving for it. 'Stay away,' they told him. 'Baaaa.'

Marek did nurse the ewes when Jude wasn't looking. He pushed the babes away and put his mouth to the sheep's teat and sucked until he felt sick. He felt this was his right as a child of God. He was a lamb himself. Not that his meekness stemmed from weakness. Rather, he was a bridled boy, gentled to be a servant to God. And as God's meek servant, this sheep's milk was his inheritance. Anything could be cajoled into sense if he thought enough about it. As father and son now walked through the woods toward the pasture, Jude was troubled by the number of shoeprints he saw dotting the path. He hoped they were not the tax collector's. He had paid all he could that spring already. Any more and he and his boy would starve.

Contrary to his father, Marek preferred winter to spring. He enjoyed the cold. He understood that God's love burned through the fire in the hearth. He liked the large kindness of that, and so he loved the smell of smoke. He liked the wet of mucus on his lip, how it would crust and pull at his skin and sting when he widened his mouth into a smile. He liked the snow on the boughs and the look of clouds, like a curtain that could be peeled back. A clear blue sky was hard to take. Marek saw it as emptiness, a place with no heaven in it. He preferred the clouds because he could imagine paradise behind them. He could stare up and focus his eyes on shapes in the clouds, wonder if that was God's face or God's hand making an impression, or if God was spying down at him through the gauzy mist. Maybe, maybe. The heavy cloak he wore in winter weighted him with comfort. If Jude loved the stinging whip, Marek loved the cold for its cruelty. He would suffer, endure it, and thereby increase his score of good deeds and humility. Without that cruel wind, there was no need for protection to be met with a fire in the hearth, there was no prayer to be answered. The oil lamp burned with precision. Its flame was female, thoughtful, like a spirit exacting its will against time. The fire in the hearth was masculine, powerful, instinctual, tireless. Marek never shivered from cold. He felt more at ease in the cold, in fact, as though his eyes could see more sharply, he could hear more clearly, everything pure and clean in the snow and crystal air.

Jude thought the spiky shadows of the trees on the snow were menacing, that the cold welcomed evil, a ghost released in every exhalation. Because things died in winter. There were no flowers, no fruit. There were no leaves on the trees. In summer, Jude was more relaxed. He went bare-chested through the field, his skin got brown and hard, his hair got light. In winter, he was stiff in his coat over layers of wool, never changed his long underwear, afraid to be naked against the chill. Marek had been born in February. Of course, he and his father never marked the occasion as the day of his birth, but the day of Agata's death. Her absence hung over both of them like a hovering bird. Marek felt the bird wasn't close enough, that it was just out of reach, that if it descended a bit farther he could grab hold of its foot and it would take him away, fly him to some better place. And Jude felt the bird was too close. If he looked up at it, it would scratch his eyes out. The difference was that Jude had known Agata. And he knew the truth about her absence. All Marek knew was that she had given her life for his own, like any good mother would do.

Back at home now, Jude fed the lambs and sent Marek to the stream to fetch fresh water. This was Marek's favorite chore because his slanted shoulders made it hard to keep the yoke steady. He enjoyed the work of resistance against his deformity. He had to torque his torso to balance each side or else the buckets would slosh and spill. He was well practiced at this game as he fetched water several times a day. A good deed, he thought it, adding to his soul's score. But this day, as he was practicing his balancing act on his way to the water, he tripped over an exposed tree root and fell, and one of the buckets hit and split. Never mind that his chin was bludgeoned and his front teeth had cut into his lip. He wiped the blood on his sleeve and looked at it. Was it not the same color as the bandit's blood? 'Father, help!' Marek cried out dramatically, hoping his pathetic voice would carry across the pasture. But secretly, Marek was a little pleased that he was bleeding and that surely the broken bucket would be reason enough for Jude to give him a sound beating when he got home. Pain was good, Marek felt. It brought him closer to his father's love and pity. He fingered his chin and his busted lip, then found a rock with a sharp edge and sawed a bit at his cheeks to make them raw and bloody, as though he'd fallen much harder than he had. He jabbed at his forehead with the sharp point, mussed his hair and hat, then continued on his way to the brook. It would be much harder to balance the yoke with only one bucket full. Good, Marek thought. I deserve this hardship. He lived for hardship. It gave him cause to prove himself superior to his mortal suffering.

Jude always had hard feelings after visiting Agata's grave. By now, the lie he had told Marek—that Agata was dead and buried under the poplar tree—had come to feel somewhat true. Agata was as good as dead, and there had been so many tears shed, so many flowers laid on that spot under the boughs. His descriptions of Agata's screams and the smell of her blood as it seeped from her womb across the hearth had the integrity of real experience. He never felt guilty for the lie that followed. He was too proud to confess the truth of Agata's disappearance. But she was out there, he guessed, somewhere. She hadn't died in his arms like he'd said so many times. She was just gone, invisible. For years, Jude had expected her to return, her breasts dripping with milk, desperate and sorry and weeping at her stupidity for fleeing in the middle of the night like that, taking only her coat and Jude's leather gloves because it was winter, he guessed, and her hands were always cold. Jude had been up holding Marek in his arms, the strange and tiny creature—not quite human, he looked—with bulbous eyes that wouldn't open, a shallow breath that had Jude panicked at every silence. 'The babe is going to die,' Jude said, and he loved babes. He was distraught. This is what must have moved Agata to leave, Jude believed. She couldn't stay to watch the baby die. She was only a child herself. And Jude had loved her like a savage, like an animal, promised her the moon and stars and all of God's protection as long as she stayed in his sights. 'Be my wife,' he'd begged so many times. 'The baby is going to die.' Stupid, stupid words. He scared her away. She lay shaking and bleeding on the floor. Jude threw her coat at her. 'Quit your shivering,' he'd said. If the baby had indeed died, there may have been some rationale behind his stupidity. He must have turned inward for a moment, just a moment, and when he awoke to the room, she wasn't there. He wrapped the baby under his coat and ran outside, the lambs bleating. He called for Agata across the pasture. It was snowing, the dark air blurred by the haze of whiteness in the moonlight. He could have chased after her, searched the woods, but the tiny creature was cold. It was dying, he really believed. And then, as though Marek knew that his father needed some kind of reply, he cried, his mouth a sucking wound of flesh, the tongue pink and quivering. 'Babe,' Jude cried. He went back inside to the fire and kissed the baby, cleaned the blood from its face. The placenta was lying in a puddle by the hearth still. Jude threw it into the fire and it hissed and steamed.

When the sun came up, he went to Ina's cabin with a lamb to pay her to nurse the baby. She refused the animal but said she'd take care of Marek whenever Jude needed.

'Why does he look so strange?' Jude asked.

'Your girl tried to kill it, that's why,' Ina said. 'She came to me many times for herbs to get it out of her.'

And that was it. Agata was dead to Jude.

Jude petted the newborn lambs now in the afternoon shade and tried not to think about Agata. 'The poor creature,' he told himself, fingering the ear of the runt of the last litter. He had sixteen babes and five ewes and one ram. The ram lived apart from the rest in a small pen at the southern end of the pasture, under an awning of pines. Jude didn't care for him the way he cared for the females and the babes. When he fed the ram, he simply threw some hay over the fencing. Water was dumped once a day into a leaking trough. The ram seemed indestructible. And he was strangely complicit in his own imprisonment. He never tried to break through the fencing, although it was made of weathered branches and old wooden boards and was very near ready to collapse on its own. Marek wasn't allowed to go inside the ram's pen.

'He will think you're a sheep and try to fuck you or kill you,' Jude said. 'That's all he knows how to do.'

'Why does he not kill the ewes then?' Marek asked.

'What a stupid question,' Jude said, sincerely appalled. 'A man doesn't kill his lady. How else will he live on but in his children?'

'Will you live on in me?'

'I hope I will. And you'd better have a son of your own some-day soon.'

'Soon?'

'You're thirteen years old. You've got hair on your pubis. You could be a father any time you like.'

'But I want to be a son, not a father.'

'Well then.'

Marek and Jude always watched the mating rituals. Jude liked to guess which of the ewes was in heat first. After so many years, he had grown sensitive to their smells. He was usually correct, which made him all the more upset when he'd watch the ram mount and fuck the ewe. She did not like the feeling. Jude knew that. It was an invasion and a penalty for her sex to be so brutalized, and then so burdened. Jude felt sorry for the ewes and fed them extra wheat when they were with child. But he hadn't felt so sorry for Agata. He had felt proud of her swollen belly. He had loved her, had infused himself into her, unloaded so much into her womb, which was built for him by God. When he ejaculated, he groaned, and felt in that moment that this was the language of God Himself, the groan of creation. He remem-bered how Agata turned her head as he released his grip on her neck and moved her face to look back at him from where it had been pushed into the hay pillow. She was crying. And Jude thought, Good girl. That's my good little girl. You are mine now. The white that dripped from his greasy penis smelled like a summer rain, iron in it, tangy. 'I love you,' Jude said, and sat back against the wall. Agata had cried—she was still a child, after all—and Jude took her by the arm so she could wash herself outside with water from the lambs' trough. Later she fell asleep inside by the hearth, her feet bound by rope to the round rock that would later mark her false grave. This had been their nightly ritual. He discovered, not long into their love affair, that she was with child.

When Marek returned from the stream, bruised and bleeding, toddling through the door with the broken pieces of bucket, Jude put down his work of darning a sock and picked up a shovel and threw it at the boy's head. Marek felt the blow to his right ear, and his vision went white. He heard the singing of angels. The wooden pieces of the bucket silently clattered to the floor, and Marek lifted his hand to his ear, which was numb and hot to the touch, and then Jude started punching. Marek fell to his knees and bent his head low to protect his face while Jude hit. And then he took his hand away from his ear to allow Jude to deliver a few more blows. And then he lifted his face to Jude, and Jude hit him across the nose and again on each cheek, like a king with a sword on a knight's shoulders, and then Jude kicked Marek's left knee so that he fell to the side, and then Marek stretched his legs and rolled on his back so that Jude could kick him or stomp him wherever he liked. If my father kills me, Marek thought, I am sure to go to heaven. Another blow to his head made him turn and gag. A tooth skipped out of his mouth and landed in a little shard of light coming through the doorway, the last of the sun between the trees. He watched the light play on his glistening tooth. He'd seen a lot of blood today. That was all right. Blood was the wine of the spirit, was it not? He licked his lips and sucked the blood back into his mouth, comforted with the knowledge that the damage Jude had done to him would warrant a whole night of praying, repenting, that his father would cry and beg God to forgive him, and Marek would become hypnotized by his father's remorse.

And so it was. Once he had caught his breath and taken a sip of water, Jude calmed, then cried. He wiped the blood from his son's face and held him in his arms, kissed his strange, swollen face, and told him the story of Agata's sacrifice again. 'She died for you,' he said. 'You see the blood?'

Marek was happy.

Ina had lost her vision when she was only seventeen. She suffered a high fever due to a malady that had torn through the fiefdom. The entire family fell ill very quickly, one by one, mother, father, and her two little sisters. Ina fell asleep, shivering and sweating, and when she awoke, she came to nothing but the black light of her blindness and the stench of her family's dead bodies in the bed around her. Such stories were not unusual at the time— illness spread very easily in the region, as it was only a day and night away on horseback from the coast, where all the pestilence came in on ships crossing the sea. They said it was the rats to blame. When Ina was little, before Villiam's grandfather installed guards around the bounds of his province in an effort to keep out the bandits, traders and pilgrims passed through the village on their way to Iskria and Bordijn, bringing with them rashes and pneumonic contagions. Travelers often stopped in Lapvona to trade work for food and shelter, or simply to see how other people lived. Lapvona was a special place, known for its good soil and fine weather. And the villagers were kind and generous people, often taking in visitors and giving freely of their stores of food. They could afford to do so as their lord was fair and God-fearing. Taxes were low. There were only a few dozen families in Lapvona when Ina was a child, and they all worked and lived together peacefully until the plague took half of them to heaven. That changed everything. The houses were burned down with the dead inside for fear that burying the bodies would infect the ground. The survivors became infected with fear and greed. Guilt was extinct in Lapvona thereafter. Perhaps this was what allowed the village to move on after so much loss. Even their dear lord, Villiam's great-grandfather, had perished, leaving his twelve-year-old son, Villiam's grandfather, to manage the village.

Ina was the only sick person to recover from the plague.

When she staggered out of her home, the villagers were about to strike the flint. 'God rest their souls,' they said, then gasped at the sight of the sick teenager, her dress dark with sweat, her face bleached of color, roving blindly and calling out:

'Where am I?'

A woman screamed. The men backed away, afraid of infection.

Ina spoke to the voices in the darkness. 'Am I alive or dead?'

This question made the people of Lapvona very suspicious. Nobody would answer. They weren't sure what to say, anyway. If she was alive, how had she miraculously survived the illness? Had she seen death? What devilish germ might she have brought back with her? Why did God spare her, only to leave her orphaned and blind? Wouldn't death have been more merciful? Maybe blindness was penalty for some profane ill within her soul. And if she was dead, was she a ghost now, there to taunt and torture them? Was she an angel of evil? Only Jesus could rise, the priest, Father Vapnik, had told them. The people were perturbed. They told Ina to sit still on the dirt, then made a circle around her with small stones and proceeded to set the cottage on fire. The rest of the villagers came out to stare from a distance. In her weakness, Ina begged for water and food. 'Should we give it to her?' Nobody dared. They wordlessly agreed that it would be better for everyone if she were to succumb to her illness safely, within the circle of stones. They were afraid. A few people turned away, coughing in the smoke, not wanting to watch her die. But she wouldn't die. She only begged for food more passionately.

'She sounds like a howling sheep,' someone said.

'Yes, the kind with horns,' another said.

It wasn't until Father Vapnik heard of her situation that she was offered a cooked potato. A neighbor threw it at her, and she ate it. Eventually Father Vapnik directed the village carpenter to fashion a long pole by which Ina could be prodded this way and that, to get her safely away from the others. Nobody wanted to take her in. She was thought to have some kind of hex on her.

They closed her in the anteroom of the church, used in the past to incarcerate madmen when they were throwing fits. Nobody in Lapvona had gone mad in a century, but the room still held the charge of dread and insanity. Ina could feel it. Villiam's grandfather, traumatized by the death of his father, took the priest's advice and ordered Ina to be sent to the nunnery. No man would ever marry her anyway. She had been betrothed, but the boy and his family were ashes now. Father Vapnik arranged for a horse to take her up to the convent once she had recovered enough. She slept and ate, stuck in the anteroom, and touched her body with her hands to remind herself that she was real, she was alive. Emboldened by the church's charity toward the blind girl, a few people left food and jugs of water for her, and eventually she regained her strength, but not her eyesight. Ina understood that nobody wanted to hear of her sorrow or her fear or loss or anything to indicate her passion or dispassion for life.

And she knew that the nuns would make her do some menial work, the kind that a blind girl could do without mistake—probably scrubbing laundry or grinding wheat. She didn't want to spend her life gripping dirty rags and plunging her arms into cold lye water or turning the handle of a crank for hours each day. She had indeed seen death and she was not afraid of it. What scared her were other people and their immovable selfishness.

The night before she was to make her journey to the convent, Ina couldn't sleep. She stayed up eavesdropping on Father Vapnik discussing things with the vicar in the chapel.

'We'll need to bring in new families to offset the deaths,' the priest said. 'Maybe this is a blessing. The new lord is so young and pliable, he'll do whatever I say. And we can build a more robust village. The northerners are good-looking, aren't they?'

The vicar agreed, adding that northerners were more compliant in their disposition as well. 'They are good farmers,' the vicar said. 'They don't waste time praying and singing like ours do. Northerners are reasonable people. Sturdy.'

'We could become quite rich in due time,' the priest said. 'There are churchmen in Kaprov with jewels in their crowns.'

'Yes, Father.'

Ina coughed and they hushed. Then Father Vapnik said, 'What do we have to hush for? She's only a blind nun, if that.'

When the men had left and the church was quiet, Ina felt around for the door. They had not locked it, so low was their esteem of her will. So she ran out into the night. Better to live wild in the woods than to be enslaved by the nuns, she believed. A few people taking their midnight constitutionals saw her stumbling and feeling her way through the village, but they didn't bother her. They simply got out of her way as she staggered with her arms out toward the woods. Nobody knew where she went. Or rather, nobody wanted to find her. Father Vapnik lied to his congregants the next Sunday, said that the horse had taken Ina up the mountain and left her safe and sound at the nunnery. Those who had seen Ina escape into the woods said nothing. They never gossiped about the priest. To do so was blasphemous. So Ina was soon forgotten.

After some time in the woods, crawling through the wet leaves and cold spring rain, attuning her ears to the slightest twitch in the air, the scattering of pollen, every noise and smell, young Ina began to develop an uncanny fluency in birdsong. She could interpret every peep and warble. It was this language that guided her toward shallow puddles of dew when she was thirsty or a slug when she needed food. Eventually, she understood the world through sounds and echoes, relying on the birds to tell her whether a man or animal was coming her way, where to hide, where to find berries, where to dig for truffles or wild carrots or potatoes, where to find shelter from a storm. It didn't take long for her to forget what things looked like. In a way, the forgetting eased her grief. She forgot her parents' faces. They became, in her mind, lost ideas. Her dead sisters, faded dreams. Thus, the darkness was a benefit to Ina's heart.

One day she found a cave hidden by a willow, and this

became her home for decades. During that time, Ina became an expert in survival, listening to the birds who loved her. She lived for years off mushrooms, wild apples, eggs, and rain. Comfortably, almost happily. She built fires, slept curled up with the darkness in heaps of willow leaves, steeling herself from anything outside but the birds, who sang her songs and picked the mites from her hair. She didn't think about people or her past, only the movement of air and the shadow of sound it carried. Quite often, she heard the bleating cries of babes.

When she was in her forties, something dripped from her nipple. She didn't notice it at first. Having abandoned her vanity at such a young age, she had felt her breasts were relics of a past life; she would never need them. The substance weeping from her nipples was such a surprise at first, she thought they were misdirected tears and tasted the secretion. It was not salty, but sweet and creamy, but with the nuttiness of the scent of her own skin. Milk, she understood it to be, had filled her bosoms. Was she a victim of divine conception, she wondered, remembering for the first time in years the story of Jesus Christ the Lord and Savior? She remembered one image in particular, after the Crucifixion: Jesus, bloodied and dead, falls into the arms of Mary. Her nipples hardened thinking of that embrace, and her breasts ached. But she couldn't remember whether Jesus embraced Mary who was His mother, or Mary who was His lover. Father Vapnick had told the story many times when she was little. She touched her breasts and let the milk squirt out into her cupped hand. She squeezed and squeezed until her palm was full and warm, and she drank it. And then she bent her neck and lifted her breast to her mouth—she was thin enough that her bosoms had no real integrity, were just bags of fluid. She nursed herself. She drank. It was a nourishing sup. She was not at all embarrassed to do it. And then, miraculously, the black light faded. She regained her vision, not perfectly, and only temporarily, but she could see enough to remember the world as it had appeared to her as a child, and to recall her longing for society. It lasted only a few minutes. This was what led her, eventually, to reenter Lapvona, however on the fringe she would stay. Day by day she nursed herself and ventured down bit by bit to the village, wondering all along if she now somehow held in her womb the Christ Child, though it never grew or came.

In the many years she had been away, everyone she'd known in Lapvona had died. New people filled the village and nobody recognized her. They only saw a nude, wiry woman with heavy bosoms, her hair matted and full of leaves and twigs, her skin covered in dirt. They assumed she was a refugee from a village ransacked by bandits.

'How old are you?' a young man asked her.

It hurt her throat to answer, she hadn't talked in so long. 'I don't know.'

To Ina's surprise, the people of Lapvona didn't reject her. On the contrary, they treated her as an elder, and many villagers volunteered food and clothing. Ina accepted their hospitality and found herself soon well employed as the village wet nurse. She moved into a foxhunter's cabin in the woods. People saw her arrival as prophetic. There had been a blight on the farms in recent years, and from the resulting malnutrition, the mothers could not produce milk to feed their babes. It was as though Ina's bosoms had heard their cries. Many babies would have died that year had it not been for her milk. In the years that followed, she was very useful to the women, and in turn, the women became more useful to the men. A child could nurse on Ina while its mother worked in the field. Sometimes Ina resented this turn in her life and missed the freedom of her cave. At other times, she felt that her milk gave her life meaning, made her human again, and she enjoyed the villagers' dependency on her gift, remembering the past generation that had abandoned her in her grief and suffering. She felt, in some small way, that she had recovered a sense of family. 'Maybe some of me will get into these babes,' she thought. 'And so they will all be mine.'

Ina bounced the babes on her knees, fed two at a time in the gentle light through the trees. Nursing continued to have a miraculous effect: for a few minutes after her milk was drained, she regained her eyesight, and could see beyond shapes and colors to every cobweb and scuff of dirt. She used the minutes of vision to go outside and watch the wind in the trees and the birds fly overhead and the bright green moss and wild lettuce, everything. Sometimes, she would close the babes in the cabin and wander through the woods, looking for glimpses of herself in puddles or on a flat rock that she urinated on, anything to tell her what she looked like on the outside. She did this over and over with the babes, her breasts filling soon after they were emptied—she closed the babes inside; she went out. She picked herbs and listened to the lessons of the birds in how to identify the medicinal qualities of each flower and grass and shrub and fruit. She experimented on babies who had colic or rashes or fever or lameness. She also practiced eating certain plants—calendula and comfrey, catnip, fennel—to see how the infusions into her milk could affect the babes' moods. She developed a tincture for herself that enhanced her vision. It was Euphrasia and mint. She ate valerian to keep the babes asleep longer.

The mothers brought her food and clothing, spoke kindly, offered her puppies from their litters, kittens, flowers. They thought her milk would be more nutritious if she was happy. Ina could have made friends with these women, but she was only comfortable with the babes. She had been hurt too badly to trust anyone grown up. She didn't like to go to town. The plot of land on which her family's house had once stood had been split up and taken over, replotted. The old mulberry tree had burned and died and been cut down to a stump and was now used as a place to ax firewood. The village reminded Ina too much of what she'd lost, and there was no herb that could heal her loneliness. When she asked the birds what to do, they answered that they didn't know anything about love, that love was a distinctly human defect which God had created to counterbalance the power of human greed.

Years passed like this—babes born and brought to her with varying regularity according to the success of the harvests. Another ten years gone. And then ten more. Lapvona grew. The northerners had mixed with the Lapvonians. More cottages were built, with their small croft gardens, but otherwise every last bit of land was growing something to be exported for the lord's profit—wheat, barley, oats, pulses, fruit, root vegetables, nuts, and rapeseed. The manor on the mountain doubled, then tripled in size. Guards protected the roads leading up there. No longer were travelers permitted to pass through. Only the guards were allowed to leave the province to haul the harvest and honey to the sea, where they were sold for a great fortune. A few more decades passed. The lord died and his son, Villiam, took over.

Now Ina was as old as a person could be, a wrinkle of waxy skin and a nest of white, brittle hair. Marek continued to visit her. Ina felt sorry for him, for his twisted body and strange mind. She felt somewhat responsible for his malformation, as she had been the one to counsel Agata when she was pregnant and wanted to destroy the baby. Ina had tried to abort the baby herself, even, a hand up the girl's sheath, clawing at the tiny thing inside, but the baby had persisted. Ina thought maybe Marek was something like her, attuned to a different nature. So as a babe, and long after, he was allowed into her cabin to nurse. He had been the last babe to taste her milk. Now there was no milk left, and Marek was grown, but he still came to suck. Ina could smell his manhood stink up from his loins when they lay on the small bed, but it didn't trouble her. The time they spent together was peaceful for both of them. With Marek sucking her nipple, they drifted off into a realm of quietude, like being adrift on the sea, although neither had ever seen the sea. Marek did some chores around the house in exchange for time at Ina's breasts. His sucking did not restore her vision, but by now Ina was tired of looking at things anyway. She had seen it all.

The day after the hanging, Jude woke up before dawn and stood over Marek, who was asleep on the floor, bruised and wheezing from the beating. Jude went out to relieve himself and marveled at the low reach of stars that shone over the manor at the top of the hill. He imagined his cousin was stressed, enraged. Each time the bandits came through, Villiam must suffer a great blow to his pride, Jude thought. He believed that he was lucky to live so close to the manor, because the guards would surely protect him from invasion. They had a clear view down to Jude's pasture from so high up. But of course, nobody at the manor cared about Jude and his lambs. The clearing of the pasture was only a convenience of security. The guards would see anyone trying to sneak up the side of the mountain from Jude's land, but they would not protect it. They had no reason to. The bandits would never storm the manor. If they did, they would be met with open arms.

When Jude went back inside, a noxious smell had been loosed in the cottage. Marek had shat his pants. Enraged at this unruliness, Jude shook the boy awake, told him to go wash himself in the stream, and was thus relieved again in his heart—thank God—that he had been right to act with violent hatred against the boy the night before: Marek was a pest. His mother had been smart to abandon him, and God knew it was Jude's great sacrifice to allow the creature to live out his meaningless life. As usual, Marek was heartened by his father's renewed disdain, as this made God love him more through pity. But he was weakened in his body. He stumbled in the dimness out toward the stream and washed himself in the cold water. He felt he needed to be restored somehow that day or else he could grow ornery and act out in a way that would displease the Lord. This happened from time to time when his suffering clawed at his inner darkness—he acted savagely, kicking at the lambs and trolling around the village, wishing ill on people. At times like those, Ina was the only one who could ease his spirit.

So later that day, while Jude was out in the pasture, Marek made his way through the valley to her cabin.

'Come in, Marek,' Ina called out, detecting the strange rhythm of the boy's feet on the path. She could hear his breathing was not quite right. She was glad that he had come. She could soothe him and he could do her some favors. She liked to be demanding, and Marek liked to be subservient.

'Fetch some water from the well, Marek. I'm thirsty,' she said, not moving from where she'd been perched on the floor, counting out her potatoes. She had reached sixteen potatoes, had them lined up in front of her, and then had lost track of her counting.

At her age, in her loneliness, her mind was like a memory of a mind, echoes of birdsong. She'd done everything so many times in her life, she drifted between now and then, often getting lost in between. Her need for food and water was almost trivial, but not quite. She liked to believe on some level that she was inhuman, that God had granted her life after death with one caveat: she might live forever. The slow hell. Marek's visit broke up the monotony of this timelessness.

He fetched the water, set the small pail down next to Ina, and dunked a cup for her to drink. He held the brim of the cup against her lips.

'What's that smell?' Ina asked.

'I was sick at night,' Marek said, unashamedly.

'No, I smell blood.'

'Father beat me.'

Ina sipped and sighed and stretched her legs slowly out on the floor. Marek moved the potatoes out of the way.

'Will you rub my feet, Marek?'

Marek rubbed her feet. It hurt to crouch down. He was sure a few of his ribs had been broken, and his busted jaw made it hard to move his mouth to speak clearly. His tongue was swollen so that when Ina asked, 'Will you cut me a piece of the bread you brought, Marek?' and he answered with a woeful lisp, 'Sorry, I didn't bring you any bread, Ina,' she understood that he had been brutalized sufficiently to deserve her comfort. Of course, she already knew he'd brought no bread.

'Bad boy,' she said. 'Help me up.'

Marek lifted Ina up off the floor as best he could. They shuffled together toward the bed.

'Take off my dress,' Ina said, standing before him. Marek
lifted the scratchy brown fabric, revealing the old woman's small,
childlike legs, her swollen knees, her crumpled torso. 'Tell me,
Marek,' she said. 'Why did your father beat you this time?'

Marek liked to make a better story than the truth for Ina. 'I
kissed the bandit in the pillory.'

'And why did you do that?'

'So that father would beat me.'

'Child of pain, don't you know the man is bent on cruelty?
He used to suck me dry and then some, my nipples would bleed,
and then he'd suck some more.' This was true. Of all the babes
Ina had nursed, Jude had been the greediest.

'Is my father a good man?'

'He's good, yeah,' Ina said flatly. 'Why do you always do
things to make him angry?'

'So that I can come to you.'

'You like my pity?'

'Yes, Ina.'

'Lie down on the bed.'

Marek lay down. Ina smiled and did a little dance. She was
not without humor. Marek smiled and laughed at the absurdity
of her body. It was something like the absurdity of his own.
They were both small, Marek disfigured by birth, his spine
hinged forward so that his little shoulder blades stuck out from

his back like sharp wings. He looked like a bird. Ina was small from age, her spine bent and her chest caved in toward her pelvis. Her loose breasts were more like flaps than breasts. Her nipples hung like little pebbles. She lay down next to Marek, fitting easily into the space left by his body on the bed, her head above his on the hay pillow. Marek curled up, took her breast into his mouth, and sucked. His mouth had stopped bleeding, but the cuts in his gums and tongue were sore, and his jaw ached as he drew the nipple into his throat. But soon the sucking soothed him away from his pain and he was adrift, and so was Ina. They stayed like that, Marek's saliva dripping from the corners of his mouth like Ina's milk used to. A bird sang through the open doorway. 'Someone is coming down the hill,' it sang, but Ina didn't move. She was not going to interrupt the moment with alarm. Marek lifted his head.

'Hush and suck. It means nothing to you, just a pretty song.'

Marek nodded and hushed and sucked. He felt at home. He knew every inch of Ina's body by heart: her face like a desiccated apple, her large drooping ears, her pale and tender scalp, the billow of white hair fixed stiffly on top. He knew her breasts, of course, and her arms, and her wrinkled belly. Ina's pubis was covered in thin white hairs as soft as fine grass. She looked like an angel to Marek. He sucked some more, softer with his mouth, and moved his tongue back and forth over the hard little nipple, hoping it would bring Ina some pleasure. If he did it right, Marek knew, her pubis would pulsate and emanate a smell that Marek could only identify as orange blossoms and pine. He had tasted it once, had asked Ina could he suck the milk from there as well, and Ina said yes. But never again. She said it wasn't good for Marek's health to suck from there. 'Maybe when you are older,' she said. But he had sucked enough then for Ina to lie shivering on the bed, drained in the black light of her blindness. Never again. She cared too much for the boy to so abuse him.

Now she thought of Agata, her woe and petulance. Wordlessly, the girl had begged Ina to rid her of the babe inside her, as if there were some fantastic future for her if only she could stay flat bellied and young. Ina resented Agata's fear of motherhood. She didn't have a high opinion of the girl. The birds had told Ina about Agata, tongueless and wandering the woods. The birds thought, perhaps, that Ina would take pity on the girl. They told her the whole story: Agata had found her way to Lapvona from her bandit village in the west after being impregnated by her own bandit brother. When her father had found out, he had cut out her tongue and banished her as a whore. Cruel, yes. And what bad luck later to have been captured by Jude, an insatiable dog if ever there was one. But Ina thought Agata wasn't very brave to have been so horrified by her expulsion. Ina had survived her expulsion, after all. And she hadn't fallen into the arms of any man along the way.

It had been Ina's idea to tell Agata to go up to the nunnery when she showed up in the cold night, bleeding through her skirts. 'They'll suck the blood right out of you,' Ina had said, and pointed up to the hill where the abbey was. And there she went and stayed for all these years. Ina didn't tell Jude or Marek where Agata had gone.

Marek wandered home now, taking the long route through the valley, his heart beating slow and strong after his time in Ina's arms. His jaw still ached, but with a sweetness attached to the pain now, and not just the pounding of his father's fury, which was a different flavor, like hot stone. The afternoon sun was high. The heat in the air made Marek feel dizzy and his vision spotted with white. He paused under an oak tree to cool himself and further delay his return to Jude, who he predicted would be suffering the contradictions of his feelings: disgust and remorse for having beaten Marek so badly. Maybe one day Marek would be big enough to push Jude away. He could imagine toppling him to the ground and pressing a knee on his chest, bashing his head against the ground. That would be something.

Out of nowhere, as though God had heard his thoughts and wanted to punish him, a pebble hit Marek on the shoulder. He scrambled up from the ground and pinned himself against the tree and looked around, squinting into the sun. A laugh came. It was Jacob, Villiam's son. He carried a bow and arrow on his back.

'Hi, boy,' Jacob said.

'I didn't hear you,' Marek said.

'That's because I've got on new shoes. They're for hunting.

They quiet my step.' Jacob approached Marek, who still clung to the tree. 'Do you want to try them on?'

Jacob was a year older than Marek, tall and strong. He was dressed in fine spring silk and linen. His boots were red leather tied with cerulean blue satin laces. His hair was thick and black, and his skin was pure ivory. He had not one freckle, while Marek was spattered with brown splotches all over. The two had known each other for many years, since Jacob had grown old enough to leave the manor and since Marek had grown old enough to leave Jude's purview of the lambs. They had a friendship, one of taunt and abuse, and one in which Marek could act somehow other than the subservient object of Jude's indignation, but subservient still, as was his true nature.

Jacob was incapable of indignation. He understood that about himself, and that it was a privilege of his wealth and breeding. His father, Villiam, was the same way. Never in Jacob's fourteen years had he seen the lord so much as clear his throat in anger. Even at his most impulsive and cruel, his father spoke with humor, as though it were all a game. When news reached Villiam that a bandit had been captured and put in the pillory, he simply laughed and told the guards to have good fun at the hanging. 'It isn't every day that we get to play keepers of the peace.' And he wanted to hear all the details: How big was the crowd, were people crying, did they throw any food of value? Did they go back to work right away? 'Tell the villagers that God wants them to redouble their faith now, and that this spring harvest will be a testament to their goodness in the face of villainy. And let the bandit hang for a day. Good if some birds come and peck at him or something. That will make people feel that justice has been paid.'

The only true pain familiar to Villiam and, by extension, his son was the complaint of boredom, but it was never without certainty that the boredom would soon be quelled. The young man always emanated a jocular wit, as if to tempt the fates of humor toward him. Villiam emanated something of more insidious intensity, which was like absurdity and irreverence. His judgments and ideas veered toward immorality, delivered through the personage of a calm, well-oiled, funny mask. Jacob thought often of the difference between him and his father. Why was his father's persona so creepy, like a serpent disguised as a man? Villiam liked grotesque topics of conversation, nasty comedy always conveyed as colloquially as a passing fancy. He liked games and tricks. Even during meetings with his accountant and advisers, he demanded songs and dances. He liked to be entertained. He was dogged in his pursuit of diversion and demanded it of those around him. Jacob had different interests. He was an explorer, a hunter. He had already amassed a number of mounted animal heads and was teaching himself taxidermy. He had stuffed creatures in his room at the manor. Sometimes he wore a necklace of rabbits' feet around his neck.

Like Marek, Jacob had not inherited any physical attributes from his so-called father. Villiam was not handsome, had a long, crooked nose and cheeks that were pitted with scars from a rash that still often broke out across his face. Jacob had no intimate knowledge of his father's body, but he could imagine it: he was bony and sickly, his skin wet with sweat that stank of vinegar and scented oils, his buttocks grossly loose, and his penis a small white bone that gleamed like an ornament of alabaster handled too much. Better to leave Villiam's private habits in private, Jacob thought. He often wondered why his mother, Dibra, had married Villiam in the first place. She had come from a distinguished family in Kaprov, the northernmost fiefdom. Her brother, Ivan, was ambitious, and he had a strong army, she said. All Villiam had were his bandits. 'My brother could come slay Villiam anytime he wants,' she had said.

'Why would Ivan want to kill him?' Jacob had asked.

'Lapvona dirt is good dirt,' Dibra had replied.

'Is that why you married my father?'

'For the dirt, yes, my love,' Dibra had said unjokingly.

Jacob didn't know that Marek's father was his father's cousin. The two boys couldn't have been more different. Pressed to find a similarity between them, one could say they did share a desire to know the land. Jacob wanted to leave Lapvona one day, not to be a lord elsewhere but to be an explorer. Marek's sense of his own future was as stunted as the growth of his body. He still looked like an eight-year-old, and his delight in the trees and flowers and rocks was sincere. He couldn't imagine maturing into a man. Maybe, Marek thought, he could skip manhood and go straight to being a wrinkled elder like Ina. But for now he was trapped in his childhood. Jacob liked that about him. It made Marek easy to manipulate.

'Why are you hugging that tree? Is it your girlfriend?' Jacob asked.

Marek let go of the tree.

'I don't have a girlfriend, Jacob,' Marek said kindly. 'Do you?'

'Lispeth, my servant, is like a girlfriend sometimes.'

'What's a girlfriend?' Marek asked.

'Someone you want to marry.'

Jacob sat down in the spot of shade under the oak where Marek had found the cool air a moment ago, and Marek sat to the left of him, the humble side, where the sun shone down and made Marek hot and dizzy again.

'So you like my shoes?'

'They look like cliff birds,' Marek said.

'Do they?'

'Red and blue. You must be so happy.'

'Because of my shoes?'

'You deserve fine shoes, Jacob. You're fine yourself. You're a prince.'

'I'm not a prince.'

'But you seem like a prince.'

'Whatever,' Jacob said, bored of Marek's flattery. 'Where can we find some of those cliff birds?'

'They have nests at the top of the mountain, on the outcroppings, where the trees branch out over the cliff.'

'I want some,' Jacob said simply. 'Take me to them.'

'Are you going to eat them?'

'No, dum-dum. I'm going to break their necks and gut them

and stuff them and put them in my room with all my other stuffed animals.'

Marek liked birds because he felt they were liminal creatures between heaven and Earth, and by liking them he was aligning himself with ascension. Jacob liked them for the way they looked.

'Do you really want them, Jacob? It's hot out, and at the top of the mountain, the sun can burn your skin.'

'Are you in bad shape or something?' Jacob asked. 'I see you are sort of bruised up. What happened?'

'I fell,' Marek said.

'Clumsy,' Jacob said, knowing full well that Marek's father beat him. Nobody had ever laid a hand on Jacob. He liked to think that if someone did, he would have a great time fighting back.

In front of them, a little starling with spring plumage landed on a patch of sun-warmed grass and pecked at the pink head of a worm.

'Come on, Marko,' Jacob called.

Marek complied. He got up and led the way to the mountain, still woozy from Ina and the sun like a weight he carried on his back. Jacob moved lithely, with confidence, as though nothing in the world could ever get in his way. He had a further advantage as he was not hindered by carrying his bow and arrows. Marek volunteered for that.

Hearing Marek wheeze, Jacob offered him a sip from his canteen, but Marek refused. He had never taken anything Jacob offered. Marek knew that God took pity on the poor and hungry. He would rather faint than give God any reason to suspect him of indulgence. Jacob drank freely and whistled a song as he walked steadily up the mountain. Marek didn't care about Jacob enough to warn him against extravagance. Jacob's father was very close to the priest anyway. Marek guessed that Villiam could use his wealth to influence God's will. That was the way things worked, Marek thought. If you didn't have money, you had to be good.

'What are you whistling?' Marek asked. Jacob's song had a quick rhythm, like a joke. It made Marek nervous as he scanned the path up the mountain for snakes and sharp stones. The soles of his shoes were thin and wet, the leather eaten away under the ball of his right foot because he stepped more heavily on that side.

'Do you like the song?' Jacob asked.

'It's funny,' Marek answered.

'This guy my dad knows comes to visit sometimes, from the south. They have good songs there, so he sings to us after dinner.'

'Why are the songs so different?'

'Because the people are different.'

'But why?'

'People from the south are more relaxed. They have a sense of humor because they don't have to work as hard. They take more time to think about things.'

'If they don't work hard, how do they survive?'

'I don't know. Maybe they're rich, and rich people have more time.'

'You're so lucky,' Marek said, not understanding himself.

'Even if I sat still and did nothing,' Jacob said, 'I'd get all my father's money when he dies.'

'I hope your father doesn't die.'

'Pff,' said Jacob. 'How much further to the cliffs?'

'We're halfway there,' Marek answered.

'I don't care about riches,' Jacob said. 'I'd rather run away.'

'Where would you go, and who would take care of you?'

'I'd go to some strange land where the people don't know me. Everyone knows me as Villiam's son here. It's boring. If I ran away, I would change my name.'

'What new name would you choose?' Marek asked.

'I'd choose your name. Marek.'

Marek blushed. It was the most flattering thing Jacob had ever said to him.

'Because they'd think I was a nobody,' Jacob explained. 'Your name has no dignity. So people would treat me like a normal person. You're the lucky one, Marek. Nobody expects anything of you. I'm going to be married next year to my cousin in Kaprov, and I'll have to sit around with her father so that he can do more business with mine. It's all so stupid. I don't care about any of it. If I had my way, I'd live like you, like a beggar.'

Marek didn't defend himself, but he knew he was not a beggar. Everything he ate came from the land, and what Jude bought in trade for his lamb milk. The money he made selling his flocks to the northerners paid for the taxes he owed to Villiam and the monthly dues at the church, though they never attended, and the rest went for things like shoes and clothing, tools, rope, although there was rarely much left. Neither Marek nor Jude had ever begged anyone for anything, except God for His mercy and blessings. There were no beggars in Lapvona. Everyone had a skill and a purpose.

'My father hates beggars, but I think they are free,' Jacob went on.

Marek bristled at what he thought was Jacob's naive hubris. He told God in his mind, 'Forgive him his insolence,' but only so that God heard him. Marek didn't really care about God forgiving Jacob.

'How much did your new boots cost?' Marek asked.

'How should I know? How much would you pay for them?'

'Ten zillins?'

Jacob laughed. 'This is why I envy you, Marek. You don't know the meaning of money.'

They walked silently for a bit across the dark side of the mountain, and Marek's sweaty shirt cooled as it clung to his chest. He watched Jacob walk ahead of him, the soles of his new shoes slippery on the dirt, his shiny trousers gleaming with the dust stirred at each step. Marek's pants were worn thin at the knees and rolled up around the ankles. The material was stiff with dirt and stained and scratchy. Marek had only one pair of pants. Every time he saw Jacob, which was once a month or so, Jacob wore a new outfit, his garments perfectly fitted to his body, which was, month by month, taller and stronger and more beautiful, Marek thought. On any other day, he would have been happy to climb the mountain with Jacob, but he felt weary from last night's beating and his time with Ina. He believed that Ina was like a mother to him, and that, had Agata not perished, he would have received the same closeness from her instead. He presumed that every child—he wasn't sure when a person stopped being a child—sucked its mother's tit to soothe its nerves, even with no milk to be had. He assumed Jacob did this as well. Jacob was so certain, so calm. And so Marek assumed that Jacob's mother's breasts must be much finer than Ina's, and instead of envy toward Jacob for his good fortune, he felt anger, as though Jacob's fortune were an insult to his own. Maybe it was the dark light and the smoothness of Jacob's stride that pierced Marek's heart with a disdain that he could not shake. 'God, please relieve me of this temper,' he prayed as he walked, but he was burning inside even as he was cool on the outside. Just then, they turned into the sun again and they were steps away from the cliff where Marek said the bird nests were supposed to be.

'Can't you walk any faster?'

In the sudden eye-blind of sun from shade, Marek hadn't noticed that Jacob had gone on far ahead of him. Marek tried to run, but he tripped over a rock and hit himself in the chin on the ground. He accepted the pain gladly, as he understood that God was exacting punishment for the hatred Marek had felt in his heart just then. He got up, his ears ringing. His head rushed with blood. When he regained his balance, Jacob was yelling in the wind. 'Show me where those birds are!'

Marek picked up the rock he had tripped over. It was heart shaped and heavy; he could carry it in one hand. He ran up the rest of the path to where Jacob stood, now overlooking the cliff. Just as Jacob turned and said, 'I don't see any nests up here. Why have you brought me—' Marek flung the rock at him. Jacob, quick on his feet, stepped backward to avoid getting hit and swiveled his body toward Marek. So smooth were his movements, so quick was he, that these maneuvers happened simultaneously. He sprang from the cliff's edge, pitched toward Marek, his face happy with fight, but his foot slipped—his new shoes were too slick—and he skidded backward and tried to catch his balance with one foot tensed on the broken root of a tree sticking out over the cliff, but he couldn't. He fell. He fell and said one word as he flew down through the air: 'No!' and Marek heard him land on the plateau below.

Had God seen? Marek looked around. The wind stilled for a moment, then stirred again. There were no cliff birds, no nests on the cliffs. Marek had lured Jacob up for nothing. A joke, he'd thought. The only birds who lived up so high were vultures. He took a step toward the cliff and peered over the edge. Jacob had landed on a stone outcropping. He lay on his side, as if in a casual repose, but as Marek squinted down he saw that a sphere of blood was widening across the rock like a halo around the boy's head.

'Help!' Jacob cried.

Marek couldn't move. The blood was black as sap, and Marek

felt his knees buckle and shake when Jacob cried again, 'Help!' as he rolled onto his back. Now he stared straight up at Marek. His face was split and flattened on the side that had hit, and an eyeball was hanging from its socket. Marek got down on his knees as though he would pray, and he did—'God, forgive me!'—and curled up on the dry hot ground. He could hear Jacob crying out, 'Help me!' His voice was not clear and strong as it used to be, but gurgling and shortened, like a poor person's voice, a beggar groveling in the shit and piss outside a rich man's window. 'Marek?'

Marek was quiet. He watched the sky fill with thin gray clouds.

'Help?'

Marek was grateful that the sun had been subdued. His skin chilled, his heart slowed. Eventually he couldn't hear Jacob crying out and wheezing anymore. He took another look over the edge of the cliff. A few birds had landed on the outcropping and were blithely sipping at the blood that had pooled in a shallow of rock. This turned Marek's stomach. He stepped back from the edge and vomited into the dry dirt: clear saliva came out, like a fountain. He realized that he hadn't eaten anything since breakfast. It was now late afternoon. Jude would be wondering where he'd gone. If his father thought Marek had wasted the whole day at Ina's, he would be angry again. And Marek knew Jude was already tired from the work of being enraged last night, so this new rage would be a passive rage, one that was too steely and cold to come out with the passion of violence, but would be pure evil. It was a feeling that left Marek alone and jumpy. And on a day like this, having killed Jacob, he did not want to be alone. So he decided to run down the mountain as best he could—despite the burning acid in his throat and his hunger and fatigue and the throbbing in his head coming from his jaw and the soreness of his broken ribs. He had left Jacob's bow and arrows at the top of the mountain. Maybe he would come back and get them one day. If the bandits came to the pasture, he could protect the lambs and his father. Wouldn't everyone be surprised if this small, twisted creature came to be their savior after all? These were his stupid thoughts as he ran.

In the prestorm air, Marek could smell violets blooming, their bitter perfume lifting from the low ground into the wind as it swirled around the mountain. And from the ground there was also a warm iron smell. The mixture was heady and made Marek feel woozy again. The caw of vultures careening overhead woke him up and he ran faster. By now Ina would have heard what he had done to Jacob: the birds were singing all about it. Would they tell Ina about the rock? Marek wondered. Or just that Jacob slipped and fell? He considered running back down to Ina's to seek shelter from the coming storm instead of returning home to Jude. As he reached the bottom of the mountain, he turned and looked up. Clouds were already covering the sky. If he turned south, he'd go to Ina's. If he turned west, he'd go home to Jude. Thunder struck then, and it made Marek's decision for him.

Jude had seen a lamb get struck by lightning once, he had told Marek. 'The smell of its cooked flesh carried through the prickling air, a horror worse than death,' Jude had said. 'Don't get hit by the light, son. It will cook you.' So Marek turned west and ran down to the pasture through the tall grasses now slapping against him, wet with rain and churning in the wind.

Jude knew what kind of storm this was. Not a spring rain, but a reckoning. Maybe God was angry that he'd beaten his son so hard the night before. Or maybe this was the hanged bandit's spirit come back to wreck the land. Either way, he smelled the iron stink of blood in the air and he knew it was vengeful. Something bad would happen. He herded the lambs inside the cottage through the front door. He counted them again and again, saying, 'Get in! Go!' The babes obeyed, ignorant of the threat of the storm, crushing up against each other and baaing with complete trust and faith in Jude as he pushed them in. The ram would be left in its prison outside. It was indestructible, Jude thought, but the ewes and babes were sensitive. He got them all inside and told them to hush. 'Lie down and rest until this is over.'

Marek finally appeared, wet and trembling, his panting breath stinking of bile and his eyes pathetic and fearful. The rain was falling hard by then. It was seeping into the cottage through the doorway.

'Don't be a baby,' Jude said. 'Get in and calm the lambs.'

Marek found a place to squat between the babes and petted their heads and cooed at them, trying to forget that he had left Jacob up on that rock. His father watched the storm through the crack in the door, looking out as if someone were coming, waving his hand behind him to hush the lambs. Marek was good. He petted the heads of the babes and hushed them some more. He was an innocent, he told himself, a child. If some stray impulse had resulted in horror—a simple rock was all it was— someone should be comforting him, in fact. A child makes mistakes, yes, but accidents are God's purview. Was Jacob's death really Marek's fault? Hadn't the little prince been vain to walk up the mountain in such slippery shoes, and hadn't he been perverse and greedy to want to catch a wild bird, break its neck, and stuff it with sawdust? Marek had invented the cliff birds, yes. But he hadn't really lured Jacob up the mountain to kill him. He had only wanted to see the boy's disappointment.

Jude watched the storm hover over the mountain and then change its course toward the north, and he saw only a few flashes of light out that way. 'I think the worst is over,' he said.

Marek took some comfort in his father's relief. He sank his hand into a bag of grain and ate it raw, grinding his teeth so that the grain turned to paste. He drank from the bucket with his cupped hand. His jaw hurt and he was quiet.

By early evening, the storm had passed. The clouds cleared and the sun glowed pink and purple. Jude opened the door and watched the light flood the pasture. The horizon was hazy with rainbows. He smiled.

'Come on, my babes,' Jude said, clapping his hands in delight at the soft golden light angling over the mud. Let the storm torment the northerners now, he thought, they deserve it. They were the ones who ate his sweet creatures, after all. The babes followed him into the sunset and grazed in the balmy air, their feet sticking in the mud, until the sky was low and dark blue.

Alone in the cottage, a nervous dread seeped into Marek—it was the truth hitting him at last. The sun was setting and Jacob was still out there. Was he really dead? Marek thought of the spilt guts of the bandit, then of Jacob's crushed head. 'Help!' Jacob had cried. And Marek hadn't helped him. He went outside, desperate for something, anything—an embrace or a blow to the head. He trudged through the mud toward Jude, trembling, tears budding from his eyes, his face mottled with sweat and dirt. Jude turned and looked at him. Could Marek be just another babe to care for? Oh, that would be nice, wouldn't it? To be pitied just once? Didn't God owe him that, after all the horror he had endured?

'What?' Jude said, pulling a broken root from the ground. He wiped the mud from his hands on his pant legs and looked up at Marek impatiently. 'What?!'

'Something terrible has happened to me,' Marek began.

As they trudged up the mountain the next morning, Marek played the events of the previous day over and over again in his mind. He had not told Jude the truth. Rather, he had begged his father for protection from what he called 'an evil wind' that picked Villiam's boy up off the cliff and into the air—'like a bird catches a mouse by the skin of its neck'—and dropped him on the stone outcropping. 'I was so afraid, Father! There was blood! I couldn't do anything, I was paralyzed there, terrified that the evil wind would come for me next!'

'You poor boy,' Jude said coyly. 'What scent had the wind? Was there myrrh in the air?'

'Oh yes, Father. And fire! And the smell of burning flesh! Lightning must have struck Jacob.'

'Burning flesh, eh?'

'Like a lamb struck by lightning!' Marek offered, hoping to garner further fright and sympathy from Jude, who he knew had been so disturbed those years ago when the same had happened to one of his babes. But Jude had invented the story of the lightning. It had been merely an excuse for his overprotectiveness of his lambs. He himself had been afraid of storms since his parents drowned. They sent him into a panic. He had collected his babes inside the cottage for the comfort of their closeness. No lamb had ever been struck by lightning. God could never be so cruel.

'I should beat you dead if you're lying to me,' Jude said when they stopped to catch their breath. But his fists were too tired from the work they'd done already.

'I'm not lying!' Marek cried, shielding his face from his father's hand.

Oh, but his insistence was suspect. Jude prayed in his heart that the boy was lying. Jacob was his cousin Villiam's son. Their fathers had been estranged, but there was still tragedy in hearing that someone of his own blood had died so young.

'You're telling stories to trick me again,' Jude said. 'I don't believe you.'

'No, he's really dead! He's there! Let me show you!'

'Let's get going,' Jude said, and they kept walking.

Now they were halfway up the mountain. Marek was quiet, marching along. He remembered the first time he had met Jacob, years ago. It had been winter, Jacob a dot on the snow-covered horizon as he approached in his red wool cap, his fine coat, his red leather gloves. They were only five and six then. Jacob had seemed to Marek like a magic boy, impervious to the cold. He was so healthy and strong, his nose didn't even drip. Pale as the snow. The two boys loved the winter. The cold whip of wind on their eyeballs made them hungry to trample through the snow to discover something. A few years later, Marek had shown him where to hunt elk, wolf, lynx, and beaver. Waxwings, black woodpeckers, and white-tailed eagles were harder to shoot, but they were around in winter. Jacob had an easy time with white fox and bunnies. Marek didn't like the blood and killing, but he liked to assist on the hunt. Jacob had enjoyed his company and guidance. They'd had fun together, and Marek had felt lucky to be valued for his knowledge of the land and its animals.

These memories made his heart feel warm. But when he detached from the memories and looked around at the morning grayness and the looming height of the mountain before him, the rising sun, his heart felt cold, like a sweat chilled by a sudden wind. It was a terrible feeling, the boy's first experience of nostalgia: the pain of his past. Until now, time had had almost no meaning. The sun rose and set. The church bells donged, but he didn't bother to count them. Just the thought of the church pained him. The thought of the road filled him with longing, as if he might never go back there. He might never again trudge through the snow into the whiteness of the pasture. He might never again smell the smoke of fire burning in the cottage chimney. He might never see another winter. He may never see people again. He would be punished for what he'd done to Jacob. He was worried Jude might kill him.

Jude was worried, too. He had spotted Jacob before on his walks through the pasture toward the mountain but had never spoken to him. He'd seen him and Marek walking side by side, and the sight of them together had been hopeful somehow, as though the conflicts of past generations were ameliorated by these boys who intuitively shared a kindness toward one another, not even aware of their relation. The hopefulness confused Jude. He had gone through bouts of despair and anger about his lot in life, especially when he was younger, before he had found Agata. He had felt that God had deprived him of his great-grandfather's fortune, had made him suffer for his grandfather's stupidity: nobody ever told Jude what his grandfather had done to get himself exorcised from the family. Jude's own father had been too proud even to speak of it, regaling them instead with boasts of the godliness of their pasture and their babes. 'The Earth will provide all we need in this life. Anything extra is a sin.' Jude had balked at that idea in his youth. Once his parents had died, any wishful thinking about money had faded completely. He understood that his destiny was to be small, a keeper of small animals, a man of the land, not of riches. And he had learned to accept the religious truth that his father had preached, that God favors those who are poor and powerless. Or he tried to accept that. Every day he looked up from his pasture at Villiam's stone manor and tried to feel sorry for him. His cousin must carry the heavy burden of worry over the welfare of the entire village. Jude tried to think of him as a martyr. And poor Jacob, who would never know penitence or humility. God save those with money, Jude had tried to think.

But a life of poverty had not earned him an easy way. The more Jude went hungry, the more he mourned his beloved Agata, the more wrenching became the yearly goodbyes to his sweet lamb babes. The more he watched Marek grow ugly and twisted, doughy somehow despite the lack of proper food, the more Jude wondered if his grandfather hadn't made a grave error. What good was a life of struggle with no guarantee of heaven? He watched Marek shuffle ahead of him up the mountain and wondered how he had ever committed himself to this strange, ugly creature. Agata had been beautiful, hadn't she? All Marek had of hers was the fiery red hair. Poor Jude. Poor me. For what he suffered through on Earth, he had better reap rewards in death, he thought. If the boy kept him from heaven, he would kill him.

He would throw him off the cliff. These were Jude's thoughts as they walked up the mountain. 'Kill the creature and walk away.' But he wouldn't. He couldn't. His own boy, no, God forgive him for the vile thought. Jude tried to shift his focus away from God and onto Marek's story. He knew the boy was lying, but he couldn't identify the lie. So he used his own lies to try to tease out the truth.

'This wind, you said, Marek—was it warm or cold?'

'It was cold, Father,' Marek said, gasping from the effort of climbing uphill. He had barely eaten more than a handful of grain the day before, too nervous to think of requesting any of his father's porridge that morning. 'Like winter, it was so cold it hurt my skin and felt like a burn from fire.'

'Aha. So it was a wind from the north.'

'I think so,' Marek said.

'This is very troubling,' Jude said. 'Very bad. Forgive me, dear boy, but I'm afraid this omen will be the end of me. I never told you the story of my death, did I?'

'But you're alive, papa. What are you talking about?' Marek was alarmed.

'Do you believe Ina's visions?'

'Of course I do,' Marek said.

'Ina told me the story. It came to her the day we buried your mother. Just as we were smoothing down the dirt, a cold wind from the north came and picked up one of my babes and dropped it from a great height down on the rocks of the stream. Ina said that there would be three winds such as that. The first would kill a babe. Thank God the wind didn't come for you next, Marek, or else I would have killed myself with sorrow.'

'Don't say that!' Marek cried.

'The second wind would kill one of my kin.'

'But Jacob isn't your kin, papa. I am. I'm your only kin now. You said so.'

'Jacob is my kin. Villiam is my cousin. I never saw any point in telling you . . .'

Marek was happy to hear this. He had always thought of himself as a creature without history, a bloodline blurred by loss, meaningless. If Villiam was his father's cousin, that meant Marek was a cousin, too.

'Then why are we so poor?' he asked his father.

'How dare you think of money at a time like this?'

'I'm sorry,' Marek said, and he was. He was already crying, grateful that he was walking up ahead of his father. He knew that Jude couldn't stand the sight of his tears.

'My grandfather committed a grievous betrayal and was exorcised from the family wealth, and so will we be forever and ever. And I am sorry you have suffered so, my boy.'

'No, I am sorry,' Marek said.

'Ina told me that the third wind would come for me soon after the second, and that it would lift me off my feet—just as you described the wind lifting Jacob—and drop me from a great height into a pit of fire.'

'What fire?'

'The swidden. The northerners are always cutting their

forests and burning them. Great fires, they burn for years. They think they'll get good earth that way, so that they won't have to trade so much with us in Lapvona.'

'The wind would carry you all that way?'

'Oh, it could carry me to the moon if it wanted.'

'And would you get hurt in the fire?'

'I will perish.'

'No!' Marek cried.

'If the wind killed Jacob, it will come for me next. I'm only grateful that it took Villiam's boy and not mine.'

'But father, the wind didn't take Jacob.'

'You said it did. Don't lie now just to comfort me.'

'No, I will tell you the truth.' Marek stopped on the trail, the sun rising behind him. Was it the glow of the swidden? Could he already feel the fire coming for his father? No. No. Ina's prediction had not come to pass. Marek knew this for certain. 'It was I who killed Jacob. I did it. It wasn't the cold wind. I threw a rock at him and he fell off the cliff. I will show you how it happened. You won't be swept away, Father. Please forgive me. If Ina's prediction comes true, it'll be me that is killed first. Let me jump now and let the wind take me. Anything to spare you from the swidden. Oh God!'

Marek burst into tears, and Jude slapped him across the face. Another tooth broke loose in Marek's mouth, and he swallowed it and choked.

'Hit me again, Father!' he begged. He got down on his knees and prayed. 'Please, hit me!'

But Jude was too worried about what would come next to raise his fist again. 'You aren't worth the wind beneath my hand,' he said.

Marek lay on the hard dirt and splayed his arms and legs.

'Then stomp me. Kill me, papa. I beg you.'

'Get up, you idiot,' Jude said. 'It's not up to me to punish you. We'll take Jacob to his father and let him decide how you ought to suffer for this.'

Marek fully expected he would be put to death. And part of him was glad—he might finally see his mother in heaven, he thought.

The puddle of blood that Marek had watched seep out of the boy's head was now pale pink and watery, and it had stained the back of Jacob's white shirt. His black hair was curly from yesterday's rain, but dry, and from afar he looked fevered and pale, as though he had slept through a nightmare. But there was no life in his face. His lips were blue. The right side of his face was smashed like an apple that had fallen from a cart at high speed. His right eyeball was stuck to his torn cheek. The left eye was open and still. Jude looked down. Then he turned to vomit, but all that came out was a cry that echoed across the valley.

Like the idiot he was, Marek put a hand on his father's back and asked, 'Is he dead?' as if his father might determine this all to have been a joke, a staged horror. Jude breathed heavily, too distracted by his heaving to slap Marek's hand away. 'He is, isn't he?' Marek continued, trying to make his voice soft and sad. 'Poor Jacob. He was such a nice boy. He always wore such beautiful shoes. I guess they're ruined now.'

Jude had seen death before, of course—villagers slain by bandits or ravaged by illness. He had seen the bandits hanging, their innards spilling. He'd seen his own parents dragged from the lake, bloated and rotting. But the dead boy's body was a horror he hadn't imagined, the body flattened on one side, the wretched look of slow agony in his clawed hand, the other arm broken at an insane angle, the hand bent backward. Jude knew he would have to climb down somehow to retrieve the body.

'Stay here,' he said to Marek, part of him wishing the false story about the evil wind might come true and dispose of both of them without a word.

'Should I follow you?' Marek asked.

Jude was too perturbed to reply. He didn't care what Marek did. It was at this moment that he loosened himself from the creature that was his so-called son. Villiam would surely kill him. Jude would spit on his body as it swayed from the gallows, denounce him completely, disown him, or else the villagers would turn against him and he'd be hanged next. His only hope would be to ingratiate himself with Villiam. 'I am your cousin,' he would say. The good lord couldn't kill his own flesh and blood. But Marek, a bastard murderer? Executing the boy was only fair.

Jude walked back down the path and explored the area of the

mountain where the cliff evened into a slope. There was a trail there that he guessed was a passage worn by wild goats. Lapvonians let them wander unchecked, as their meat had been deemed inedible by the northerners. They said the wild goats were noxious. Jude had always seen the flocks clomping up and down the mountains and tried to ignore them. But now he was glad for them, as the path they had worn spun around the mountain. The path was long but indeed led to the outcropping as it looped back around. All Jude had to do was climb the face of the rock to get to the boy's body. He said a prayer before gripping the edge of the sharp crag and pulled himself up.

Marek stayed behind, sitting with his legs dangling off the cliff. He peered down and watched his father turn and vomit again off the outcropping. The man had no stomach for it. Perhaps it was this kind of weakness, the same as he had for his babes, that had plagued his grandfather and divested the family from the lord's fortune. Maybe there was a way out, Marek wondered, and fingered the rock beside him, the very rock that he had thrown at Jacob. 'If my father was to die, nobody will know what I've done,' he heard his mind say. He picked up the rock and kissed it, not thinking of its impiety, but automatically, as though it were a dying bird. Just then, Jude grunted below, wrestling the stiff legs of the dead boy.

Jude had never seen Jacob close up before. He saw no similarities between Jacob's features and his own. He was a strong boy, yes, but that was likely because he had grown up well fed, and not starved with scurvy, itching with mites, and filthy his whole life, like Jude. Jacob had had hot milk before bed and had slept in a cloud of feathers, not a scratchy mattress of hay. Marek was right about his shoes—they were the finest shoes Jude had ever seen.

'Papa!' Marek called down.

Jude ignored him. He pulled Jacob's feet over the side of the outcropping. One of the boy's legs dragged—it had been broken at the knee. Jude climbed back down onto the goat path and turned his back to the rock and reached up with both hands and pulled the boy's body down by its feet over his shoulder. Jacob was heavy and stiff. But he smelled like violets and rain. Holding Jacob's thighs against his chest, Jude tracked through the brush toward the main path and started down the mountain. Balancing the weight of the body would take concentration if he was going to keep his steps braced correctly on the slippery dirt. He focused on his breathing. He had a long way to walk to Villiam's manor. But he felt no need to stop for food or water. The dead boy on his shoulders was like the hand of a herder pushing him along.

Marek loped down the mountain trying to catch up with his father. He wondered if Ina could bring the boy back to life. He looked out at the morning for whatever birds might be out there. Could he communicate with them somehow? Could they be sent to Ina's to fetch some herbs? Could they return, find Jude, and drop the herbs in Jacob's open mouth and have him suddenly revive, his eyeball sucked back into its socket, his bones heal, his clothes clean? Was there any chance Ina knew how to turn back time? Marek knew that the answer was no. Only God could do that. If only his mother were alive, he thought, she would hold him tight to her chest and defend him. 'You can't take my son, he is perfect and beloved. To harm him is to damn yourself to hell, Villiam. Leave us alone.' Jude would not defend him. Poor Marek. He slipped as he ran down the mountain, then gained enough speed that he could see Jude's back and the dead boy over his shoulder, Jacob hanging upside down, stiff-necked. His dangling eyeball bobbed up and down with each step Jude took. Would it be unkind to wonder what would happen to Jacob's shoes? Would they be buried along with him? If Marek could wear them to hell, his feet would be protected from the flames, at least.

Villiam was asleep in his four-post bed. He dreamt that the bed was made of human flesh, a living thing of fat and soft baby skin. He was under the covers, caressing his fine silk sheets. He had never known injury or hunger, yet he was rawboned and his body often hurt from its own frailty against the cushioned chair or the fine velvet settle. Bed was the only softness that gave his body peace. He was a glutton, ate for an entire family, stuffed himself at every meal and in between. But he was never full and had barely an inch of flesh on his bones. He didn't take walks or do much but sit and be entertained by whoever was at his service on a given day.

He had spent the night before eating and drinking in his

room with his accountant, Erno, and his head guardsman, Klarek. They were supposed to discuss the reallocation of funds for new tariffs paid to Kaprov. Ivan, Villiam's brother-in-law, had raised duties and now Villiam had to pay more for his guards to pass through his fiefdom on the way to the sea to sell Lapvona's crops and livestock. There wasn't enough money in the coffers to make up the difference; the lord had spent too much that winter on furs and wine.

'Next month, tell the villagers that the spring harvest was intercepted by bandits and take all the money from the sales at the port,' he said. 'Use what you must to pay off Ivan, and bring the rest back to me.' Erno nodded and left. Erno and Klarek, like all the northerners, complied with Villiam's requests without reserve. There was something in their temperament that made them especially well suited to amoral servitude. Villiam never tried to hide his cruelty or silliness around them. This was what saved him from fear of God's judgment. His life was plain for all to see, though not all did see it. No villager was allowed past the drawbridge at the manor. Most had never even seen Villiam. The guards carried out any punitive action the lord directed if a family had failed to pay its taxes or had voiced some grievance to the collector or priest. Oftentimes punishment consisted of a little poison in the family's well, just enough to make the wife and children sick for a week. The priest would say that God punished those who didn't uphold their responsibilities as citizens. This was the way Villiam governed. Surreptitiously.

Villiam had spent the rest of the evening asking Klarek over and over to do the comic trick of crossing his eyes and sticking out his tongue. Each time, Villiam laughed so hard that the wine spurted from his nose, and he'd need a long moment to recover before he'd ask Klarek to do it again. They stayed up until dawn just horsing around. The night had been no different from most nights. He never spent time horsing around with his wife. He despised Dibra, in fact. She was a bore and a nuisance. Marrying her, his parents had said, would be good for business. Of course, like so many other things, they had been sorely mistaken. 'Her brother, Ivan, is trying to ruin my life,' he told Klarek. Klarek understood this and pretended to pity him. 'You poor man,' he'd say every time the wine spurted out of Villiam's nose. Servants came in now and then to tend the fire—it was cold in the stone manor even in the spring—and to mop up whatever Villiam had spilt and refill his cup and bring a new plate of food. Villiam's tongue was wide and thin, more like a bit of cloth than a muscle. When he chewed, the taste of food struck him powerfully and immediately and then disappeared. Sometimes food got stuck in his throat and he'd choke and cough, ringing his bell for a servant to come in and slap him on his back. More than once, someone had to reach into his throat to pull out a chicken bone or a peach pit. The man had no sense about what to swallow.

Villiam believed that his appetite was nothing but a physical symptom of his greatness. He needed more because he required more, because he deserved more, because he was more. Food was not the only thing that he could not get enough of. He needed company at every moment of the day. His team of servants was trained to be placid and witty. Villiam was not the kind of lord to care much about female beauty. The servant girls all cut their blond hair short and wore caps. No, Villiam wanted to be entertained, cajoled, mystified. He often had visitors to the manor, people from as far as Iskria and Torqix, who did magic tricks like pulling quail out of jewelry boxes or smoking intoxicating herbs and exhaling apparitions, or so they said. Villiam's favorite daily activity was to watch people do impressions of him. This was a requirement of the servants, to fill any moment of idleness, and so they practiced as they cooked and cleaned, working continuously to come up with language and gestures, the best new joke about Villiam's character and physical countenance. It was not that Villiam enjoyed humiliation, but that he enjoyed the humiliation of others. Father Barnabas supported him unquestioningly, did impressions, sang songs, told stories, anything to make Villiam laugh or cry. And Villiam did cry. He was not a stony lord. He was sensitive, so much so that a sad tale could throw the whole estate under the shadow of Villiam's sorrow. Everyone would work tirelessly to cheer him up. When Villiam suffered from fear or insecurity, the priest summoned nuns from the convent at the top of the hill to demonstrate miracles.

Villiam's days had a casual discipline to them. He woke in time for lunch—a feast—then played games all afternoon, barely disturbed by an occasional meeting with Erno or Klarek. In the evenings, he was bathed and dressed for dinner. He liked to look good. Yesterday he had taken a tour of the grounds by carriage.

Father Barnabas came along so they could have a private chat about the state of the village. Villiam was fond of the priest. Father Barnabas had a room at the manor and stayed there most nights. The two men often gossiped about what the priest had heard in his Saturday confessional. Yesterday, on the carriage excursion, Father Barnabas had said that the families of those slain by the Easter bandits were refusing to work in the fields until the next Sabbath. Luka, the horseman, could hear them over the clomp of the hooves.

'Let them grieve, I think,' the priest advised.

'One day is enough,' Villiam said. 'Tell them tomorrow to get back to work.'

The priest nodded. 'And how is your son today?' he asked. 'I saw him walking through the pasture this afternoon. Is he still feeling restless?'

'Restless and rude,' Villiam yawned. 'Jacob is very boring.'

Villiam wasn't very fond of Jacob. The boy was unwilling to be wowed by his father's eccentricities. He called his father 'a spoiled brat' and refused to visit with any girls that Villiam invited from nearby provinces to entertain the boy. Villiam was also a little frightened of Jacob. He was larger and stronger than Villiam. They couldn't have been more different. Jacob liked hunting, was built more like a servant than a lord. His mother worshipped him, and Villiam resented that. Dibra was not like her husband. She was perfectly content to spend her days riding her horse with Luka. Her quarters were on the opposite side of the manor from Villiam's. Husband and wife met once a day for lunch and barely spoke to one another. Villiam had a general distaste for the female voice. All the singers who traveled from afar to perform for Villiam were male.

'Do the trick with your eyes again, Klarek,' Villiam had requested one last time that evening, the words drowsy with wine. The carriage tour had tired him out.

Villiam had fallen asleep and dreamt of Klarek's mouth forming words that floated like puffs of smoke across the fire, lips dripping of wine and melted suet. He woke up in the morning to Jacob's servant, Lispeth, poking him in the shoulder, her finger digging into the thin flesh covering his scapula. He felt it and went back to sleep. But she kept pressing, and the pressure sent a pain through a nerve down to Villiam's foot and up to his head, and he rose with a cry and an immediate request for suet dumplings.

'What have you brought me and why am I awake?'

'Something horrible has happened, my lord.'

'What, no more suet? Go get some and wake me later.'

'No, not that. Please, come down and see.'

The girl was crying, which Villiam found moving.

'You're crying, poor girl.'

'Yes.'

'Let me cry along with you, for God's sake,' Villiam said. He made the sign of the Cross over his bare, bony chest and began to weep.

'My lord,' Lispeth said, wiping her eyes. 'You must come down.'

She was used to Villiam's befuddling eccentricities. 'There's so much more to cry over downstairs,' she said.

Villiam sighed and pulled the silk robe from her hands and tearfully requested she do a little dance as he got out of bed. This was not unusual. Lispeth curtsied and stepped from side to side, lifting her arms aloft and crying as Villiam pulled his long, bony legs from under the cover and stepped into his red velvet slippers.

'Fine, fine,' he croaked. 'Now a bit of wine. I'm sorry the dancing didn't cheer us up.'

Villiam preferred wine from the north until midday, a sweet white wine that was crushed by blond children. The stronger, drier white wine was crushed by teenaged boys from the south, and Villiam liked to drink that after his repast with Dibra in the late afternoons because her company bored him so, made him feel limp and trapped. Why had he married her? Because he'd needed an heir. Villiam's mother had insisted he take Dibra as his wife shortly before she died. 'Her father won't try to steal our dirt now,' was all she'd said.

'How about a little song?' Villiam asked Lispeth.

Lispeth stopped dancing. 'Later, my lord. It's Jacob.'

'What about him?'

'Come and see,' she said and ran from the room to lay out the red carpet that Villiam demanded be rolled out for him every morning, through the hall from his bedchamber and down the central stairs to the great room where the servants would line up to say good morning, however late he'd gotten up, and to tell a joke that each of them had invented overnight.

Now Villiam tied his robe clumsily and shuffled out of his room down the hall as the red carpet rolled farther and farther. He was still half asleep, his throat parched. He heard a cry come from down in the entry room, like a wounded animal, or a monster. It was Dibra. Villiam flinched and paused, considered plodding back upstairs. But then he heard another voice, a small child's. 'I'm sorry!' it said.

Villiam hurried toward the entry room, delighted and curious to see what young visitor had come and upset Dibra enough for her to wail so dramatically. He nearly tripped on the tails of his robe down the red stairs. 'No! No! Nooooo!' Dibra cried, a bit less convincingly now, as though the strength of her performance had weakened as Villiam drew near. She was forever disappointing him. Villiam was so accustomed to being entertained that any drama, however real it was, seemed to him as one staged for his private amusement. He had been living in perpetual diversion for so long, he could only conceive that this demonstration within his home was a farce. While tales of bandits marauding through the village may have given an honest lord cause to bang a fist on a polished table, Villiam's hand was forever limp and unsurprised. He knew it was all planned, all theater. Death wasn't quite real to him. He never once left the manor to see where the dead were slain or buried. He barely left the hilltop at all.

What theater was this now? Villiam's excitement grew. As the scene appeared from below, a bit more with each step he took down the stairs, the cast of characters was revealed. First Lispeth, crying with her hands covering her face. Then Pieter, the front guard, and Luka, the horseman, bent over, hunched, as though God Himself were admonishing him. Villiam slowed his step to prolong his pleasure as the play unfolded. He peered down. Next he saw Dibra on the floor, her skirt splayed out, her arms collapsed under her head as though someone had just pushed her down. Dibra had never been good at physical comedy. Her wails were far too exaggerated. She didn't understand restraint at all. For this reason alone, Villiam supposed, they were well paired. But now another character appeared as he reached the lower stairs. He looked farther into the room, into the shadows, at what looked to him like a faun, so ugly and goatish was its skull, and the body so small and contorted, as if it had tried to fix itself of its animal form to stand upright. The twisted figure moved Villiam; he had a special taste for freakishness. The creature spoke.

'If only God had taken me instead!'

A bit too fervid for Villiam's taste, but he supposed the priest must have approved of the script. Was he here? No, not yet. Father Barnabas must be sleeping in. Villiam finally reached the bottom stair and shuffled past Lispeth and the men. He did not stop to address Dibra, who was wrenched in despair, her body shuddering on the floor, a lull in the audible exclamations. Good that she knew to hold her sobs while Villiam passed so as not to distract him from the direction of the drama. Well played, Villiam conceded. And he approached the ugly little creature, who immediately fell to its knees before him. Villiam cleared his throat and assumed a tone that was low and indignant and self-controlled, as he thought his role to play was that of a stern lord.

'And who are you?'

'I'm the wretch who killed Jacob!' the creature cried and reached his weird arms out to grasp Villiam's calves. Villiam could feel the hands close tight around his bones, narrow as saplings. He almost fell over trying to step away.

'Please, my lord. Have mercy. Or I'll burn in hell for this.'

'Who is this, Lispeth?' Villiam asked.

Lispeth wiped her face and ran to curtsy at Villiam's side. The creature wept, its sorrow loosening its grip on Villiam's ankles.

'He came with his father,' Lispeth said, pointing to the dark recess of the room. Villiam looked, squinted.

'Step into the light,' he commanded.

Jude had only stood in the great hall for a matter of minutes, but he was already shivering from the cold of the stony air against his sweaty skin. He was in a strange rage, vibrant and ignorant of any future. He could not imagine how life would go on after this and he didn't want to. He focused on balancing the weight of the dead boy on his shoulder, which had become tiring after the long walk. He did not like people to see him struggle. His stomach growled, and he was suddenly aware of the pungent odor of wild garlic. Jude wondered to himself if he should be ashamed of the odor, assuming it was coming from his own sweaty body. But it was not him. It was Jacob, the delicate stench of his decomposing body now cleanly detectable in the coolness.

The smell made Jude's eyes water, as did wild garlic when he ate it in the fall, picking it out from between the other weeds in the pasture close to the ram's cage. He believed that garlic was good for virility. Ina had told him that once.

Finally, Jude took a step into the light so that Villiam could see him. Villiam was immediately perplexed by the resemblance between this stinking peasant and himself. They both had their great-grandfather's broad nostrils, pores stretched so wide, Villiam sometimes thought about filling his with tiny rubies. But Jude's eyes were more open than Villiam's, Jude's forehead more manly. His jaw was wider and his chin dense with brown hair, the opposite of Villiam's loose-skinned, bare chin. The frail man could barely grow a mustache thicker than Jacob's—a few hairs above his top lip. But both men's lips were thin, downturned, the color of unripe plums. Villiam stared at Jude, mesmerized, as though their similarities were a magic trick.

'He looks like me,' Villiam said. Nobody agreed or disagreed.

Next Villiam circled around Jude, searching to make sense of the large doll he carried. The doll's face was terribly disfigured but still recognizable.

'Doesn't that doll look just like Jacob?' Villiam asked, sincerely impressed.

'Yes,' Lispeth answered.

'But this one's dead, is that it?'

'Yes, my lord.'

'And how is that?'

Villiam was asking Jude. Jude could not look him in the eye, both because he was carrying the man's dead son and he was terrified of whatever punishment could come forthwith, and because Villiam seemed insane with denial. 'Is that an eye hanging out?' he asked and chuckled. He turned to Lispeth.

'I did it,' Marek said. 'I did it.'

'I see,' said Villiam, turning his attention to the creature. 'And what do they call you?'

'Marek,' Marek said.

'What are you, Marek?' Villiam asked.

Marek couldn't answer. Jude spoke finally, his voice cracking from thirst. 'He's a boy,' Jude said.

'Yours?' Villiam asked him.

Jude nodded. He seemed to be overcome with temper for a moment, as though the weight of the body on his shoulder was all that was holding him back from rushing at Marek and strangling him to death.

'I'm your cousin,' Jude said instead, staggering a little. 'Our grandfathers were brothers.'

'I didn't know my grandfather had a brother.' This was true. Villiam's father had never once mentioned any relation outside the manor. But Villiam wasn't suspicious. He played along.

'My name is Jude.'

'Why don't you set down your prop? You look tired. Lispeth, bring this man, Jude, my cousin, something to drink.'

'I'm fine,' Jude said.

'Is that so?'

Nobody knew, even as Villiam instructed Jude to set Jacob

down in the side room, whether Villiam had lost his mind with grief or simply did not believe that the body there, half smashed and stinking, was really Jacob's. Villiam was a happy person. He was immune to such tragedies. It wasn't real. It was impossible. But he accepted it somehow, as a game. He sat down on a chair and thought a moment.

'I suppose we'll need to negotiate an exchange,' he said finally, crossing his legs. He looked at Jude. 'Ah! I have an idea. I'll take your boy, and you can take mine.' This would surely upset Dibra, he knew.

'Papa!' Marek cried as Jude shook Villiam's limp, bony hand. But that was it. The trade was a fair one. An eye for an eye.

Then Jude was gone, carting off Jacob's stiffening corpse, not a word to the boy he had raised for thirteen years. No matter, Jude said to himself, balancing the weight on his shoulders and angling through the open doorway. Marek was not his son anymore, and in fact never had been. Yes, Agata had come to Jude already pregnant. Thank God. Finally, the truth was a comfort to the man.

# SUMMER

Jude woke up late, having been trapped all morning in a dream in which he wandered lost in a maze. The walls were made of limestone, the air heavy with the blood smell of iron. Each time he turned, hopeful that he had found an escape back into the forest, he was met with another wall. The sun was high and strong, and sweat dripped into his eyes. Bright white lights eclipsed his vision. In a shaded corner, he stopped to collect himself. His feet were bare and cut up from the coarse brambles that grew up between the stones. A puddle of water was stained with rust, and he kneeled to drink from it. He slurped voraciously, his thirst finally relieved after ten handfuls of brown water. Now his vision cleared and his head cooled enough to assay his surroundings with more certain intelligence. There was an iron gate at the end of the passageway. Thank God. He could climb over it. He cupped his hand and dipped it into the puddle again, but now the water was not brown but red. Blood dripped from his hand. He let it go and it splashed onto the stones. A sudden pain in his groin made him double over. A baby cried. Then thunder struck, and in an instant, the sky was filled with heavy gray clouds. 'Thank God,' he said out loud. 'Rain.' But then the short gate at the end of the passage disappeared. He turned and turned, following the narrowing path. He had seen the gate, he was sure. He had seen the flow of green trees swaying through the bars in the prestorm breeze. There was his freedom, but he couldn't find it.

His thirst returned as the dream faded. He lay face up on the floor of his cottage. He was neither tired nor refreshed—his constant hunger had lulled him into a state of perpetual dreaminess and agitation. He couldn't remember falling asleep the night before, only the darkness of the room and the way his mind made it darker, how the ground seemed to be drawing him downward. Whether he fainted into sleep or simply fell, it didn't matter. He was starving, but he was still alive.

The summer heat did not retreat at night as it did in summers past. And there was now an infestation of flies and bees in the pasture due to the drought and subsequent death of all flowers. The bugs were attracted to the moisture of breath exhaled by living creatures, and perhaps to their blood as well. A few nights in early June, when Jude had tried to sleep outside with the lambs, he'd woken up with dozens of bees collecting themselves into his nostrils and mouth. Fortunately, Jude was immune to bee stings. He'd been sorry to watch the bees die, pulling each tiny tooth from his withering skin. Since then he'd kept the doors shut and slept in the baking heat inside with the lambs. It made the air harder to breathe, but at least they were safe inside. They were thirsty and hungry, but nobody could get to them. By August, that was a dream in itself.

He could hear the bugs buzzing this morning. They were waiting for him, but he figured they would die out soon, like everything else. He was alone in his cottage now—no babes. Through his single window, the sun beamed in a solid ray, as though it were shooting out from the palm of God. It made Jude think of Marek. He closed his eyes. There wasn't a single bird singing.

It had been months now since the last rain in Lapvona. Not since the night Jacob died had a single drop fallen from the sky. The late spring harvest had been carted off to the north as usual, but then bandits had intercepted it—all was lost. Then the summer crops had failed completely, leaving the villagers with little money and nothing to buy with it. They traded their stores of goods among themselves until there was nothing left. The whole village was starving, and the wells had dried up. Jude had wasted weeks digging for water in the pasture, upturned the soil enough to spoil the dead grass for grazing. He'd been desperate, not thinking clearly. Villagers had come to him early on with grains and potatoes, jams, dried summer fruits, asking if he would trade one of his ewes or a few babes for food, but he'd refused. 'Eating meat is a sin,' he'd insisted. He held out some hope for his own garden, pulling the carrots from the dry dirt when his patience waned, but they were just little strings. Nothing could grow. His lemon tree had lost its blossoms and leaves and dried out and died. His strawberry bushes dried and died. Jude prayed for rain, like everybody else. Maybe something will grow back, he hoped, after just one storm. Just one. For a long while, the ram, by some miracle, had seemed immune to starvation. He paced and drank his paltry ration of water, which became harder and harder for Jude to carry from the lake, since all the streams had dried up. The river had dried up completely by mid-June. The ram slept with a frown on his face, wasting.

Jude had spent all his energy walking to the lake and back each day for months, carrying the single bucket of water, sweating the whole way. It had been too much to make the babes walk so far to drink. The villagers had all abandoned their homes and taken refuge by the lake, many of them spending all day sitting waist-deep in the water, as if staking out their claim, their hold on life. They could only gossip about food—where wild things once grew, and where there were animals that hadn't yet succumbed to the drought. Jude spoke to no one at the lake, and no one spoke to him. Since he had refused them the meat of his babes, the people had turned against him. 'He's gone mad,' they said. 'Traitor,' they called him. And they wondered what had become of his boy, Marek, who had been the subject of some gossip in the village in brighter times. 'What an ugly child,' they'd said. Now they said, 'His father probably chopped him into bits and fed him to his precious lambs.'

There was little to discuss by July, and those who had fed were too ashamed of what they'd put in their mouths to speak of it. Dead bees, bats, vermin, worms, dirt, and even old, desiccated cakes of animal dung had filled their bellies. Jude had stopped eating almost completely after the lambs had died. He lost his appetite out of sorrow, and then their rotting flesh attracted flies, which he found cruel and stupid, his beautiful animals teeming with maggots, the lowest of God's monsters. He buried the lambs in the pasture while the indestructible ram watched, steam puffing from his nose. The villagers found out and some of the older men came to demand Jude pay for his crime of starving the village of the only meat left. He had nothing to give them but the few objects inside his home—his stool, a few bowls and knives—which they took, although they were useless. And then they took his ram, slaughtered him on the spot while Jude hid inside his cottage. He could hear them portioning out the meat. He hated them. He had nothing left then, only his ravaged brain that held memories in fragments, without words, small, desperate thoughts lifting off the smell of the air. He remembered Agata and Marek. He remembered his babes. He spent all his time trying to remember, as if memories could sustain him.

Now it was August. Jude lifted his bones from the floor and felt the blood rush from his head. Was he going blind? he wondered. He got up and shuffled painfully to the door, opened it and nearly inhaled a swarm of flies and bees. He clapped his hands over his mouth as they flew in, chewed them up, and tried to swallow. The bugs were sticky in his throat. He had no saliva to help him suck them down. He inhaled and choked and coughed, his vision spotting. Finally he leaned in the direction of the lake, hoping his legs would follow. He had never liked the lake. It wasn't a refuge for him, but rather the thing that had killed his parents. He knew water was necessary for survival, but this one body in particular was laden with horror. Now he couldn't afford to be horrified. If he wanted to live, he would have to join the villagers in making his home there, though he was loath to. Some said there were fish in the lake, but no one had caught any. A few had gone mad trying to catch one. Since the drought began, the levels had fallen, the banks dried. The lake was smaller now at least, Jude thought.

Jude did not miss Marek, although the thought did cross his mind—in the late-night haunts of hunger so strong they drove him to near madness, too—that if the boy were there with him, he would have taken some pleasure in watching him starve, yes. Such dark thoughts would have disturbed Jude had he the energy to be disturbed. He still prayed every morning and every night. Still beat himself with the whip on Fridays. Still believed that there was indeed a God out there watching him, measuring his suffering. If you died from famine, you were guaranteed passage into heaven. This was common knowledge. Jude had been through a drought before, watched faces wither into skulls, whole farms die, but never one like this, so sudden, so hot, so destructive. No clouds. No wind. No life. Only Jude's raspy breath. He turned away from the sun to cool his face for a moment and caught sight of Villiam's manor on the hill. Marek was up there, he knew, and that was all he knew. Whether the boy was alive or dead, Jude could only wonder.

The ground was rocky and the dirt lifted into the air as a hot breeze blew. Dust clung to the lashes of his eyes. It hurt to blink. His clothes were stiff and scratched him as he moved. His skin hurt. His teeth were loose. His joints ached. His bones were sore. At least his feet were in better shape than the rest of him. The colorful leather boots he'd taken off Jacob's body were well worn by now, but they fit him like gloves. He thought maybe he could soak them in the lake and try to eat the leather, if it came to that. For weeks now he had lived only on mud. If Marek had been with him, he thought, maybe the lambs would still be living. Marek could have carried water from the lake. This was a comforting thought for Jude, as he could rest his mind on hating the boy, blaming him for everything. It gave him strength to pity himself, a man starving alone while his son lived in the lap of luxury, or so he could imagine.

Up at the manor on the hill, Marek was still asleep in his bed. He had been sleeping later and later into the day as the season deepened, now into the afternoons, as he had no work to do, no water to fetch, no chores, no fear that Jude would turn to him enraged that he had left the door of the larder open or that he had not shoveled the lamb shit well enough or that he was chewing with his mouth open, something that Jude complained was a habit of arrogance, and he would hit Marek in the back of his head so that he would choke on his food and have to spit it out. And then there'd been the accusations that Marek did not appreciate his blessings. 'Do you know how hard I have to work to feed you?' Marek didn't need to know now. Jude wasn't feeding him. Villiam was. And Villiam worked not at all, it seemed. By some miracle, the drought had not disturbed life at the manor—there was nothing to worry about. Villiam had told Marek that life was for enjoyment and that he would now have to be broken of his boorishness. This was hard for Marek, as he was so addicted to suffering. Sleep made it easier. He could sleep and feel no guilt. Villiam thought Marek's waking martyrdom was a kind of barbarian vanity. 'God doesn't reward misery,' he'd said. 'Just ask Father Barnabas.'

Marek had met Father Barnabas the afternoon he arrived at the manor. He had expected the priest to be a large, virile northerner—he'd imagined that any man of authority must have blue eyes—but he looked like an average Lapvonian, only dressed in a long black robe. It intimidated Marek, as he'd never spoken to anyone so educated before. What Marek couldn't tell yet was that the priest was a charlatan. Yes, Father Barnabas had been educated at the seminary, but poorly; he'd been a terrible student. He loved not the Christ but himself and the thrill of keeping people in line. He liked wearing his habit, and he liked the preposterous authority that his position granted him. Since his assignment in Lapvona, he had not given any real sermons. He simply translated Villiam's rule into language that sounded vaguely religious. If the Lapvonians had any sense, he thought, they would have noticed long ago that the bandits only raided the town when there were rumors of villagers hoarding foodstuffs after a plentiful harvest. They didn't understand that their crops were not taken as necessary taxes, but were simply sold for profit so that Villiam could continue to live so well and rule them. The little gift of religion Barnabas allowed the villagers on Sundays—the church gave out drops of wine and little oats for the Eucharist—was enough to fool them into accepting their poverty and enslavement. The priest had no sympathy for such stupid people. And yet he didn't see the hypocrisy of his disdain, as he was stupid, too.

Father Barnabas's head was soft at the top, as though the fat in his face had traveled upward and collected there. His forehead was narrow and wrinkled and jutted out over his brow so that his dark, pinched eyes were always cast in shadows. His nose was thin and pointy, and his cheeks were flat. His mouth was down-turned, like he was perpetually smelling something that displeased him. Maybe it was the stink of the servants, Marek thought. It was impossible not to notice that the servants all smelled distinctly of cooked cabbage. Even Lispeth, who was young and pretty, had breath that smelled sour and hard. Often when a servant passed, the scent of rotten eggs lingered. This was because the servants' diet consisted mainly of cabbage, while Villiam, Dibra, Father Barnabas, and now Marek were served every imaginable food from the manor's lush garden, farm, kitchen. It had been immediately apparent to Marek that Villiam had a very different appetite than his father's. Food disappeared into his mouth to no effect, as though the lord contained a great void inside of him. It made sense to Marek that Villiam was able to evade the shock and sadness of seeing his beautiful son smashed and dead, laid out on the floor. It was as though he had swallowed his son whole and sent him into that darkness. Nobody spoke Jacob's name, and Marek gathered that he must never mention what had happened. According to Villiam, Marek was his son now.

On the day he'd arrived, Villiam had instructed Marek to pick a servant out of the line to be his personal attendant. He'd chosen Lispeth because she was around his age, and he recognized the mole on her forehead. Jacob had spoken about her often. 'My servant, Lispeth, has the prettiest mole,' he'd said.

Lispeth followed Marek everywhere, bathed him, dressed him, opened his curtains in the morning, and blew out the candle at night. While he slept, she sat in a chair at the ready, waiting to attend to any need should the boy wake and make a request for food or drink or diversion. It seemed that Lispeth didn't need to sleep, or wasn't allowed to. Marek felt sorry for her that she was so enslaved, but after a while he enjoyed the attention. He had not yet worked up the courage to ask if he could nurse her, but he'd studied the faint swell of her breasts under her gray uniform. He missed his time with Ina, but he was not supposed to venture away from the manor. Villiam told him not to go down into the village. Even the guards barely ventured down there. 'Hunger is what makes people violent,' Villiam explained. 'It turns them into animals.'

Marek loved animals. When he lived down below, his days were full of birds and mice, deer, rabbits, the lambs, of course, moles, squirrels, chipmunks. Each species was stuffed and displayed in the next room, which had been Jacob's. Marek went there often just to look at the animals. He recognized the ones he had helped Jacob hunt. Now he thought of these animals as old friends—they were all that was familiar to him in this new life at the manor. The first time he'd been served a piece of meat, freshly slaughtered from the manor's farm, Marek had vomited it up onto his plate, which Villiam found hilarious. And from then on, Villiam had requested feasts of various meats simply to watch the boy chew and sweat and even cry sometimes at having to swallow the stuff. Lispeth always kept a bucket nearby to catch any of her young master's vomit at the dining table. Marek had gotten used to the sport. Dibra rarely joined them for meals at all. Since Jacob's death and Marek's subsequent adoption, she had barely come out of her room.

It was not God's mercy that had saved the manor from drought, but a tactic long used by lords in seasons without rain. Snow melt from the higher mountains, which fed the streams and rivers—as well as the wells and cisterns—was diverted by a dam to flow into a reservoir hidden inside a grove of pines on the far side of the estate. The moat was always full of water. There were flowers blooming on the lawn at the manor. Everything was fresh in the garden still.

Marek often dreamt of his old life, of the sun through the trees at the edge of the pasture, of walks through the fields and down the road into the village. He dreamt of small moments, of his father's shadow, of the sound of a lamb stepping up from sleep and butting the door with its head. He missed the soft feel of grass under his feet, the wind, the winter fog in the morning, the clouds. He missed all these things, and although he was of course permitted to go outside and walk the grounds, to lie in the gardens, Marek couldn't bear to revisit the old world of nature. He felt too ashamed, and too guilty, and too superior all at once.

'Good morning, Marek,' Lispeth said now as he rose out of sleep. He had gained weight and grown since he'd come. He felt heavier each morning when he lifted himself up from the bed.

'Good morning,' Marek croaked. Lispeth was by his side immediately with a cup of sweet wine. He'd gotten used to her strange smell.

She brought a wet cloth to wipe his face and used her fingernail to scrape the white scum from his teeth, the sleep from the corners of his eyes. She helped him dress and combed his hair, then knelt before him and slid his feet into his summer slippers, made of thin leather.

'Thank you, Lispeth,' he said.

'Your father is downstairs,' she said.

Villiam was eating grapes in the great hall, keeping his mouth full so that he could stay silent while Erno whined about money. Villiam's servant, Clod, was drawing his portrait.

'It would take a miracle to get the land back for a fall

harvest,' Erno was saying. 'I've been taking an inventory, and I still think that if you sold off some of your wheat, Ivan might be more forgiving on the interest you owe him.'

'Please, Erno. It's Sunday. It's evil to discuss money on the Sabbath, don't you know?'

'It's Tuesday, my lord,' Erno muttered.

'Every day is Sunday in God's kingdom.'

'Then when would we work?'

'Please, Erno. Clod needs to concentrate.'

Erno plucked a cluster of grapes from the platter and took his leave.

'My son,' Villiam said when Marek appeared, happy for the diversion the boy could offer. Erno was so serious. He had no humor to him, even though he did look funny lately, his head oddly large, his fingers spindly.

'Sit by me, Marek. Let's have a picture of the two of us. Two generations, side by side.'

Marek complied and sat beside Villiam. 'Are your bones hurting you today?'

'If I say yes, will you tell me a riddle?'

'Yes, Father,' Marek said. But he had no riddle prepared.

'Then yes, they ache terribly. I'm near to death in pain, ha ha ha.'

Clod stopped drawing and turned the paper around to show Villiam. It was a ridiculous caricature. Villiam slapped his knee in glee, then winced from the pain of the slap, then held himself around the middle and laughed for a long while. Finally, he wiped his eyes, found his breath, and in an instant he was bored and expectant, so he turned to Marek again.

'All right, what's the riddle?'

Marek's mind went blank. He said a little prayer in his mind, but his prayers had become strange since he'd come to the manor. He found himself praying to his own mind rather than to God. 'Think of something good,' he prayed.

'Quick, Marek,' Villiam said good-humoredly. His voice was never mad or cutting. He was a kind man, Marek thought.

'What is brown in the winter, brown in the spring, and brown in the summer?'

'Hmm, let me think. . . . Give me a clue, Marek.'

'It's also brown in the fall.'

'I've got it,' Villiam said. 'A brown dog.'

Marek smiled and nodded. Villiam slapped him on the shoulder.

'Getting stronger, eh?' he said.

Marek believed that Villiam truly valued his company, and that the man's insistence on lightheartedness was a way to alleviate Marek's guilt over Jacob's death. This generosity softened Marek's need to self-flagellate. The times that he'd tried to hurt himself at the manor, he had been caught. The first time it happened was the first night. Villiam had handed him over into the care of Lispeth, and she had spent the evening bathing him, cutting his matted red hair, clipping his nails, and applying salve to his cuts and bruises. Marek had been stony with her, trying not to feel the gravity of the day's events. But then, the kindness of the salve was too much for his shame to bear. When Lispeth's back was turned, he picked up his old shoe and started swinging it over his shoulder so that it hit him in his back. Having just finished his bath, Marek was naked and clean for the first time. He was beside himself, crushed by Jude's abandonment and disgusted with the filth that Lispeth had sloughed off his skin. Marek deserved to be punished, not attended to by the dead boy's girlfriend. The pain of the shoe digging into his twisted ribs and spine released what felt like a spirit of hurt, as though it had been lodged within his body and was now set free.

'Oh please,' Lispeth muttered in irritation, grabbing the shoe from his shaking hands. Marek let go and crouched down, both to hide his genitals from the girl and to expose his back for more lashings.

'Then you do it!' he sobbed.

Lispeth wasn't moved by this at all. Rather, she was nauseated at the sight of the boy's body. It had been hard enough for her to bathe him, holding the memory of Jacob's beauty in her mind, how his skin felt under her wet fingers, how his muscles twitched at her touch, how he stretched his arms overhead for her to scrub his armpits so that their faces came so close. He'd stared at her and made her feel naked, too. They had never kissed or touched much outside of the bathing and dressing, but a few weeks before Jacob had died, he held her hand for a moment under the table while he was practicing his penmanship. It had been a mindless movement, as easy and natural as scratching an itch on your neck or swatting away a fly. But as soon as her hand was in his, they'd both held their breath and turned inward. They felt the pulse of blood in each other's fingers, and just the slightest movement of a thumb or pinky was ecstasy. It had been so intense that Lispeth had closed her eyes and dropped her head, and Jacob's mouth had opened and his gaze had drifted away from his ink and paper into the corner of the room. Then a bird flew into the window and Lispeth gasped and took her hand away and got up and went to look at the glass, where there were tiny yellow feathers stuck like a butterfly. She remembered the look Jacob gave her when she turned around, his hand still held midair where she'd left it under the table. It was a look of shock and love, something true that had been growing underground for years and was finally breaking through. She had blushed and smiled, then cleared her throat and circuitously made her way around the table and back to her chair. She folded her hands in her lap and bowed her head. Jacob took his time to collect himself, said nothing, and looked back down at the paper he'd been writing on. A puddle of ink had pooled under the pen. He crushed the paper in his hands and pulled a book into its place. He pretended to read to himself until Lispeth said it was time for lunch.

All of that, years of longing and the wish for a future, and now Jacob was dead because of this deformed child who had no regard for life, even his own. Lispeth had looked down at his naked body hunched and dripping wet from the bath. She held the shoe behind her back and wanted to beat him in the head.

'Get up, my lord.'

She had brought him his supper privately that first evening, in his new room, and had showed him all the objects as he ate his potatoes and drank his milk, skipping the lamb roast and blood sausages.

'This is the chamber pot. This is the cabinet.'

Lispeth was fourteen, the same age as Jacob. She shared an understanding with the other servants that their lord Villiam was an ill person, a man who had never grown out of childhood, who would die early because of his underdeveloped strength, and whom they were glad was not vindictive or ambitious. The servants were especially grateful to be at the manor during the drought. The guards who patrolled the village occasionally brought back stories of suicides, madness, blasphemy. They said that the bandits were watching from the hills, that Villiam had instructed the guards to stand down if the bandits came, to let the bandits finish the villagers off, because why not—he could repopulate easily once the rains returned. 'He just wants us around to protect the manor,' was what the guards said. Klarek kept them ignorant of Villiam's real rapport with the bandits.

Marek and Villiam chatted now as Clod drew their portraits. Marek was asked to report his dreams to Villiam every morning, and he was smart enough to withhold anything that might give rise to stress. For instance, he had dreamt one night that bandits had stormed the manor and hanged Villiam by a rope from the chandelier in the great hall. He dreamt of Jacob's broken body coming back to life, shooting at rabbits and eating them, fur and all, as he walked purposefully into a lake of fire. The dreams he did share with Villiam were more playful. 'I dreamt there was a bird that had a voice like a man, and he would say everything a man would think but never say.'

'What did he say?'

'I love poop,' Marek said.

Villiam thought that was rather tame.

'How about "I'd like to cover my testicles in custard and have the servants clean me with their tongues?" Yes. What a nasty little bird!'

'Very funny,' Marek said.

'What else, Marek?' Villiam asked.

'I'd like to marry my grandma.'

'Disgusting!'

'Then my father would be my son.'

'That's very clever. Who would be in charge?'

'I think it would be confusing,' said Father Barnabas, entering with a yawn.

'For the father or the son?'

'Exactly.'

Villiam preferred Marek's face to Jacob's: it was narrow and fleshy, funny, the nose was crooked and limp, his lips moved like a fish when he spoke. His red hair was unnatural, a joke color, Villiam thought. He turned to look at the boy, his new son, and petted him affectionately on his lopsided cheek. The boy's face had healed since he'd come to the manor, his jaw a little asymmetrical, his bottom lip scarred with a white line where it had split and seamed itself. He looked more confident in his body now that he had more flesh, almost portly. Villiam admired this in him. It made the boy look as spoiled and rich as he now was. Villiam wished he could be portly, too. 'You're a good son,' he said to Marek as he patted his hand.

This kind of sweetness was what gave Marek the faith and courage to adapt to his new life. He had never been treated so nicely by anyone. Even Ina had been withholding, always a bit rude, as if nursing him were a sacrifice she made out of pity, rather than care. Villiam actually seemed to enjoy Marek's company, his strangeness and funniness. Marek grew less compulsive about his fear of God. As Villiam was powerful and unafraid, Marek believed that pleasing Villiam was akin to pleasing God. And Father Barnabas always agreed with whatever Villiam said.

'When the drought is over, we'll invite more northerners to live here. Lapvonians are all too serious and dark-haired anyway. Don't you think, Father?'

'That's true. They're stern, ugly people. Some more lightness wouldn't hurt.'

'And maybe some red-haired children will add to the fun,' Villiam elbowed Marek in the ribs. 'If there are any pretty young girls looking for a roll in the hay. You like hay, don't you, Marek?'

'Hay is itchy,' he said, and Villiam frowned. So Marek corrected himself. 'And I like to itch.'

'There he is, the little wolf. I bet you'd like to sink your teeth into Lispeth, too.'

Lispeth had been sitting in the corner, listening to the entire exchange, as was Clod, who had put away his drawing materials when the priest arrived.

'Oh no,' Marek said, looking at Lispeth and then the empty face of the priest, who, in turn, looked at Villiam, awaiting a sign as to whether to smile or frown. 'Lispeth stinks too much of cabbage,' Marek said.

Villiam chortled, then cackled, then bent over chuckling until he had to hold himself around the ribs to keep them from vibrating too painfully. 'Ouch! That was funny, Marek! Now Lispeth, come. Let us sniff you.'

Marek was sorry he'd said anything, but he had only told the truth.

'Maybe she should eat some cakes,' Marek said. 'Then she'll smell sweeter.'

But Villiam was too busy sniffing Lispeth like a dog. 'Turn around, put your arse in my face,' he said.

Lispeth did as she was told. Villiam leaned forward so that his face pressed against her backside. He inhaled deeply, then sat back and sighed.

'You're right, Marek. Cabbage, and something a bit worse than that. Shit, I guess.'

'Now now,' said the priest.

'I'm sorry, Father. What ought I say instead of *shit*?'

'*Excrement*, my lord.'

'Excrement. Is that like sacrament?'

'It is like sacrament, yes—for the Devil,' Barnabas replied.

Villiam's irreverence seemed to do nothing to displease Father Barnabas. When he was around, Villiam's humor took on a more aggressive tone, more perverse and humiliating, as though the priest were in on the joke.

'Lispeth, I think you've stepped in sacrament. Come, show us the bottoms of your shoes. Stand upside down if you must,' Villiam teased.

Lispeth never seemed to mind Villiam's humiliations. She understood that the lord had no shame, so she felt no shame around him. She assumed this was the reason Villiam picked on her so much. In truth, Villiam hated Lispeth because she reminded him of Jacob.

'Throw this at Lispeth, son. See if she can catch it,' Villiam said now, handing Marek a grape.

Lispeth stood up and readied herself for the game. Clod was busy burning the portraits he'd drawn in the fire in the hearth at the other end of the great room—Villiam didn't like to hold on to his portraits. Pleasure and fun were not cumulative, he believed. Everything had to be done again and again for it to have any worth. All that mattered was the matter at hand.

'Go on, Marek,' Villiam said now. 'Throw the grape. But wait, no. Lick it first.'

Marek licked the grape.

'All right. Throw it.'

Marek lobbed the grape at Lispeth, who caught it in a quick fist.

'Can she eat it?' Marek asked Villiam. 'Have you ever had a

grape before?' Marek had only tasted the wild grapes that grew on the vines along the path to Ina's house.

'Don't eat it,' Villiam said. 'Come bring it back and Marek will throw it again.'

Lispeth did as Villiam said, placing the grape into Marek's open palm with a curtsy. Marek could see that she had retreated from her spirit. She got an empty look in her eyes whenever Villiam abused her.

'Now Marek, put the grape down your pants and give it a good rub.'

'Down my pants?'

'Do you need help with your buttons?'

'No, sir.'

In fact, Marek did need help with his buttons. After several months, his fingers still fumbled.

'Help the boy,' Villiam said, and Lispeth knelt before him and unbuttoned his pants. Marek held the grape out, waiting for Villiam's next instructions.

'Put the grape in there. Get it under your sack and give it a good slap.'

Marek moved his hand toward his pubis, hesitant to defile the grape.

'Oh no!' Villiam cried. 'Never mind. I have a better idea. Put it up your arse.'

'Up?'

'Not all the way. Just get it at the hole and rub it around a little.'

Marek moved his arm lower.

'No, from behind. Here, let me do it. Stand up and bend over.'

Marek stood and turned. Nobody but his father, and maybe Ina, had ever touched him there, and then not since he was a small child.

'Perfect,' Villiam said, holding the grape under his nose. 'Here.' He handed it to Marek as he sat back down, impatient while Lispeth buttoned his pants closed. 'Now throw it to Lispeth. But this time, Lispeth, try to catch it in your mouth.'

Marek hesitated.

'Go on.'

Lispeth walked back to her spot and turned around, set her head back, bending at the knees and bringing her arms out by her sides. She had played this game before.

'Throw it!' Villiam cried.

Marek threw it.

Lispeth ducked her head, moving like a lizard on its hind legs. She caught the putrid grape in her mouth and swallowed it.

'Well done!' Villiam said, pleased. His smile faded as soon as Lispeth had returned to her chair in the corner, his ennui like an itch that was only relieved while it was being scratched.

'What'll we do next? Marek, tell me a story. A funny one. And make Lispeth the main character.'

Villiam was well aware that he was punishing the poor girl because she carried Jacob's ghost. Any reminder of the dead boy brought such displeasure to his mind that it would go dark and blank, as though it had walked into a wall. Of course, Jacob's spirit was everywhere. In his old clothes, which Marek wore—they were all too big and had to be tailored. Nothing had been removed from Jacob's room after his death. He remained there, in his stuffed animals, the weird rocks and bones on his desk, his papers, his maps, his childhood drawings still pinned inside the walls of his armoire, drawings of horses mostly. Marek hadn't felt anything eerie or vengeful in Jacob's objects, but he did sometimes imagine he felt a presence in the room when he visited. Of course, it was actually Lispeth and her memories of Jacob. She projected him back into the room so she could watch him sit and write or talk at the window, or turn over in bed. She was his ghost, in fact.

'Begin now,' Villiam said, repositioning himself on his pillows and sucking on a fig. 'More wine, Lispeth,' he muttered. 'Marek, get up and stand before me so I don't have to turn my head to look at you while you tell the story.'

'What sort of story would you like, Father?'

'I don't care. Something strange. Something scary. Should we close the curtains? Lispeth!' he cried as the girl was bending with the decanter to refill his glass. 'Turn off the sun. I think Marek's story will be better in the dark.'

Lispeth went to the windows and unhooked the heavy curtains from their catches so that they swung in a puff of dust across the glass. The room was nearly pitch black. Marek stood across from the settle and felt himself dissolve into the darkness, floating. He cleared his throat and heard Lispeth take her seat in the corner. The chair creaked like a bell donging to signal the beginning of an incantation.

'Once upon a time,' Marek began.

Jude didn't want to spend any more time at the lake than it took to dip his body into the cool water, gulp as much as he could, and find a hidden place to scoop enough soft mud into his mouth to fill his stomach. Other people made him nervous. The mud drowned his hunger but did not alleviate the pain in his belly or the ache in his bones. He knew that he was dying. He had no need for life anyway, he thought. Ought he pronounce his demise to the villagers and say goodbye? They were scattered along the shore, some naked and covered in mud, which was supposed to have healing qualities, some squatting in the water, and others under little tents they had fashioned from tablecloths and sticks. If Jude had been more keenly aware, he would have noticed the silence of the scene. No babies cried. No one spoke. In the blur of his fatigue, Jude couldn't recognize anybody but Klim, a blind man, who gripped the leash of his dog as he stepped cautiously toward the water. Klim looked very thin, thinner than Jude. His knees were like fists, his feet like huge scraps of tree bark. He moved stiffly and uncertainly, pulled by the canine, whose skin sagged from its sharp ribs. Jude could see the dog strain against the rope, desperate to drink.

Jude stepped back in the water and let his body rest from the heat for a while. Klim was edging closer and closer to the shore. The dog pulled. 'God help them,' Jude said to himself, remembering Marek's piety and how it had annoyed him. He splashed water on himself to forget the thought, and as he wiped his eyes, he saw Klim trip and fall on the bank of the lake. His dog broke loose and galloped into the water. Klim cried out to it—the first time Jude had heard his voice—a searing caw like a bird being torn apart by wolves. Klim turned onto his back, his blanket fell beside his emaciated body, his blind eyes opened to the sun, and then he died. The dog gulped water, unaware, then returned to its master, sniffing and licking him with growing panic. Then it sat by his side and began to howl, drawing the attention of the villagers. Jude could not stand by and watch them do what he feared they would do: slaughter the dog and eat it. He could see it in the way the people turned their heads, bloodthirsty. And what about Klim? Would they eat him, too? Before Jude could think, he barreled through the water, determined to get to the blind man before the villagers did. Others were running from their tents and the shadows of the trees on the other side of the lake, hearing the howling dog. Jude arrived first. The dog started barking and nipped at Jude's wet leather shoes. He picked up the dead man and hoisted him over his shoulder—half the weight of Jacob, he thought—and plodded away as fast as he could back through the woods. He heard a yelp as the villagers got hold of the dog.

. . .

'I was thinking today we could play a little game,' Villiam said, already bored and tired of Marek's story. Marek had barely gotten through the preamble: 'Once upon a time, there was a man whose name was Villiam, and he was the greatest man in the land, and among his servants was a fine girl named Lispeth, and one day Villiam was sitting eating grapes, and his son Marek came in . . . ' It was very dull.

'Never mind the story, Marek. Let's have a battle,' Villiam said. 'Who can eat the most sausages while Lispeth holds her breath?'

'All right.'

'Clod?' Villiam called for his man. 'Get us some sausages. Enough to feed a hundred people.'

'Yes, my lord.'

'In the meantime, Lispeth, sing us a song.'

Lispeth curtsied and sang while Marek and Villiam waited for the sausage. She sang very quietly, so that Marek had to strain to hear the words. Villiam picked at his cuticles, only vaguely aware of the song, just enough so that he would not have to endure the silence as he waited for his food.

> *To sing I must, of that I would rather not*
> *so bitter I am toward he who stole my love*
> *for I loved him more than anyone;*

*my kindness and courtesy make no impression on him*
*nor my beauty, my virtue or intelligence;*
*so I am deceived and betrayed,*
*as I should be if I were ugly . . .*
*One thing consoles me: I never wronged him,*
*And if love could bring him back*
*It would, so much I have to give.*
*I am glad that my love is greater than your vanity.*

'Sing it again,' Villiam said, yawning. 'A little louder this time. Clod! Hurry up with those sausages!'

Marek wished he could be more like Villiam, dumb and numb to other people's sorrow.

Lapvonians had not taken kindly to Klim while he'd been alive. They thought he was a jinx. He had lived alone in a hovel in the corner of the village and came out once in a while to pick through the trash on the road for scraps of food. He had looked sickly even before the famine. His dead hands flapped like fish against Jude's back as he plodded through the woods.

Jude knew that his hunger had driven him to madness, otherwise he would never have picked the blind man up in the first place. He would have just shouted at the villagers to respect the dead. But his reasoning had left him. Klim's body felt like an effigy, something that could be put down and looked at, a sculpture of a man, like Jesus on the Cross. Maybe Jude could take Klim as his own personal Jesus. Jude had never been inside the church in Lapvona. He had only smelled the burning myrrh on the rare Sunday morning he passed by during Mass. He never wanted to join, never felt that he would be welcome there. Ina had said that there was a cross on the wall with a wooden Jesus nailed to it.

Without intending to, Jude now found himself on his way through the trees toward her cabin. But now the shadows under the summer sun were not of swaying, lush branches but the stark, still stalks of dying cottonwoods. There were no grapes hanging from the vines that trellised across the boughs, not even a shriveled raisin. The dirt clouded up like smoke with each step through the woods. The last time Jude had visited Ina was shortly after Marek's departure. Ina had understood what had happened, of course, and was sorry for Jude that he would have to live without his boy. But there was something strange in the way she had pulled her bosom out from her dress that day, something resentful about it. And although she had long since ceased her production of milk, there was a miserliness with which she held her nipple out for Jude to suck, as though she were doing it begrudgingly, sacrificially. Jude had held it against her. Now she owed him some actual generosity—a sympathetic ear, a nipple, and a place to rest. Maybe Ina would even have something for Jude to eat. It didn't occur to Jude that the old woman might be struggling in the drought like everybody else. She had always seemed without needs. He had never watched her eat food, although each time he'd come he'd brought her a basket of vegetables and a bucket of lamb's milk, unless the babes were still nursing. He had no idea how old Ina might be. Maybe a hundred years old, he would guess.

He found a bit of shade where Klim's body could lie while he went in to see her. He knocked on her cabin door and pushed it open, expecting to see the old woman as she usually was, squatting on the floor examining herbs or mushrooms or picking mites out of a tiny grouse. But now Jude gasped at the sight of her as he looked inside. Ina was still alive but had been reduced to a crumpling of skin and bones in the corner of her bed. Her body had flattened, deflated. Only her skull had any volume. Her face hung on it like an old rag from a nail. Her blind eyes opened, spreading the wrinkles. Her mouth spoke.

'I have nothing for you, Jude,' she said.

Jude was quiet, stunned.

'But if you would bring me something to eat, I might spare a suck, if you can find a nipple.'

Jude stepped into the dark of her cabin and looked around. Every vessel, usually filled with leaves and herbs and dried flowers, was empty. Even the ashes in the hearth had been swept out. There were teeth marks on the wooden bedframe. Tiny fragments of bones were littered on the floor—the bones of birds, Jude thought. Had she eaten the sacred animals who spoke to her? Jude overturned a bucket, shook out the dead spiders, collected them into his thin palm, and approached the bed.

'Here, Ina,' he said and fed the little spiders into her mouth—a cavern of white, bloodless flesh—one by one. She chewed. Jude sat and listened to the bones of her jaw creak, her teeth grind the stale legs of the insects, her dry tongue scrape the roof of her mouth.

'Are you better now, Ina?' he asked after she had swallowed and gagged and coughed, her head rolling back and forth on the bed, which was emptied of hay. It was a stupid question.

'Bring the blind boy and cook him.'

'You're crazy, Ina. I saved him,' Jude said.

'He's dead,' Ina said to him. 'And you're dying. I can smell it on you.'

'I won't eat a man, no,' Jude said.

'Then cook him for me. I'm hungry.' She was serious. 'And then I can nurse you, I'm sure.'

'What about heaven, Ina? Don't you want to go?'

'It doesn't matter,' she said. 'I won't know anyone.'

Jude paced, the mud and water in his stomach sloshing. He didn't want to have to cook the man. He had taken the body for just that reason—to save Klim from being eaten.

'There isn't much meat on him,' he said lamely, trying to deter her.

'Go get him,' Ina said, her head rolling like a fallen apple on the ground. 'I'll eat him raw, I'm so hungry. Do it. Now.'

Lispeth had failed to hold her breath for very long. The huge gasps of air made her lightheaded, and she fainted a bit, then revived and held her breath again. Villiam had beaten Marek in the eating contest, of course. The score was 71 to 30, and Villiam could have kept going had Marek not forfeited the game by vomiting into his bucket.

'Delicious,' Villiam pronounced. 'We should do that more often. Clod?' he called. 'I think I'll take a nap. Carry me up the stairs.'

Clod was very tall and strong, his thick hair, beard, eyebrows, and eyelashes so pale blond, they were nearly white. He towered over Villiam naturally, but was so attuned to his master's need to feel respected that he bent from the waist like an old man and bowed his head as he approached him at the dining table. He hoisted the frail lord gently from his chair and moved smoothly out of the room.

'What will you do with the leftover sausages?' Marek asked Lispeth, who was now carting away the bucket of vomit.

'We will feed them to the chickens.'

'Why won't you eat them?'

'It is against our God,' she said, 'to eat the flesh of His creatures.'

Marek gasped at this bit of purity. He had forgotten purity. It had been brushed aside and replaced with a desire to please. He was immediately embarrassed.

'It is against my God, too,' he said halfheartedly.

Lispeth said nothing. Marek took a last glance at the shiny, brown muck of regurgitated meat in the bucket as she took it away, and then he burped and got sweaty and hot with shame.

Jenevere and Petra, the other female servants, came in to clean the rest of the mess. Marek watched in a daze, his mind strangely clear, but perhaps not altogether lucid. He thought he saw something hidden beneath the cover of calm in the servants' faces. Underneath the placid kindness, he saw, was disgust and pity. The flatness and ease with which they performed their services were not in deference, but in charity. They were not doting servants to Villiam, they were slaves in their hearts to God. And they were judgmental observers. Who could blame them for having judgment? Marek was jealous of their power. He remembered the pride that he used to feel as Jude's son, like a noble witness to that precarious soul that couldn't help itself but sin. And the more abuse he took from his father, the better he was in God's eyes. He had always known that virtue was determined in relation to others. He was on the losing end now. Each time Lispeth slopped his vomit out to the chickens, God was watching and sent her another blessing, taking a blessing away from Marek in turn.

Marek got up, wiped his tongue with a napkin and rushed through the manor to the large doors. 'Let me out,' he said to Pieter, who did not hesitate to unlock the doors and lower the drawbridge. Marek winced, moving from the dark cool of the stone manor to the bright sun. The air was hot and teeming with bugs from the water in the moat. The level was higher since he'd arrived that spring. How different life had been that day. And how tricked he felt now that the servants were so secretively cruel and pious. He could feel their satisfaction, like a rash on his skin. The worse he behaved, the more God loved them.

The land around the manor was green and aflutter with butterflies and bees humming around the flowers. The stableboys
were bent over in the garden, filling baskets with vegetables.
Luka was feeding carrots and apples to a steed by a trough of
gleaming water. The cows grazed the dark, rich grass. Bunny
rabbits slept on their backs under the shade of a tall pear tree. All
was well, it seemed, though it was hot. Marek followed a path up
the hill to gain a view of Jude's pasture. The last time he'd seen
the pasture was the day he had climbed the hill to the manor
with Jude carrying Jacob on his back. Marek had grown stronger
since then. His breathing was easier now as he climbed, his feet
in their supple leather slippers digging into the hot wet soil. At
the top of the hill was a grove of peach trees. A ripe peach fell at
his feet, and he stooped down to pick it up—it was pink and
yellow, red streaks nearly splitting it open. The fragrance made
him swoon. He bit into it, and despite his previous nausea from
the sausages, the sweetness sent him into a state of heady relief.
He leaned against the peach tree and sucked the fruit, the juice
dripping down the heel of his hand onto the lap of his fine satin
pants. No matter, he thought. Lispeth would bathe him and
clean his clothes. Every day there was a new set of pants and
shirt, specially tailored to fit his own strange body. So quickly had
he forgotten his shame and unhappiness. Sugar was the cure. He
sucked the juice as though it were milk from a lamb's teat.

The sky was cloudless as he stood and walked to the ridge of
the hill and looked down. At first it was all a haze in the heat,
the air vibrating and blurring. And then a breeze hit him like a

slap in the face, and his vision cleared for a moment. Lapvona came into focus. It was all gray. The trees were bare. The roads were nearly white with arid dirt. He saw no water in the streams, only pale rocks. There were no animals being herded through the lands. He could see Jude's pasture, a graveyard of dry dirt, no lambs, no movement. He looked down at the peach in his fist. A worm squirmed out of the flesh, a small pink thing that seemed to rear its head toward Marek, then burrowed back into the flesh of the peach, drunk on the sugar of its home. Marek was horrified. He threw the peach over the ridge and watched it roll along the soft dirt. Crows quickly descended on it.

Marek felt himself grow faint. He turned and vomited the sweet peach and saw another worm crawling through the chewed flesh at his feet. He vomited again, the last of the sausages. It burned his throat and he gagged, heaving more and more. A voice from below spoke to him.

'Shall I carry you home?'

It was Lispeth. She had followed him up the hill.

'No, Lispeth. You shouldn't do anything for me anymore.'

He caught his breath and started back down the hill to the manor. Lispeth followed.


Jude had not eaten Klim yet. He had, however, chopped dead trees outside Ina's cabin and built a fire in her hearth, then stood, sweating and licking the sweat off his arms from thirst as he waited for Ina to change her mind. He couldn't bear to look at her, her body so mangled in its emaciation. Her head tilted blindly toward the floor. She raised her eyebrows as though she could see a fine meal spread before her. She smiled and sniffed at the sooted air. 'Take off his clothes and burn them in the fire. Then chop him into pieces.' Jude recognized her madness. It was the same insanity that he'd seen in Agata while she was in labor with Marek, a female power, evil, something he would never understand.

He should let her die, he thought. The old woman had lived too long already, prolonged by the tricks she played with nature. Every time she'd felt the slightest pang of illness, she'd gone out-side and the birds had dropped herbs, shat seeds, sang her songs to cure her. She's been spoiled enough, so let her die, he thought. She's got no milk left anyway. All women were villains, users, he told himself, remembering the bloody baby in his arms and his rage at Agata, that cunt, that selfish child, what he wouldn't give to have seen her die on the floor for real. Take the baby with you to hell, he would have said. And Ina had tried to help her. She was like all women: only concerned with their own comfort. He could be strong if he just kept his anger close. He had almost convinced himself to walk away. But then Ina started to gag and cough. It was too pitiful. He felt too sorry. Comfortable or not, the poor woman had nursed him. After his parents drowned, she took him in and healed him, fed him. She taught him how to gain strength from within himself. She gave him his life. God knew that. So Jude surrendered. Klim was already dead, he reasoned. Wouldn't God favor a sacrifice to save the life of an old woman? Feed the blind to the blind. It had a certain logic to it.

Jude went back out into the woods, cooler in that heat than by the fire in Ina's cabin. Smoke puffed out the chimney and hung in the air like dark clouds, the wind so slow, a cruel joke. He sat by Klim's body and prayed and cried for himself and licked his tears from his palms and thought of Marek, the bastard who had brought on the drought, he was sure of it. This anger provided him with courage. He gently lifted the dead man's legs and twisted the torso so that the body lay on its side. Now, squinting through his tears, he pulled the left arm out, lifted the ax, and brought it down on the wrist. It broke at the joint, and the dry, loose skin split, but not all the way. Jude had to hold the ax by the blade to cut the tendon and the rest of the skin clear through. He didn't want to touch the hand. It didn't bleed, but the hand seemed suddenly more particular to Klim now that it was separated from his arm, as though it had come back to life and could sense its detachment from Klim's body. Jude blamed Marek for having forced him into such depravity. This was how he could weather the horror: blame Marek. He picked up Klim's hand by the pinky, carried it inside and threw it on the fire. Jude listened to the skin hiss and cook.

'Don't leave it too long or it won't taste good.'

Ina's mouth seemed to chew the air, her dry tongue reaching to her lips as though she were tasting something already. She started gagging again. Her eyes—which were green and young looking, as though she'd plucked them from a little girl—glistened in the light from the fire. Jude reached into the flames and drew out Klim's hand with a stick and set it on the bed next to Ina's crumpled body.

'Aaaah,' she said.

'It's too hot, Ina.'

'I don't care about that,' she said. 'Put the thumb in.' She opened her mouth wide.

Jude put Klim's thumb in her mouth. Ina sucked it and chewed it. Jude watched. After a moment, she seemed to gain strength and could lift her arms—like broken twigs. She pulled Klim's hand away, ripping off the flesh of the thumb with her teeth. She chewed the flesh and swallowed and sighed. Then she chewed the flesh of his palm.

'I'm happy you feel better, Ina,' Jude said, 'but I have to go now.'

'Oh no,' Ina said, now sucking the meat voraciously. Her body was coming back to life. 'I'll need more right away.'

How peaceful the boy was now, lying asleep with no shame, naked on his soft mattress that Lispeth stuffed and restuffed and batted every day, goose feathers fluttering up into the room and into her mouth and up her nose. She had wiped his arse with a rag wetted in a bit of warm milk before putting him to bed.

There was shit in the chamber pot for her to cover with a cloth and carry downstairs. Of course Lispeth had no appetite for the food the family ate at the manor. The gardener used the shit to fertilize the food, to grow the hay to feed the animals. Villiam, Dibra, and Marek ate their own shit at every meal. And so did the priest. And maybe he was eating Villiam's shit directly out of his arse, she wondered. Who knew what the two men did at night alone? They certainly weren't praying. She imagined Villiam's bed: blood smeared, shit smeared, semen shot on the canopy. Clod would never tell.

Lispeth watched Marek's face as he slept, so spoiled and dumb, his top lip curling up and his bottom jaw hanging open, an oaf. He disgusted her. Poor Jacob, she thought. Even smashed and bloodied and dead, he was more attractive than Marek was alive. She didn't know where Jude had buried him. That poor man, she thought. Everyone down in Lapvona, she knew, was doomed.

Later, in the middle of the night, Marek awoke nude and tangled in the bedsheet. Lispeth was asleep in her chair. She hadn't pulled the curtains closed or prepared his bedside mead, which he always drank if he woke in the dark. He sat up and looked around the room, remembering the events of the previous day. He was tired, but hungry.

In the moonlight, he got up and walked naked to the window, lit a candle, and ventured out down the hall, wrapped in his sheet. Through the darkness he heard voices downstairs, the thumping of feet across the great room, and the front door creaking open. A rush of hot night air whooshed in and up the stairs. Marek followed it. Perhaps this was a dream, he thought. But his dreams were usually more dreamy. It struck him now that his dreams were never quite right. They seemed to occur in a space without time, in death, he thought. He heard a night bird sing its aeolian melody. That was the problem, he realized. He did not dream of birds. Without birds, there was no time. He moved carefully down the stairs, his bare feet chilled on the stones. The night bird cuckooed. A jubilant voice outside mimicked it. 'Cuckoo! Cuckoo!' The front door had been left ajar, the guard was gone. Marek pushed it open and followed the voices across the drawbridge into the dark.

It was less hot now, but still hot enough to break a sweat moving slowly up the slope of the hill. The voices were singing a song now, and he knew it was Villiam's singing—the nasal twang of his voice was unmistakable. He sounded drunk, and so did the other man with him. It wasn't Clod, whose voice had a northern depth.

'Goddamnit!' the other voice cried suddenly. 'I stepped on a thorn.' It was Father Barnabas.

'Don't be a baby,' Villiam crooned. 'Come on. Let's go.'

Marek followed the blue light of the moon up the path the two men had traversed to the reservoir, which he'd never seen before. He crouched behind a rosebush and watched them disrobe and turn, naked, toward the water.

'Ready?' the priest asked. Villiam grunted. And then they ran in tandem and jumped into the water. Marek had never been allowed to jump into the lake down in Lapvona. Jude forbade it. 'You'd drown, no question.' But Villiam and Father Barnabas floated and dunked and came up and splashed at one another like little children. They laughed and swam. Marek smiled for a moment, cheered by their glee. Then he listened to them talking.

'Father, what do you say when the people ask why it is so hot this summer?'

'Oh, I say it's because the Devil got out of hell and is on the loose, hungry for innocent souls. His fire has dried up the land. God has shut the gates of heaven to keep the Devil out.' Of course, he told no one that Villiam was hoarding water in a reservoir up there. It was perfect water, clean and pure and cold as ice as it trickled down from the far mountains in underground streams.

'Isn't that a good story,' Villiam said, splashing a bit feebly. 'You really are a good priest.'

In a ray of moonlight, Marek spotted Father Barnabas's black robe hanging from the branch of a tree. Under it were his stockings, shoes, and hat.

By nightfall, all that remained of Klim was his head, neck, and torso. Jude had first eaten the man's narrow bicep, his first ever taste of meat, and it had ignited in him the hunger and the strength to go back out and chop the man's leg from the pubis and roast it, foot and all, on the fire, snapping at Ina to shut up, to keep quiet. If she said the wrong thing, he knew, the nightmare would end and he would wake up starving. Jude could feel his own muscles relax after months of gnawing and tightening. Even his teeth, which had been aching, felt harder. His vision was clear despite the darkness of night—oddly, eating the blind man's body had improved Jude's eyesight. Had Ina's vision been restored? He hadn't been paying attention. As soon as he'd started eating, he'd turned into a wordless animal, grunting and squatting before the fire, eating the stump of Klim's leg, gnashing his teeth at the small muscle, as the rest of the leg still cooked. Ina had her fill, regained her ability to move and stand and walk, then fluttered in the shadows behind him, dancing with her broom. He didn't want to think of her—he wasn't sure he could trust her. Something felt strange now that she had tricked him into eating human flesh. She seemed anxious to get rid of him once she was up and about. She swept up the bird bones and pretended to trip over Jude, who was licking his fingers. He had blood on his hands, sticky and brown.

'You should go home,' she said.

'But I'm still hungry,' he said. 'How about some milk?'

'Don't be greedy,' Ina said. 'Come back next time.'

'What does that mean?' Jude asked.

'It means goodnight.'

Jude got up and went out, lugging the rest of Klim over his shoulder.

. . .

The priest's clothes smelled of burning resin and sweat, and the blackness of the garments made Marek feel he was invisible in the dark. He had never worn black before and he did enjoy the sensation of walking unseen. He spotted a plum tree on the path down the mountain and stopped to fill the priest's pockets so that he would have a bit of sweetness to chew if he got hungry. It had been so long since he had come this way, and then only once, uphill with Jude and the dead boy. On the way down, the slope of the mountain looked much gentler, a gradual descent into the dark sway of heat. It was odd how the air was thicker the lower he went, and the heat in these flatter reaches at the bottom was like a wall he broke through with every step. He felt some-how that the priest's clothing protected him, that the man's sweat had cooled the clothes. He might be in a dream, he thought, but the priest's shoes were too big. That small trouble kept him rooted. The guards on the road tipped their hats as he passed.

Marek had had fantasies of visiting Jude many times. They were not joyful reunions, but waking dreams of going down to beg his forgiveness. Jude rejected Marek even in his brightest reveries, ignored him as he toiled in the field with the babes while Marek ran around trying to get his attention. 'Look at me, Father!' he would scream. But Jude was always blind and deaf, his head ever tilted at the ground where the lambs grazed. 'Please!' Desperate, Marek would hit himself in the head with rocks. In one particular fantasy, he ran to his father and used his own fingernails to slice at his wrist, held the blood to drip onto Jude's shoes. Jude simply kicked some mud onto his shoes and kept going, his staff digging into the ground rhythmically and steadily while Marek bled to death in his shadow. Wouldn't it be nice to bring his father some plums now, to show him that his sacrifice had not been for nothing?

When Marek reached the bottom of the mountain and looked out at the dark pasture, he saw his old home and smelled the stench of death floating on the slow breeze as he walked toward it. The ground was not feathered in soft grass as it had been that spring, but was stiff with dry dirt, and he stumbled over mounds of broken ground. He knew the stench of death from the attacks by the bandits. The spilt blood of the slain villagers last Easter had carried a bit of carrion stink, but their stink was human and sweeter than what Marek smelled now. He kicked at the dirt as he walked and exposed the desiccated head of a babe. The stink was coming up from the ground, the air gamey, as though the hot dirt had cooked the little lambs in their graves.

Maybe now that his babes had perished, Jude would appreciate his son's return and give him a warm embrace. 'I'm so happy to see you.' But when Marek kicked open the door of the cottage, holding the priest's sleeve against his mouth to keep the flies out, he found it empty. He shut himself inside. It was smaller than he had remembered it, and emptier still. Marek sat on the bare bed and pulled a plum from the priest's pocket and ate as his eyes adjusted to being home in the dark. The sweet fruit made him feel sad and hazy. He lay down, smelling the stench of his father and missing him. He would wait there, he thought, until Jude returned.

Agata had escaped from the abbey two nights ago. The nuns had no food left to feed her; she was free to fend for herself. So she began to creep away, sleeping first in the abbey courtyard, then against the abbey walls in the dead grapevines, and then outside the walls. She didn't want to go with the other nuns down to the lake. They'd been cruel to her since she had appeared thirteen years ago, young and bleeding at their doorstep. They made her do the worst of the work at the abbey—cleaning the latrines, slaughtering the animals, sleeping with the dogs at night. God had not appeared to her in all that time. So she preferred to stay faithless rather than hold on to a fantasy. It was easier to live like that. She had lost everything. Her home. Her innocence. Her freedom. Her bandit family. Her ability to speak. She was empty. 'I am an object in the room,' she had told herself. 'That is all that I am.' This belief spared her the agony of her own intelligence while she was a slave to the nuns.

She wasn't sure where she would go, or whether she could survive the journey. She was already too hungry and thirsty to make sense of her thoughts. When she looked up and saw the distant flames of the guards' torches around the manor, she resigned herself. She would go up there. There was nowhere else to go anyway. It was stupid to take the shortcut through Jude's pasture, but it was an honest mistake. The scorched land didn't resemble the lush land she had remembered, not at all. Even the sound of the ground beneath her feet was different.

By the time Jude reached the pasture, his hunger was renewed. He could roast Klim's head, he thought. He could taste the blind eyes and eat the brains. That would keep him full enough, and then he could sleep through the worst of the heat. But he'd get thirsty. Perhaps he could skin Klim and sew the skin into a pouch and use it to carry water home from the lake tomorrow. He'd need a sharp blade to do such work, and good light. At home, he had an ax and a few dull knives. He would need to find a good rock to sharpen the blades when the sun came up. He could find one. God would help him. Maybe the chipped edge of Agata's gravestone would work, he thought.

Jude found his ax in the dry dirt in the pasture, past the graves of his babes. It had been only weeks since he'd buried them. Had they been guarding him from his own depravity all along? He put Klim down and used the ax to chop off his head. He could burn the broken chair in the hearth and roast Klim's head and eat it, sleep, then sharpen the knives to skin his torso in the morning. Yes. He picked up the head and carried it under his arm. The torso he heaved up and carried across his shoulders.

Jude felt a sense of accomplishment as he reached the door of his cottage. The flies swarmed him and the body, but he didn't mind. He sidled inside in the dark, shut the door, then let Klim's torso fall to the floor.

Once his eyes had adjusted to the dark, Jude saw not Marek on the bed, but a figure in a black robe and stiff collar. He froze, panicked. Word from the villagers at the lake must have reached Father Barnabas somehow, he thought, and the priest had come to wait for Jude here at home to punish him for his cannibalism. Would he be put in the stocks and tortured? Would they burn him at the stake, or hang him? In the dark, the priest rolled away, his back turned. Jude held his breath and silently tiptoed back out the door, still holding Klim's head under his arm.

A tremble of the ground woke Marek in the corner of the room. For a moment, he forgot that he had ever left his father's home. How many times had he slept there? How many times had a noise or vibration roused him while it was still and dark in the room? His father always got up early. Marek turned and felt the cool black linen against his body. These weren't his clothes. The stiff collar pressed against his throat. Still, he was not sure what was real. He opened his eyes and let them adjust from dream to darkness.

'Papa?' he said. He must have awoken this way a hundred times since Jude had left him at Villiam's, a soft moment of the mind. Lispeth always answered, 'No.' But now nobody answered, and the hard bed beneath his body reminded him of where he was again. He was home. 'Papa?' he said again.

Marek pushed himself up, thirsty and confused. He could have sworn he'd felt Jude in the room. The door was slightly ajar and the flies were crowding in. He could feel the bed calling back to him to lie down, to stay still in the heat. Marek forced himself to get up anyway. Nothing moved but the flies. Marek stumbled toward the swarm, adjusting his eyes to the moonlight through the open door. He saw Klim's torso, a headless, armless, legless thing made of collapsed ribs and a spine whose bones were exposed at the bottom, like a little tail sticking out from the flesh. Taking this flesh for his father's, Marek fell upon it. How had he not seen it before? Had he been so blind in the dark when he'd come? What monster had cut his father down to this? He remembered his promise to Jude. 'I'll feel guilty when you die,' and so he did. His guilt was a lonely horror, desperate but dumb. He got up and backed away from the severed torso and went out. In the pasture, everything was still, the moonlight thin and low. Had he not looked up at the sky to beg God for guidance, he would have seen Jude scurrying into the woods on the far side of the pasture, running from guilt of his own.

When Jude was deep between the trees, he stopped to listen for anything above the distant buzzing of the flies, but heard nothing. No wind, no birds. He half expected that a hand would descend from the sky to grip his shoulder and yank him down into a booby-trap grave. He turned to look behind him, above. It was only when he caught his breath that he realized he still held Klim's head in his hands. The man's jaw hung open, his tongue thin and gray between sparse brown teeth. His nose was smashed and broken. Jude had not been careful in his butchery, grappling with the body, letting the head hit and drag on the hard ground. Under the moonlight through the empty branches, Jude saw Klim's eyelashes flutter under his own breath. He startled and screamed, silently—like in a dream—and threw the head into the undergrowth and ran further away, deeper into the woods.

Was this a dream? If so, when had it begun? Had he actually left his cottage that morning, or was he still there, trapped in the maze of blood? Or had he fallen asleep by the lake? Or had he died and woken up in hell? White orbs began to appear in his vision as he ran, like fireflies, but cold, white. Sprites or ghosts, he didn't know. They moved steadily toward him, widening as they got closer. 'They will absorb me,' Jude thought. 'This is what death looks like. White lights coming for you through the trees.' He closed his eyes as he ran away from them, but the lights were still there. They were inside his eyes. He ran faster and repented in each breath—'God, forgive me.' And he felt something push him from behind, like an icy hand at the small of his back. The coolness was delicious, a seduction. Perhaps it was just the wet of his shirt smacking his skin, but it was enough to cause him to run even faster. He ran until he could no longer breathe. The lights followed him.

Finally, he stumbled and fell and found himself facedown in a bed of wildflowers. He lifted his face into the moonlight and the miraculous scent of wild basil and crocus. Had he arrived? Was he through to heaven? Was this where the lights had been chasing him? How else to explain such flowers growing in the dust? He rolled over and looked up at the sky, a closed circle of black night surrounded by bare trees. The white lights retreated upward into the stars.

Then, as in a dream, he began to feel that he was not alone. Narcissi glowed in the moonlight like lit candles illuminating a female figure draped in black, her long skirt trailing over the flowers up ahead. Jude felt no fear or surprise. It was as though fate had brought him into this miracle. 'Agata?' he called. The girl's head turned.

Even after all his ire, his spite, his disgust, his struggle, the movement of her head toward him filled his heart with longing. Here was his girl: thirteen years older and dressed like a maiden of death, all in black, like the priest; her face was thinner than he'd remembered, but it was her. Her green eyes were sunken and hollow under her black hood but they were the same. They gleamed at him in the moonlight like a wolf's as they had so many years ago when he'd found her wandering the woods, a child. He had to have her. He rose and ran. She dropped the small satchel she carried, picked up her skirt, and ran through the flowers away from him. But Jude caught up to her easily. 'Agata!' he called again. From the pulse of her steps, Jude knew she had recognized his voice. He was dreaming, he was sure. And perhaps this assurance removed any hesitation he might have had to run at the girl and push her down so that she fell straight back and hit the ground. She struggled under her robes to get back up, but Jude pounced on her, his face meeting hers immediately, his spit shaking on her as he spoke, his head vibrating as though it, too, would separate from his body. 'Did you bring this on? This unholy terror?' he asked her. She said nothing as usual, simply turned her head away and closed her eyes. If it was Jude's dream, he could have his way, however he'd like. He felt the sweat of nausea creep up from his loins to his throat, and as he straddled the dark girl, he held her down by the throat with one hand and lifted her skirt with his other. She wore many garments, all dark and heavy. Her innermost garment was black and thick with sweat. Jude didn't wonder what it all meant. Already his penis was hard and throbbing. He held her shoulders down now and used his own knees to force hers to spread. She submitted easily, her head ever turned away, but her eyes open. Jude clumsily poked at the red froth of hair on her pubis, then stabbed at the lips to her sheath, which was clenched tight like a fist. He let himself lie on her body—she was larger, softer than she'd been as a child—and he sank himself inside her, into the small darkness. He'd last known her sheath tortured and bleeding, straining to birth a distorted skull. He pulled out, studying her face in the moonlight for any indication of suffering or pleasure. He went back in, shuddered at the pressure of her tight hole, a touch he had longed for, for so long. Would he die now? She gave a little puff of air through her nose, like something was getting snuffed out. He pressed his chest against hers and kept his hands on her shoulders so she couldn't move. He would have her in his dream that last time, mad in the fever of his cannibalism, near death, he thought, finally. And thank God she had appeared in his moment of madness. He fucked her until he collapsed, ejecting what felt like cold poison into her womb. He felt it go, and he pulled out and rolled off, spent.

Marek had not wept for long over the severed corpse that he believed was Jude's. He wasn't smart enough to understand the horror of this death beyond its immediate gruesomeness and the selfish sadness he felt in losing a father who had not loved him sufficiently. It did not occur to Marek that Villiam was to blame for the devastation of the land. It did not occur to him that Villiam had forced the village to suffer this drought, stealing what was rightfully owned by nature for his own excess and pleasure. The vision of Villiam and the priest swimming in the pool had inspired only jealousy. Marek would have liked to have been invited to swim, too. Now his father's death confirmed his sorry lot in life. He didn't even wonder where the rest of his father's remains had gone. 'I'm really an orphan,' Marek thought. This was his great revelation. And, 'My father will not know that I've brought him these plums.' If Klim's body hadn't been so badly degraded by starvation, Marek may have noticed that it was not his father's torso. But such was death—it had nothing to say. The boy saw what he expected to see.

Determined to spare his father the humiliation of rot and maggots, and to deliver him to heaven, Marek hoisted the torso onto his back and began to walk, stooped over in a way that befitted his misshapenness, to the only place he felt was sacred: his mother's grave. If he could give his father anything now, it was the dignity of a proper burial. He found a shovel in the yard and dragged it along with him. It had been months since he'd allowed himself to ponder the afterlife. There was too much risk of shame and regret in the subject. Poor Jacob. Poor Jude. Would his father be whole again in heaven? Surely God could restore his limbs and head, feed him, give him water and a comfortable place to live, and reunite him with Agata. Marek rested on that certainty.

He was tired and hot under the moonlight when he reached the stone that marked Agata's grave. He laid the torso down gently on the dry ground and began to dig.

After his dream of Agata vanished, the smell of Klim's dead body on Jude's hands separated from the heady fragrance of flowers, and he realized that he was lying in dry dirt, not a single flower about. His pants were down. What a dream, he thought: Agata dressed like a nun, trudging across the clearing. Her small body had squirmed and bucked under him, just as it did when she had lived with him so long ago. He shook the dream away and felt sick. He turned his head and his body pulsed, his throat and guts cramping as he regurgitated Klim's pinky toe, small and roasted, its little nail sticking out. If he died there in the dirt, all the better. 'Let the birds come and pick my flesh apart. Let them start now,' he thought, 'while I wait to die.' Whether it was real or not, he didn't care. He felt it was real enough. 'Come and take me,' he said to God.

But God wasn't listening. God didn't care about Jude. God was busy lifting the sun for another day.

And so the sun rose on Lapvona.

Marek was nearly done digging. He had measured the length of the torso—it seemed smaller than he remembered Jude, but this was only a piece of him, after all. Jude, herding with his staff, had cast such a long shadow at noon across the pasture. Marek recalled how his father lilted through the heat last summer. 'It will break soon,' he had said. His sweaty throat, the tight cords in his neck and shoulders, all the sores and scars from self-flagellation, Marek remembered all of it. This torso here was so dirty, he could only see the outline of the protruding rib cage, the shocking white of bone at the spine and neck, the haggard entrails. The sun was already burning hot on the horizon.

Marek had dug the hole just where Agata lay, below the chipped rock. He prayed, pushed by the mania of his effort, that he would not find his mother's bones. If God were good, He would have taken her, he thought, recounting what Jude had said. 'The Devil leaves you to rot, but God takes you, flesh and bone.' Ought he still believe that? Would Jude's torso disappear, too, once it was buried? Could Marek drop it into the hole, cover it up, say a prayer, and then dig it back up to see if God had saved him? Of course he could, though he was already tired, and digging up corpses was a sacrilege. Probably. He had heard tales from Ina of bandits unearthing the dead to steal their garments and whatever relics were buried with them. But no bandits would do such a thing in Lapvona: it was known only for its fruits and wheat and honey. All the wealth was what could grow in its dirt, not in what was buried in it.

He had cleared several feet of packed dirt, then pushed the shovel down hard, and the dirt below crumbled easily. The blade of the shovel hit the roots of the tree. He could dig no further. Agata's bones weren't there. 'Thank you, thank you,' Marek whispered. He remembered the song Ina sang while she nursed him sometimes. 'I'll be dead and you'll be dead,' a cheery song meant to soothe Marek into the lull of a certain infinity. He sang the song in his head now and kicked the torso into the hole. Now his parents were together, 'thanks to me,' he told himself. They'll be happy. It was remarkable how easy it was to fill the hole. He just pushed the dirt in with his shoe. After hours of digging, it was laughably simple. And so was death. A simple transit from Lapvona to heaven. He knelt on the grave and kissed the dirt. When he lifted his head, his thirst and exhaustion suddenly hit him and nearly blew him over, like a gale before a storm. He got to his feet and let the feeling take him away. He supposed this was God's wind, the rush of air sucking his father's soul from its dead flesh, up and away. He ran, light on his feet, up the hill now lit golden and red with the dawn, back home to the manor.

. . .

Lispeth was asleep in Marek's bed. She had spent hours in the chair, dozing, waiting for Marek to return, wishing he wouldn't, hoping he would fall prey to the ghouls of Lapvona, and then, in the haze of her exhaustion, she had crawled onto the bed. She slept deeply and dreamt about Jacob. She dreamt of him whenever she could. Most often her dreams were relived experiences of the past: sitting by Jacob's bed, watching him sleep. His face was not something she had studied, but something that acted upon her. Like wine, it took hold of her mind and drew it into a golden light, the dawn of heaven, and her body tingled and relaxed. She felt more alive in these dreams, but woke up wishing that she, too, were dead.

This night, she dreamt of Jacob walking naked across the drawbridge in the moonlight. He walked toward her, continually moving forward under the moonlight, but ever retreating at the same time, as though the bridge were pulling him back at the same pace that he walked. She could see his shoulders in the dream, the gleam of sweat on his chest, his face angling back and forth and side to side with each step, as though he were looking out for something. Lispeth thought, 'Why don't I go to him? Why didn't I ever go to him?' and she tried to step from under the great entrance of the manor onto the drawbridge, but something was blocking her. First it was a stone that she hit with her foot. Then it was a short wall that she had to climb over, but she couldn't. Finally she found herself enclosed in a small cell, and she cursed herself for having attempted to cross the bridge at all, because it was her desire to go to Jacob that had built the wall in the dream. She ought to have just waited. God would bring them together, if not in life, then in death at last. 'Maybe I should throw myself from the same cliff,' she'd said when Jacob died. But the servants had convinced her that she wouldn't make it to heaven if she did, that such a sacrifice was in service to herself, not God, and that she would turn into a ghost and live forever, invisibly. The thought of that frightened Lispeth. But she did chew tansy, as it grew rampant in the gardens to keep beetles from the potatoes, and everyone knew that in gross amounts, it could extinguish life, or at least hasten death. If her love for Jacob didn't die, she would. God would have pity on her eventually.

Marek now stood over her and watched her sleep. He had stripped off the priest's robes. He was thirsty.

'Lispeth, I'm thirsty,' he said.

Lispeth woke, her face screwed into a frown by the sad truth: Jacob was dead, and Marek was thirsty. She got up—not looking at the boy's naked body, not looking in his eyes, nor at his dirty hands, his grimy, sweaty face—and poured warm water from the jug into his cup and handed it to him. She didn't ask him where he'd gone or what he'd done. She didn't express any worry or concern, only rested on the chair and waited for his next request. It came as soon as he had gulped his water and stuck the cup out for more.

'I'm hungry,' he said.

'There is duck left from last night. I will fix you a plate,' Lispeth said, getting up. She looked grumpy. She, too, was hungry.

'No,' Marek said. 'I don't want meat. Bring me whatever you eat. A small portion.'

'I eat only cabbage,' Lispeth said flatly.

'Then bring me some cabbage.'

'The cabbage isn't cooked yet.'

'Then I will wait.'

Marek drank more water and lay on the bed, filling the space Lispeth had left. He felt the longing in her dream of Jacob like a residue: something was being pulled away but was yet right in front of him. It was his father, he thought. His whole life, Jude had been right there, but Marek could never reach him. Poor me, he thought. Nobody loves me. And he was right. He began to cry.

Let him cry, Lispeth thought. She believed then that he was crying over his tiny hunger and the agony and martyrdom of waiting for the cabbage to cook. What a baby. She didn't get up from her chair. She couldn't cook the cabbage now anyway. It would ignite a great anxiety among the servants to think that their stock of food was being crept upon. The morning light was dim through a crack in the curtains. Lispeth was tired.

'I went to Lapvona,' Marek said finally between his tears. 'And I found my father. He was dead.'

'Your father is in his chambers,' Lispeth said. 'He's had trouble sleeping lately. And so has the priest, I hear.'

'My real father,' Marek said. 'Jude.' And in saying his name aloud, Marek was suddenly a little more grown, as though the name carried with it the strength of the man himself. He felt his jaw strain, widen; his brow got heavy and drawn. It was all imagined, of course. He appeared just the same to Lispeth, who rolled her eyes at his emotion.

'And how did Jude die?' she asked.

Marek wouldn't tell Lispeth. He could see her hatred. It came through in her pallor and her limp hands. She didn't even care enough to fold them properly in her lap. She couldn't be bothered to lift her chin when Marek was speaking. In the company of Villiam and Dibra, or even among the other servants, Lispeth's posture was very different. She had a spark in her eye, a quickness to her step. Alone with Marek, she was slow and grouchy, kept her gaze blurry and evasive, as though it would make her sick to look directly at him. Her disgust showed in her narrowed eyes and flared nostrils. Lispeth and her cabbage, her sourness, and her judgment. How could Jacob have liked her so much? Marek wondered. She must have glittered under all his gold. But she would not glitter for Marek. He was too humble, he supposed.

'How did he die?' she asked again, her eyebrows raised. 'What did it look like?' Her only curiosity was in the morbid details, Marek thought. And it was true. Lispeth got some pleasure now in asking, knowing that it must sting, 'Did he die from an accident? Like Jacob?' She turned in her chair toward him. Marek's eyes were open, his face half sunk into the dent in the pillow that she herself had made. She felt him bristle. 'Did you throw a stone at him, too?' she asked and gripped the seat of her chair on both sides, fully expecting that Marek would lurch up and strike her. She braced for it.

But of course Marek did nothing. He simply turned away from her in the bed and cried some more. His self-pity was his best comfort.

'It's easy to kill people,' was all Lispeth said. That was as far as her sympathy could reach.

Since the drought, no entertainers had visited the manor. Invitations were declined or dismissed; nobody had the strength to be entertaining. But Villiam said he wanted the singer from Krisk to come, a renowned master of the lullaby. He sent Luka to deliver his fee, an outrageous sum to ensure he'd agree, and to bring the singer back. It was dangerous for Luka to embark on such a journey in the heat, but he had no choice. Nobody could say no to Villiam, especially Luka, as Villiam had known of and permitted the horseman's affair with Dibra for well over a decade. It was widely understood in the manor that Dibra and Luka were lovers, that he slept in her chambers a few nights a week, that nobody but Luka could calm her nerves or even approach her when she was in the throes of mourning early on after Jacob's death. For Luka to refuse Villiam's order would have been to admit to the adultery. The same went for any expression of grief over the death of Jacob. Had Luka expelled a single tear for the boy, anything more than Clod or the cook might give, a sentimental frown, Luka would have been openly confessing to his paternity and calling Villiam a cuckold.

In the months since Jacob's death, Dibra had rarely emerged from the still, airless room in her corner of the manor. Only Luka and her handmaid, Jenevere, went in to see her. Nobody wondered at Dibra's grief—she had lost her child. All that was left of him were the stuffed animals mounted on the wall. Only once did Dibra and Luka go into Jacob's room together, visiting the heather cock, the fallow deer, the wolf, the snipe. It was too sad. Those little noses and eyes. All the death. The world was so sweet and cruel. Shame. Luka and Dibra each felt that they had it worse than the other. Dibra had been Jacob's mother. He had come from inside her body. A part of her had died, the life smashed and dragged away, and nobody could acknowledge the incredible tragedy of that, her beautiful boy, her child who was the promise of some better life, who had said, 'When I'm old enough, I'll take you away from here.'

And Luka had been deprived of the son he had never been able to claim in the first place. For him, there was a doubling of loss. A few times, Jacob had snuck out to accompany Luka on his horse, and father and son would converse over the clobbering of hooves against the ground or snow in winter. They traded stories of animals they'd spied, vultures and crows, mice that acted funny, deer and elk and other game that Jacob liked to hunt. Luka never dissuaded Jacob from hunting. He was, technically, Jacob's servant, and couldn't pass judgment or try to impose his loyalty to nature onto the young man. He never let on that he was the boy's real father—to do so was a death sentence for both him and Dibra. The couple had often fantasized when the boy was little of riding off into the sunset with him. 'I have enough gold left in my dowry to buy a small bit of land on the coast, where the people are freer,' Dibra said. But they'd never summoned the courage to go. It seemed impossible, a fairy tale they told each other in bed at night. 'Maybe one day . . . ' Dibra learned a little of Luka's faith and why the servants worshipped only by night. 'The stars are God's, Luka told her. 'How else do you explain such light in the darkness?'

She was, to him, a holy grace, far more powerful than any priest or nun. God lived in her eyes. That was how he had fallen for her—like a religious conversion. It had struck him the moment he'd seen her, a profound, eternal love, the kind that occurred by cause of fate, against reason. Luka had been the one to fetch her from her home in Kaprov and deliver her to Villiam when she was sixteen. Luka was seventeen. He had carted up the gold-hinged trunk holding her dowry. She kissed her parents goodbye and strode out to the carriage, lifting her bridal veil to look at Luka, who held his hat in his hands. That was the moment. He was tall, with broad shoulders, eyes a bit far apart, his jaw strong and angular, his face wide and flat, his hair always shorn close to his skull because the horses had mites and the dogs in the stable fleas. 'I love you,' she had said as he held her hand to help her into the carriage. It was that obvious and simple. The ride back to Lapvona felt infinite. Time stopped, although the horses kept moving. Luka looked back at the carriage as he rode. Nobody had loved him before.

When Dibra married Villiam the next day, Luka felt that the wedding was actually for him and Dibra. He listened with the horses outside the church, avoiding the eyes of villagers hungry for a glimpse of their new lady. As the church doors opened and Dibra stepped out, her veil still over her eyes, the young lovers spoke to one another like a prayer: a silent song floated between them, a duet of devotion. And the song had played ever since in Luka's mind. This was what made him reluctant to share in worshipping with the other servants. They had no human love in their lives, he thought. They only had their God songs. If they heard his song for Dibra, he felt, they would ruin it. But since Jacob died, the song was too sad. Luka felt his own emptiness in the silence of it. He should have sung a song for God, but he couldn't. God had abandoned him, he thought, when He took his son away.

Luka didn't attend the servants' late-night cabbage dinners in the cellar. He didn't participate in their gossip or rituals, as he was wholly committed to Dibra, far more seriously than she was to him. She was a married woman, after all. She had to be practical and careful. Luka understood this, sneaking silently into her chambers after everyone was fast asleep. He tried to keep to himself around the estate, as if his very existence was a secret. He preferred to be private, an observer. He had a clear view of the grounds from the stable: from the front gate he could see the drawbridge and the main entrance of the manor, and from the

side gate he could see the kitchen door that led to the herb garden, and the path that led further into the fruit orchard. The
guards continuously walked the perimeter of the property on
foot. Luka could see them as they crossed the horizon. Dibra
warned him that her brother in Kaprov, Ivan, was a tyrant and a
lunatic, but as long as they didn't tempt him with trouble, he
would stay away. 'And Villiam doesn't care about fidelity,' Dibra
assured Luka. 'He just doesn't want to be publicly humiliated.
So be careful.' She had no idea that after fifteen years, Villiam
had tired of the charade. She wouldn't believe it, anyway. He was
so childish and spoiled, nothing seemed to bother him but his
own immediate needs and wants. Food, wine, entertainment,
money. When Dibra learned that he was sending for the lullaby
singer, she thought nothing of it. Villiam, of course, had sent
word ahead to the bandits. With Luka dead, he could continue
to play the clueless fool, and Dibra would dance around to hide
her agony. She would be stuck with it, and Villiam would enjoy
watching her play her own charade, masking her grief in what—
insanity? A mother's sorrow was tiresome, but a whore's heartache? It would be a good show.

Luka had left for Krisk at dawn to fetch the singer. As he prepared
his horse and carriage, he had witnessed not only the naked priest
wandering down from the reservoir, but Marek, too, shuffling ex-
haustedly up the hill from the village in the priest's black robes. He

thought it odd that the priest had no clothes on, but Luka had no concern for Marek. He refused to acknowledge his existence. To Luka, Marek was nothing. A scarecrow. A shadow. A spot in his eye.

He rubbed his eyes now as he rode. He hadn't slept much. It would take half the day to get to Krisk and he was tired. He chewed a sprig of tansy to soothe his unease, the sun rising behind him. He passed Agata as he rode down the hill. She looked like a typical nun coming to visit Villiam, as they did on some holidays, to perform a mystical ritual Luka knew to be hokum. But it was strange for a nun to be walking alone. Usually Luka himself went to the abbey to fetch them. And it wasn't a holiday. It was a Tuesday. He noted the young nun as odd, but these were odd times. Perhaps they had run out of food at the nunnery. She would get her fill at the manor, he knew.

Luka took the image of the nun walking alone up the hill as a sign and tried to put meaning to it as he rode, sipping from time to time from the carafe of water and chewing bread the girls had given him for the trip. He also carried a basket of fruit and lunch for the singer, who was rather fond of food. He had the gut of a sloth, which is what gave his lullaby voice its rotund softness. Luka imagined he'd be waiting, anxious, thinner and nervous and hungry, as Krisk had also suffered from drought, though not as devastatingly as Lapvona. Luka knew well that the people of Lapvona were starving, but he wasn't afraid of them. If he saw someone begging on the road, he'd throw them a grape or an apricot. He didn't like fruit himself, the sweetness was too heartbreaking for him. The guards on the road nodded to him as he

passed. Did they know that Jacob had been Luka's son? he wondered, then shook his head. Everyone knew, of course. Villiam
knew, the servants knew. Lispeth knew. Perhaps Jacob himself
had known. This thought depressed him. Maybe the nun was a
sign indeed: devote yourself to God now. You need Him.

Halfway to Krisk, Luka stopped to take a nap in the miraculous shade of a dead chestnut tree. He crawled into the carriage
and lay down. He fantasized that some maniac would burst in
and slay him, steal the horse and take off, leaving him dead to
drift up to heaven where Jacob was waiting. Finally, he could
claim him as his son. 'He is mine,' he would say. It was all any
man wanted, to point at his son as he passes and to say to the
people, 'He is mine. That is my boy. I made him. There he goes.'
Luka cried and grew tired. He turned to face the dark of the
carriage. Eventually he did sleep. His dreams were thin and
sweaty, just pictures. The brittle landscape of the plains outside
of Lapvona, empty farms he'd passed, dried worms on the hard,
cracked ground, an itch in the back of his throat. He awoke disappointed that he'd not died in his sleep. It was a luxury to die
in one's sleep, he thought. Of course, God would not make it so
easy. This was what his mind repeated—'God would not make
it so easy'—as he watered his horse a little and mounted it again.

When Luka didn't return with the singer in time for the feast,
the stableboys were concerned that the horse had given up in the

heat. But Dibra had a worse feeling. She paced as the servants set the table. 'I loved that horse,' she said to Father Barnabas, who sat, already eating the chicken. He seemed not at all bothered that the singer hadn't arrived, for there was, magically, a replacement guest—a young nun with scorched cheeks. She sat glumly on the edge of the settle. Dibra didn't like the burnt look of her face. She could see bits of flaking skin on the nun's lips. Would she offer her some salve? No.

Dibra didn't like nuns. She didn't like their modesty. Once she had married Villiam, she refused to wear a cap over her head. Her long blond hair was wild and curly and bristly, and she liked to feel it swing as she walked. Modesty was boring, Dibra thought. Perhaps this was something she had absorbed from her husband—an irritation with anything too fussy in its purity. Marek was guilty of that fussiness. Dibra disliked him for so many reasons. Everything about him was a needy, arrogant demand for pity. He always looked up at Dibra with big, sad eyes, expecting what—a warm embrace? Forgiveness? She had nothing to return but cold disgust. He was scared of her, and she was glad. He had grown a bit since he'd arrived, but he was still so stiff, so stupefied by the food and drink every time they sat together at the table, his hands trembling to pick up his cup, as though he weren't strong enough to lift it. Dibra could hear the fears in his head: 'God, forgive me for this indulgence.' The idiot. She was an atheist herself. She had once felt that there was a power in the way things happened, a kind of fatedness that she depended on, an order to life. After Jacob's death, she lost that faith completely. Life was chaos. There were no rewards. Best to make the time tolerable, at least. It never occurred to her that her philandering might have inspired God's wrath. How could a little love cause such a horrendous tragedy?

Although Dibra got irritated by Villiam's gregariousness, she didn't mind the entertainment he demanded. She especially liked the singer from Krisk. His lullabies were the best. She hadn't been sleeping well lately either, and wouldn't sleep at all now, not until Luka was back home safe and the singer was with him.

'Let's eat,' Villiam said, sauntering feebly into the room. The priest put down his drumstick. The nun lifted her head. 'Come, come,' Villiam said, as Clod pulled the lord's chair away from the long table. Villiam made a great fuss because the pillow wasn't plumped enough. 'Clod? How is it possible?' Clod beat the pillow until it was puffed up, then Villiam sat on it, like a dying king on his throne, but he wasn't dying. He was simply an insect. That was how he'd been since Dibra had married him. He moved like a spider walking on its hind legs. Perhaps this was why he preferred Marek to Jacob, she thought. Marek was also feeble. Stunted, his eyes hollow, his body always perched as though he were shirking away from a fist swinging toward him. And Villiam liked Marek for his ugliness. Just a look at the boy's face elicited a response. Jacob had been too handsome, too staid. Marek trembled, vulnerable, spittle at the corners of his lips, a scar on his chin, his red hair so terrifically red, like it had been dyed a thousand times in madder. Maybe Marek's real father used to beat him, Dibra thought, but she felt no pity or compassion for the boy. No pity or compassion would she ever feel. Not for Marek, or for anyone.

Villiam sat and immediately reached for a leg of lamb. 'Sit there, sister,' he said to the nun, pointing with the meat to the chair across from the priest. Father Barnabas was licking his fingers—he never waited for Villiam to sit before he started eating. The servants brought the capon roast and twisted bread.

Dibra sat silently at the other end of the table, trying to block out Villiam's face with the candelabra so she would not have to watch him eat. Villiam was fine with that. Dibra wasn't looking her best. She was underdressed for the occasion, and she didn't care. It was still too hot to wear the customary dining gown, so she wore a simple yellow kirtle of thin linen. Her armpits were wet and clammy, the fabric tight around her bosom, which seemed to swell unusually on the left, as though her heart had become enlarged. Ironically, she felt her heart had gotten weaker and smaller recently. She was not self-pitying, however. 'Women have lost children since the dawn of time,' she told herself. She imagined women everywhere, all the stories she'd heard of children going missing, or children dying of fever or pox, babies dying in their cradles, strangled by their own lungs. If those women could go on, so could she. But only barely. She had nothing to distract her from her grief, nothing of any consequence—no needs or habits or work or interests. There was Luka, but his loyalty made him boring, actually. Until this moment. He was never late.

'Is the singer not joining us?' Dibra asked, masking her worry as mild curiosity.

'He must be lagging on his journey back from Krisk,' the priest answered.

'It has never taken so long to fetch the singer before,' Dibra said.

'Well, today it has.'

'The horseman left at dawn as usual?'

'Who cares, Dibra?' the priest said. He was deflecting in order to spare Villiam her distress about this other man, not knowing that Luka was good as dead. 'And anyway, we have a nun instead.'

'Yes, thank God for the nun,' Villiam said and raised his cup.

'Give me a nun any day,' the priest said and raised his cup, too.

'Of course,' Dibra said and raised her cup.

Agata seemed to blush and lifted her cup. They all drank.

'What is your name, sister?' Dibra asked.

Agata opened her mouth, pointed inside, then waved her finger back and forth. The nun's tongue had been cut out, they all saw.

'Is that what they're doing to girls now, Father? Cutting out their tongues?' Dibra asked.

'I don't think so, no. She is not typical.'

'But she must have some party tricks,' Villiam said, a little concerned. 'If she doesn't talk, what does she do?'

'Maybe she dances,' Dibra said.

'A dancing nun? Of course, that's wonderful,' Villiam said with his mouth full.

Now Marek made his presence known, trudging into the great room with his ruined shoes. Nobody turned to greet him. Lispeth followed him to the table, gently pulled out his chair, waited for him to sit, and pushed it in. Like a little child, Dibra thought. Helpless and full of himself at the same time. Oh, Dibra hated him. But there was something strange about his face tonight. It, too, looked scorched, like the nun's. Preoccupied. Lispeth poured Marek a cup of wine and went out. Another servant came forth to dish out the roast lamb around the table.

Marek put his hand on his plate.

'I don't want meat,' he said.

'Why not?' Villiam said.

'I don't want to eat meat anymore.'

'Give him the whole platter,' Villiam said, nodding to the servant. 'No son of mine will starve.'

But Marek did not eat. He looked carefully in the candlelight toward the nun.

'Is she the singer tonight?' he asked.

Dibra thought his question a bit forward. Marek hardly ever spoke at the dinner table and certainly never asked anything before. It was his role to be quiet and accept without question anything that happened at the manor. Marek was surprised by his question, too, and immediately covered his mouth to apologize. He had asked it automatically, without thinking. He looked down at the plate of lamb set before him. It smelled of the pasture—dead flesh cooked in the hot dirt. He didn't want to eat it. Especially not now, in front of the nun.

'Eat your meat,' Villiam said. And to the nun he asked, 'Do you sing, sister?'

'You idiot, she's mute,' Dibra said.

'Temper, temper,' Father Barnabas said.

Dibra was hungry. She took a piece of lamb and ate it, hoping her irritation would subside. She didn't want the nun around. Her humility was too annoying. And she worried for Luka's safety. It was not like Villiam to send him out on some fool's errand and have him killed, but the famine made people crazy. The bandits must be starving, too, she thought.

'The nun dances,' Villiam said to Dibra.

Marek pushed the plate of meat away and knocked over his cup of wine. It spilt onto the plate, washing the cuts of lamb so that the meat now sat in a pool of red.

'Clumsy!' Dibra screamed.

'Now, now,' the priest said, wiping his mouth piously with the cloth. 'The heat has got everyone in a rage. Calm down, Dibra.'

Dibra sighed. Villiam lifted his cup again in absolution.

'Marek, eat your meat.'

Marek picked up a piece of lamb.

'Sister, sing us a song,' Villiam said forgetfully.

'No need to be cruel,' Dibra said under her breath. 'She's mute, she's not deaf.'

Agata turned pale now. She stood.

'Is she leaving?' Marek said. 'Where is she going?'

'Shush,' Villiam said.

Agata turned her back to the table and stood in the darkness, just out of range of the glow of the candelabras. The four left at the table watched her figure, their faces glowing in the light. She could leave, she thought. She could starve and die. That would be fine, wouldn't it?

'She's going to do something,' Villiam said.

The priest sipped his wine, waiting for the entertainment to begin. He had never met Agata before. And he hadn't requested anyone from the abbey in months. But good that the girl was here, for Villiam's sake, he thought. Without a visitor to keep him happy once in a while, he got more and more demanding. Maybe Agata could do something really strange. Maybe she could make herself disappear. A few had come with the promise of such an act, but all they had done was throw smoke and run out. Maybe this nun was the real thing. Real magic. She did have a haunted kind of look about her. Her hands shook a bit when she'd sipped her wine, he'd noticed. Perhaps she would have a conniption. Barnabas had seen people go into fits before, but they usually fell on the ground and shook and had a look of terror in their eyes. He couldn't imagine this nun doing that.

'What's she going to do?' Marek asked.

'She's already doing it,' Dibra answered.

'What?'

'Turning her back on us heathens,' Dibra answered, chewing.

'Sister, we are ready! Please, turn around, entertain us!' Villiam said. He laughed and ripped his teeth into a chunk of lamb. 'Sing!' he cried and chewed.

Agata turned to them and opened her mouth as though something might come out. Of course she could sing. She could sing beautifully. But she could not sing with words.

'Sing!' Marek cried with curious exuberance, which was so uncharacteristic of the boy's usual sheepishness that Villiam burst out laughing again. And then he began to choke.

'Oh, no,' Villiam coughed. He had sucked a chunk of lamb the wrong way down his throat. He gasped and turned red, but still laughed, banging his hand on the table as if that might dislodge the meat.

'Villiam, spit it out!' Dibra yelled across the table. Villiam shook his head violently, gripping his throat with his hands.

Father Barnabas got up and patted Villiam lamely on the back. 'Out with it. No more games,' he said.

Villiam wheezed and banged at the table. He tried to speak, but he had no breath.

'Where are the servants?' Dibra cried. 'He's choking to death.'

The priest hit him a bit harder but to no effect.

'Enough, Villiam. Spit it out,' the priest demanded calmly.

'Spit, Villiam!' Dibra screamed, lunging up from her seat toward him. Villiam waved his hands in the air, begging for help and dismissing it at once.

Dibra and the priest shook him, but he only gasped and shook them away. He stood and put his arms up above his head as though he were calling out to God. His eyes bulged. The priest and Dibra stood back, ready for him to fall down and die.

Just then, the nun came forward, three or four nimble steps—in her long habit, she appeared to be floating—and punched Villiam in the gut. He doubled over and coughed and spat the chunk of meat out onto the table. He wiped his eyes and cleared his throat, then sat down to catch his breath. Everyone returned to their seats at the table, stunned. The nun sat back down, too.

'Let's see the culprit,' Villiam said finally.

Marek picked up the chunk of meat and held it up for everyone to see. It dripped with strands of bloody saliva.

'Very funny,' the priest said.

Marek watched the nun, who was breathing heavily and rubbing her knees. She was a strange creature, small and pink, her hair as vibrant as a torch. Marek had once had long red hair like hers. Lispeth had cut it. 'Red hair is a sign of wickedness,' she had said, tugging at him with the knife. But Jude had always assured Marek that red hair had the highest value of all human hair. 'A few drops of blood from a red-haired man turns copper into gold,' he had said. 'And your piss can cure diseases if you boil it right.' Marek knew he wasn't wicked. His hair was just the same shade of red as the nun's. She had small, green eyes, like Marek's. Her hands were long and freckled, like Marek's. He watched her bite a twist of bread. Her teeth were strong and yellow like Marek's. Her chin was soft. He watched her drink, saw the flesh of her throat pulsate as she swallowed. He felt his own throat and swallowed. It seemed to move similarly. The consistency of her flesh had a pure, flaccid quality like his. And her eyelashes were long and orange. Her lips were purplish. Her ears were large with swollen lobes.

Once Villiam caught his breath, he thanked the nun, promised her fine hospitality as long as she cared to stay, and then went on eating, a bit more carefully this time, engaging the priest in a long discussion of hell, its landscape, its economy, what kind of house the Devil lived in, how he managed his servants, and how he had escaped into the realm of Earth. And then he asked, as though he might be serious, 'How long will God keep heaven's gate closed? Hypothetically speaking.' Then he chuckled. And then he frowned. 'Honestly, Father, how much longer until the heat backs down?'

'A few more months, probably,' Barnabas said.

Dibra shook her head. 'Maybe if you let some of the water go, let the rivers flow, it wouldn't be so hot.'

'It's not my fault it's hot,' Villiam said. 'Am I a god? Do I control the weather?'

'You're controlling the water,' Dibra scoffed.

'And you?' Villiam pointed a lamb bone toward Marek. 'What is your prediction for next week? Hot or not hot?'

Marek didn't answer. He was busy staring at the nun.

'Let the sister nibble in peace, Marek,' Father Barnabas said.

Marek looked around. Could they not see the resemblance? Villiam sucked the marrow from the lamb bone. The priest spooned more herb sauce on his plate and coolly took a sip of wine. Dibra frowned and chewed. Marek turned away and looked down at the pool of wine on the plate. He could see his face reflected by the candlelight.

'What's your problem?' Dibra asked him. Marek couldn't answer.

Dibra took his look of shock for forlorn narcissism. Jacob had been much the same way, consumed with his reflection. But

Jacob's self-obsession was mysteriously internal, as though he were troubled by his own soul, and he could see it in his face. Marek's face was, to Dibra, void of anything mysterious, like a mask over nothing. A curtain covering a blank wall. Still, recognizing the familiar adolescent angst made her miss her child. If she could speak to Jacob now, what would she say? Would he even listen? He had never cared what she said while he was alive. He never spoke to her as though she had a mind, but like something to operate, like a clock or compass. She hadn't minded Jacob's self-centeredness. She admired it in him, actually, felt that she could take part in it as he was so beautiful, so brave. He'd had all her best qualities. His narcissism was, to Dibra, an expression of his love for her, as well as for himself.

'Sit up straight, Marek,' Dibra barked.

Marek sat up straighter and bowed his head. He saw that wine had dripped down the front of his shirt. He covered it with a hand across his heart, a gesture that the priest misread.

'The boy got a fright,' he said dryly.

'He's a good boy,' Villiam said. 'Loves his father. I'm all right. I'm all right,' he said and coughed a little. 'No, no, I'm all right.'


After dinner was cleared away, Marek and Dibra went up to bed, trailed by Lispeth and Jenevere. Petra took the nun to Jacob's old room, which had been prepared as a guest room for the singer from Krisk.

Now that they were alone, Father Barnabas and Villiam spoke more frankly.

'I will tell Klarek to increase security around the manor perimeter,' Villiam said. 'We mustn't give the appearance of weakness now. We don't want to tempt the Devil. Or Ivan, for that matter.'

'Hear hear,' said Barnabas, raising his cup of wine.

'Will I go to hell, Father? What do you think?'

'Of course not, Villiam. You give so freely to me and others. Your food is delicious. So is your wine.' The priest poured himself another cup.

'But what if I wanted to visit for a while?'

'We all feel that desire from time to time,' the priest answered. 'But I doubt you'd like it there. It's very hot. Hotter than Lapvona. Even hotter than down in the village.'

'A dry heat is not so bad.'

'I suppose that's true.' The priest now turned serious. 'What did you make of that nun? Did she look sick to you? Did you see her face? Looks like pox or something.'

'I thought she was all right. I like redheads,' Villiam answered.

'She seemed strange,' Barnabas said.

'Then why did you invite her?'

'I didn't.'

Villiam sat back and pondered that for a moment.

'An intruder?'

'A woman? I don't think so.'

'Do you think she means well?' Villiam asked.

'She saved you from choking to death, didn't she?'

'True, true. She's smart to seek refuge up here. The villagers have been going mad, I hear. Word from the guards is they're eating each other alive. What if they try to eat me, too?'

'They wouldn't. You've got no meat on you,' Barnabas assured him.

'Will you pray for them, Father?'

'Of course. I'll speak to God directly.'

Clod stood with his back sweaty against the wall, ready to come forth the moment Villiam snapped his fingers. He listened with little interest to what Villiam and the priest had to say. Clod had never even been down to the village. He could only imagine what it was like, the drab colors of people's clothing, the smell of human waste, the ground trampled by oxen, young maids with yellow skin and rotted teeth. He had no desire to go see it, not because he was afraid of being eaten, but because he presumed the village was ugly. Clod was an artist, a servant to beauty and his own imagination. He had no allegiance to humanity at all. Villiam and he made a good pair in that sense. The other servants thought Clod was foolish because he was fanciful and a bit obsessive in his creative hobbies. They didn't respect him or his talent, even though he was Villiam's favorite. The two men were so familiar, Villiam barely had to think of Clod, and Clod came. Their minds were connected by a rod of energy, like a stroke of fine lightning that ceaselessly vibrated.

Clod hadn't liked the look of the nun, so he hadn't looked at her much at dinner. There was something strange in her face, a blankness that made her hard to see. He didn't believe that a nun was something holy—the servants' faith did not recognize holiness in human beings. They didn't care for Jesus. Flesh was mortal. God was not. God was not alive. God was life itself. And life was invisible. This was why Clod felt he had to make art, to give proof of life. Clod knew as well as the other servants that Villiam was a sinner, the priest a heretic. But a person should never judge someone else's faith. Nobody knows the truth.

Perhaps hell is a tiny place, a single flame, Clod thought now. The thought moved him, and he imagined the pureness of the flame as he gazed through the darkness at the candelabra. Just one flame could contain all the evil that has come and gone. What if it were that easy to snuff it out? Would he do it? No. He would never interfere. Just the image of the white light, the way it swayed in the slow breeze floating through the manor, that was what mattered to him. If he could draw that, he thought, and make the picture move somehow, that would be interesting. He could suspend the drawing from a string and let the wind push it to and fro. Strange, he thought next, that fire hurts to the touch. Fire gives light. Shouldn't the darkness hurt instead? Hell ought to be pure darkness. Nothingness. The thought chilled him. There was nothing to see there. He shrugged and pulled his back away from the wall, feeling his shirt stick to his skin with sweat.

Villiam lifted his eyebrow.

'My lord,' Clod said, instantly beside him.

'Come draw,' Villiam said. 'I want a picture of what happened tonight. Draw me choking. Like this,' he said and bent over in his chair and put his hands to his throat. 'Just the way it happened.'

Clod smiled. He liked to draw at night, and when he drew portraits of Villiam, he used fine parchment made of the skins of lambs and young calves. It came from the coast, was expensive, and absorbed ink fluidly, almost as though Clod were drawing on glass. He would get lost in the lines and shadows.

'Yes, my lord,' he said and went to fetch his materials.

Marek lay awake in his bed. He couldn't sleep. He had tried to tell Lispeth that the nun looked like his dead mother, but she refused to care.

'Did you see her hair?'

'It was ugly hair—is that what you mean?'

'She looks just like my father described her.'

'Who?'

'My mother,' Marek said, tears rising in his eyes. 'Maybe she's back from the dead. Maybe she's here to save me.'

'From what?'

'From you, maybe,' Marek said.

'Guilt will make you crazy,' Lispeth said. 'Just shush and go to sleep. You've been nothing but trouble all day.'

Marek was appalled that Lispeth would attack him now,

after everything he'd gone through. 'Have you forgotten that I buried my father today?'

'Maybe you'll feel less crazy if I move my chair away.'

Lispeth dragged her chair to the corner and sat down.

'Better now?'

'Yes,' Marek said.

They were quiet for a while. Marek turned his face away from his pillow. It smelled like Lispeth, of cabbage and sweat and fine blond hair and the girl's downy skin.

'Think Jacob might come back, too?' Lispeth asked.

'Go to hell,' Marek said into the darkness. 'Maybe you'll be happy there.'

'Maybe, my lord,' Lispeth replied.

'I think I'll sleep better if I am alone.'

Lispeth got up wordlessly, went out, and shut the door.

The hallway was quiet as she walked down the stairs and through the great hall. She didn't need a candle to light her way. She knew the manor like her own breath, moving past corners and through passageways, down steps and up steps, through doorways, never thinking of the manor as a place, but as the only place. Like Clod, she had never been off the hill. Luka had left, and the stablehands sometimes went down to Lapvona, but they never spoke of what they saw. Lispeth had no curiosity. She would rather travel up into the sky than down into the village, where nobody would understand her, and where everyone toiled in vain. She passed through to the kitchen and down the stairs into the cellar where the cabbage was stewing. Lispeth was hungry, and she knew this because she could feel her hands itch to join together in prayer. She thought of eating as an act of ritual, worship. God was infinite, so just a symbol counted. To eat more than a single leaf of cabbage was greedy, akin to asking for proof of God from God Himself. The thing Lispeth despised most in people, or at least how she imagined people to be, like Marek, was their expectation that faith ought to be painless. As if faith required no effort. Anyone could whip himself and say he's faithful. Real faith was earned through self-denial. Lispeth could live off a speck of dust if that was what she chose as her food. She scoffed at the other servants who ate as they cooked and took scraps from the table, picked fruit freely from the trees. Lispeth didn't. Perhaps God liked her best, she thought, because she asked for so little.

Dibra decided not to pack more than a few apples and a carafe of water on her trip to look for Luka that night. She worried that if she took any more, Jenevere would tell Villiam that she had prepared for a long journey. She didn't want anyone to come after her.

'Won't you take a torch?' Jenevere asked.

Dibra shook her head. A torch would only draw attention. She planned to sleep on the horse, let it follow its nose to wherever Luka had gone, whether it was to Krisk or beyond. She thought, maybe he is waiting for me, enacting a plan that I was deaf to hear in my sorrow. Luka could be very nuanced in his language at times. Maybe this was his big romantic gesture, Dibra wondered. Could Luka be so naive to believe that the fantasy of running away together could come true? Did he think Dibra would be swept away in that dream? She was not so romantic. But she did want to leave the manor. There was nothing to keep her there: her child was dead; she felt no loyalty to Villiam, especially now that her father in Kaprov was long dead, the risk of humiliating him eliminated; and her brother, Ivan, was so obnoxious, he deserved the stress and trouble he'd go through if she disappeared. Ivan had been the one to convince their father to marry Dibra off to Villiam. 'Lapvona dirt is good dirt,' Ivan said. 'So what if the man is a skeleton? You don't marry for love,' he'd said. She should have run off with Luka the first time she'd ever seen him. They could have gone anywhere in that carriage. Stupid to think of it now.

Dibra said nothing to Jenevere but that she wanted to take a ride on her horse once the others had all gone to bed. She was loath to imagine giving up the comforts of life at the manor, but what choice did she have, really? She would die of boredom without Luka. Maybe she could find some perverse satisfaction in living like a peasant, making love in the afternoons after feeding Luka his lunch. She could use a broom and fetch water while she waited for him to come back in from the fields. It was something. Was that Luka's plan? That they be poor? At least she would be living honestly for once, she thought. Let me be a human. Let me see the world and go naked. Maybe life is more interesting that way, with Luka or without.

'What else will you need?' Jenevere asked.

'Nothing,' Dibra answered.

Jenevere laced Dibra's riding boots and helped her fit her gloves onto her hands, which were swollen from the heat.

'Don't tell anyone I've gone,' Dibra said.

'I won't.'

'Don't tell Villiam.'

'No.'

'Good girl,' Dibra said and opened the door for Jenevere to go out. Jenevere blushed at the gesture—Dibra had never opened a door for her before.

'God bless you,' Jenevere said.

'Hush.'

She walked away through the darkness. Dibra waited until she couldn't hear Jenevere's steps on the stairs. Then she waited some more and blew out the candle by her bed as though she were going to sleep. There was a bit of light coming through the window—Jenevere had forgotten to pull the drapes closed. Dibra pulled them. The first time in her life she had pulled her own drapes. She fingered the velvet, thin and worn like silver.

The acoustics of the cellar were hard—every chew and breath echoed off the walls. Nobody ever spoke beyond a whisper, but nobody spoke at all that night. They were all avoiding talking about the nun. It was obvious to all of the servants that she was Marek's mother. The resemblance was uncanny. Petra had noticed that the woman seemed nervous when she'd left her alone in the guest chamber. The nun had refused a bath and any help undressing. She had no belongings. Not even a brush for her hair. Petra admired the woman's prudence. She looked at Lispeth now, chewing her little piece of cabbage. Lispeth's hands were like the sticky hands of mice, bony. Her face was small and tight and like an old lady's already. Petra thought Lispeth was vain. It was vain to keep your skin so close to the bone. Lispeth never complained of hunger or hardship. But Petra could see the bruise on her spirit, the little cuts of sadness. She could deny her flesh, but she was still human. Petra looked forward to watching Lispeth crack one day. It would be satisfying to see her lose her composure after so many years of rigidity.

For her part, Lispeth thought Petra was lazy. When it was Petra's turn to dust the buttery, she always drank wine and did a sloppy job. Lazy and gluttonous. She had no other opinion of the girl. She had no opinion of anyone but Marek now, the target of all her ire. Lispeth's prayer that night in the cellar was a song for Jacob. It began slowly, evenly, two notes playing back and forth, comfortably, like easy voices in a garden. Then a third note came in and overtook the melody. Lispeth couldn't contain the arrangement now. She stopped it. Silence. She chewed and tried to remember the first note, the second. The third note taunted her, loudly, like a bird squawking, and like that it attracted other notes that squawked, and by the end of her last bite, she couldn't hear the first few notes at all. They had been lost to her in the flight of her many furies. She blamed Marek. He looked just like a bird. A bird whose mother had pushed it from the nest, who'd survived but could barely fly anymore, only flutter around jaggedly and enjoy the attention it got from the snakes, it was so deranged. Then why had his mother returned? She must want something.

'I wonder if Luka will come back,' Petra said, interrupting.

'Shush,' Jenevere said.

They all knew he wouldn't.

Marek still couldn't sleep. The air in the room was stagnant with-out Lispeth's breath to stir it, and the darkness was eerie. It was too dark, Marek thought. Usually there was a soft glow of blue through the curtains that gave enough light to delineate the bed and nightstand and the drapes and the wardrobe. Now nothing was visible. There was no difference whether Marek's eyes were open or closed. He could feel his sweat lick against the sheet as he moved, a moment of cool and then he was stuck to the sheet and it was hot from his skin again. He lifted his arm to look at it and he was invisible. His muscles still ached from having dug the grave for his father. Was that not the measure of one's manliness? If you could bury your father, you were no longer a child. Was that right? Jude had said that a man is someone who has a woman. He had his mother, didn't he? She had come back for him. He hoped it was true. Lispeth's refusal had made him doubt it. He exhaled sharply and the sound—ha!—echoed and faded as if the bounds of the room were a canyon and he were lying at the bottom of it looking up at a starless sky. He had never seen the sky without stars at night. Such darkness was like a blindfold, like blindness. He thought of Ina, their afternoon nursing. Maybe now he would nurse from his real mother at last.

Agata couldn't sleep either. She had recognized Marek immediately: he looked exactly like her brother. What cruel luck that the child had survived. A miracle, really. She had taken tansy tea every day and stuffed the fresh toxic flowers up her sheath to poison the thing inside like Ina had instructed. And she'd punched herself in the stomach, climbed up and jumped down from the tallest trees in the woods when Jude was busy with his babes and confident enough to leave her untied. But Marek had been a leech, indestructible. She'd thought it was her own strength that was keeping him alive. She had assumed that he'd died once she'd run off, that he was helpless without her. She'd refused to hold him, that gnarled creature that had fed off her and made her sick for nine months. She despised it. And so she despised Marek still. He really looked just like her brother, the one that did it. She was not at all surprised when the boy came into her room. She knew he would.

'Mother?'

Agata took his hand and held it between her own, felt his

skin on hers. It was not an act of tenderness, but rather a proce-
dure, a test. The feeling of his skin on hers was the feeling of her
own young hand on hers. 'My name is Marek,' the boy said. She
threw Marek's hand away, like she'd bit an apple and a worm
had crawled out of its frothing flesh. 'Mother,' he said again. She
nodded. He fell at her feet and kissed them. Agata restrained
herself from kicking him in the face. That he had survived until
now and had been adopted by the lord, she had to grant him
some respect. He had done well for himself, it seemed. She went
to the bed and lay down, hoping the boy would go back to his
room. But Marek followed. He peered at her in the moonlight,
his twisted body contorting in wonder and fright.

'Are you alive or dead?' he asked her.

Agata shrugged. Who could answer such a question? She let
him grope her legs, his face in awe at the feel of her flesh and
bone. Her knee, her thigh. He ducked under her robe, as though
he wanted to return into her body somehow. Agata gave no resistance. He took her nipple into his mouth and sucked. A shade of
pride prickled her face, but she let him. Surely she enjoyed her
mastery over the boy in some way. Yes, there was pleasure in self-
degradation, but it was easily spent. She pushed him away and
gathered her habit tight around herself. Marek, undeterred, simply cuddled against her turned back. Finally they slept. Marek
woke up now and then when she stirred in the bed next to him.
Each time, he was astonished at his great fortune. God had taken
his father but had delivered his mother back to him, an angel.
More than a fair trade, he thought.

. . .

By morning, Dibra's horse had returned to the manor bareback, without her. Both its eyes had been gouged out. The guards inspected it for messages but found none. The carafe of water was nearly full and still strapped to the horse's tether, but the guards removed it. They had seen Dibra ride out the night before and hadn't stopped her. They didn't want Villiam to blame them for a lapse in security. So they instructed the servants to report that there had been an attack in the night: someone, a bandit most likely, had come and mutilated the horse. The stablehands had slept through it, or perhaps one of them had turned and let the bandit into the stable, the guards suggested. But the servants refused to carry that lie.

Jenevere said nothing. She hid in Dibra's room with her breakfast, which she ate herself. She lay in Dibra's bed. She was also afraid, like the guards, that her knowledge of Dibra's departure would anger the lord. It would be grounds for dismissal from the manor. She would have to find her way back north, to her parents who had sold her to Villiam to pay off their debts to Ivan. She didn't want to go back, she couldn't. Rather than lie to Villiam, she kept her mouth shut. The rest of the servants huddled in the kitchen and decided that for their collective safety, they ought not say anything. And so, midmorning, Clod knocked on Villiam's door, set his tray of breakfast onto the table, and announced simply that a horse had its eyes gouged out. Villiam grunted and ate and wondered at the news briefly before returning to bed for several hours, drifting in and out of sleep. Finally, when he had fully awakened, it dawned on him that the horse might be sending a message. It was a warning. What did a blind horse signify? He had no idea. He stayed in bed, lazily imagining what it could mean. Horses were about power, he thought. So a blind horse was about blind power. Was this a message from Ivan that Villiam's lordship was superficial? Was he angry that Villiam had not paid enough in tariffs? Villiam was too tired for a morning metaphor. He let himself drift off again.

It wasn't until midday that Villiam got dressed, bored of snoozing. He ate some more and perused Clod's drawings from the night before. Now they seemed trite to him. Clod had failed to capture the drama of the scene—Villiam choking on the meat had been much more powerful than Clod had drawn it. But maybe if he painted the entire scene, the table laden with food, the priest and Dibra lurching up from their chairs to try to save their beloved lord, that could be worthy of a frame. Yes, Villiam thought dreamily, an action scene. And the nun punching him in the gut. He described his vision to Clod as they walked through the hall along the red carpet, down the stairs, and out into the daylight. Villiam squinted and yawned at the sun as they sauntered down the slope toward the stables, stopping to pluck a sprig of tansy and rub it between his hands and sniff. The sky seemed to darken just for him as they approached the stable where the mutilated horse was being watered and brushed.

Villiam rarely passed by the stable. He avoided Luka and

anything to do with him. As he approached and saw Dibra's eyeless horse stepping back and forth on the well-trodden hay, he remembered that Luka was gone forever.

'Does Dibra know?' Villiam asked the air. The stablehands muttered unintelligibly. 'Where is Dibra?'

'She hasn't come back yet,' one stablehand said. He was a stupid boy and hadn't understood everyone's pledge to keep quiet about Dibra. The other stablehands stepped back to distance themselves from his stupidity.

'Come back from where?' Villiam asked.

'She left on this horse late last night, but it came back without her.'

'Huh.' He didn't care.

Villiam wondered at the bleeding eye sockets. The horse blinked its long lashes, neighed, then seemed to stare deeply at Villiam, who kissed it on its dry black nose. The feeling of the chapped skin against his lips elicited a thought—a revelation. 'This horse is a revelation!' he exclaimed. Then he snapped his fingers and demanded the stableboys do a little dance for him. He clapped along to the rhythm of their feet.

Villiam felt very happy. Of all those at the manor, he was the only one to appreciate that the horse had found its way home without sight. That was loyalty. Forget Dibra. She, like Luka, would get what she deserved. Villiam would not lament his wife's disappearance. No, he would celebrate. Something good was coming. Villiam believed this in his heart as much as he believed himself to be at the heart of all things.

'Hallelujah!'

And just like that, thunder clapped, and the sky filled with black clouds.

'You see?' Villiam cried. He kissed the blind horse's snout again and trudged back up to the manor, just in time to stay out of the rain.

# FALL

he rain fell for too long. The ground had been so hardened by drought that the water just collected and stood and rose. The long fields turned to shallow lake and muck, and the men of the village waded around, trying to remember the boundaries of their plots, arguing viciously through the noise of the rain, although they were exhausted and still starving. But eventually the dirt softened and the rain turned to mist, and then a fog hovered, as though God were covering His eyes while the villagers—profoundly changed by the horrors of drought and famine—shrugged off their sins, dismantled their camps, and moved back from the lake to their homes with their belongings. A few days of strong sun dried up the mud, and the damage of the floods in their little cottages was quickly repaired with materials from cottages that had been abandoned and never reclaimed. Half the population of Lapvona had disappeared.

Now the world was so fecund and humid it was hard to get a fire started. Thank God the seeds had survived, stashed per tradition on a high shelf above each mantel. The villagers began farming again, accepting the boundaries of memory, too desperate to quarrel over a foot here or there. They were stunned when the green stalks popped up in the black earth as soon as they did. None of them would have believed such a thing could happen, that life could begin again so quickly. This renewal of hope gave everyone energy, so they were swift to renew themselves too, to emerge from the depths of their fear and hunger, to cut their hair and put on their autumn cloaks and dresses and get back to normal. They laughed at the chill in the air, how spontaneously the sun had retracted, as though it had made a mistake. 'It's like it all never happened,' they said, and nobody spoke of the people they'd eaten, though the absence of certain families was acute at Sunday Mass—half the pews sat empty. The neighbors of the departed took their land over, as well as their tools and seeds.

With the cool air the birds came back. Doves, crakes, coots, swifts, smews, quail, grouse, partridge. Geese and swans returned to the lake, whose level had risen back to normal with the rains. Cranes came. And then the mice and the rats, ground squirrels, moles, shrews and pine martens. Finally the larger animals returned—bears and wolves, who paraded around at night with human bones in their mouths. Nobody remarked on this. The rains had washed the blood off their hands and refilled the streams. The rains had cleaned the village of its summer stench of death, too. Then moose and bison. Villagers had no qualms hunting and roasting the flesh of these animals now. Human meat had disabused them totally of their vegetarianism. Everyone looked happy because they were no longer starving.

To celebrate God's mercy, Villiam had sent down a shipment of grains and summer fruits to every household. That was in August, on the Day of Assumption. Erno had no say in the matter, as he had mysteriously vanished during the rains, and with him all bookkeeping of Villiam's hoarded stores. 'Lucky for Lapvona that her lord is so generous,' Klarek said. It was his job now to take a census of which villagers had survived, and what food they'd each been given. Most villagers meted out their rations to last as long as possible, until the plants had grown enough to be eaten, but they didn't stay hungry. The church provided fertilized chicken eggs and cheese from the manor once a week. A drove of oxen arrived to replace the ones that had been slaughtered and eaten. Goats, donkeys, and lambs came in from the south. The lord was so generous, he simply added the cost of these gifts to the taxes each family owed. In a year, he would turn a profit, if everything went as planned.

Jude didn't want any babes. He was done with babes. He had not returned to his home in the pasture since the night he'd raped Agata in his dream, but had retreated up to the cave that Ina had lived in when she was young, coming out only now and then to beg food from the farmers. He felt that being a beggar suited him after all he'd lost, that it was a righteous occupation befitting his destiny. He had no energy left for contemplation or prayer. He was ruined now. He knew it. Death would have been a boon, had he only surrendered to it when he'd had the chance.

Once the village had restablized, the priest returned to his
paltry duties at the church, leading Sunday Mass and visiting the
homes of those villagers who showed any lingering derangement
from the trauma of drought and starvation. He hadn't been alive
during the Great Pestilence, but had heard from his peers in
school that survivors needed divine justification for such tragedy. He made a lame attempt to comfort the people, to soothe
their guilt and the scars of their hardship. All he could tell them
was that God worked in mysterious ways. They feigned compla-
cency and thanked the priest with grains or fruit, which he accepted simply to keep up the appearance of poverty. Not one of
the villagers would confess to a breach of their faith. 'God is
mysterious, yes, but He is not cruel,' they all said. Their faith
had been shattered, but they wouldn't admit it. Barnabas felt
that their hidden shame gave him a new special power, like the
keeper of a grave secret. Everyone smiled and rejoined around
him in an effort to mask their sins. The priest liked the farce. It
was just his style. He had no real knowledge of the Bible—he
spoke no Latin, read only a little, understood nothing—but he
walked around with the Good Book anyway to give the impression that he knew it all, and at each household he opened it to
random pages and spoke in a gibberish that made the villagers
cross their hearts and bow their heads. He told everyone that the
nobility would protect them. 'Villiam knows of your suffering
and applauds your hard work. Soon you will have new neighbors.
How lucky we are that our little village will grow and prosper.'

Villiam had sent word to Ivan that he was looking for a few

dozen hardworking young men and women to repopulate the village. He hadn't heard back yet whether the man wanted to negotiate.

Despite her headaches, Ina went into the village regularly to cast spells upon the women that they be blessed with babies, per the priest's request. She gave each man who requested it a pubic massage with fake forsythia oil—all the forsythia plants had died and would take at least a year to grow back and flower. The oil she used was just the distilled yellow liquid of her own boiled urine, but it worked just as well. 'It only takes a little bit,' she said, dabbing her piss on the tip of each member and rubbing the perineum with her soft, wrinkled thumb. The men all grew large with excitement and got hungry for their wives. Nobody commented on the strange look of Ina's eyes, but all were astounded that she had regained her vision. She claimed it was the miracle of her own medicine. In truth, Ina had replaced her old blind eyes with the eyes of Dibra's horse.

The horse eyes showed her things doubled in size—an apple, her own hand, empty space itself swelled and enlarged, and it made Ina feel that she was witnessing it all close up, without detail, blurry, as though she were huge. She saw color, but not the minor components of an object: the face and shape of a rock, but not its crevasses or its bits of moss or dirt. A man's face was a large looming fact, and she couldn't focus on any one feature—the wrinkles around his mouth, or the hairs in his beard, or the knobs of warts above his eyebrow. Every person was a skin-colored blur. She still depended on the sensitivity of her fingers, on her hearing, on the feeling of heat as her hand drew close to the man's genitals to know where to dab the urine, where to rub. When she blessed the women's bellies, she looked into their faces, which appeared so close, she felt that the domes of her eyes would kiss the domes of theirs.

'I haven't bled in so long,' all the women confided, as if it were a secret that a starving body could not live up to the moon.

'Eat more,' Ina said simply.

The wet air was always filled with the scent of baking bread. Of great concern was the chopping of trees and the drying out of firewood. The cold of autumn arrived. If you asked anyone, the Devil had gone back to hell. Grigor, the elder who had lost his grandchildren during the Easter pillage, and who had cut off the pilloried bandit's ear, did not trust Ina's lessons or anointments. Although he had nursed from her breasts as a child, he feared her. He had survived at the lake off bloodsuckers and mud, had been weathered through his sixty years of toiling the soil to have gained enough cynicism to distrust anyone who claimed to have special powers. Since the horror of Easter, he had become particularly sensitive to death—its nearness, its obligations, its consequences. He had watched so intently the flesh of his own body feed on itself over the summer months, something in his mind switched. He became open to change. First of all, he had come to suspect that life in Lapvona was not what he'd thought it was. He had worked so hard to feed himself and his family, for the love of God, believing it would earn him a seat in heaven. Now he knew he had been working, in fact, to make heaven on Earth for the lord above. Of all the residents of the village, Grigor alone questioned the rations delivered back in August. Where did they come from?

'Oh, God has blessed us,' his neighbors exclaimed, too afraid to wonder.

His own son and daughter-in-law were too hungry to entertain his distrust. 'It's food, Father,' they said. 'Eat it and be merry.'

'I'm not hungry,' Grigor answered. He could be persuaded to take only a few spoonfuls of wheatmeal before bed. He was often sleepless with hunger and worry. He shivered under a thick quilt stuffed with his dead grandchildren's clothes. He considered returning to the lake, being a strangebody, an offbeater, someone who refused to work on the farms. There were a few such people in Lapvona. Ina was one of them. But why was she suddenly mixing with the villagers and encouraging them to breed? What was she after, nosing her way into people's homes, taking their food and drink in exchange for the inspiration of lust? Where was she getting the lust from? Grigor wondered. Was that from Villiam, too? He warned his son and his wife not to let Ina in the house. 'Whatever you do, don't let her touch you.' But she had gained entrance anyway one day while Grigor was out. Ina promised to help Grigor's daughter-in-law, Vuna, conceive. 'Just let me in for a moment. I will do it for free. Just a cup of water, if you please. My eyes feel dry.' When Grigor had found out, he'd slapped the girl across the face. 'You've put us all at risk now. She'll turn us into animals.'

'Don't you want a descendant?' Vuna asked, rubbing her cheek. 'I'd think, old as you are, you'd be happy to have a grandchild.'

'My grandchildren are dead,' he said flatly. 'You can't replace them.'

'They were my children,' Vuna said coolly. 'And I'll replace them if I want.'

Grigor was immediately sorry for hitting Vuna, who had suffered so horribly. Her hair had fallen out completely during the famine and was growing back now like the fuzz on a peach. The poor girl. Grigor hid his face in his hands. It wasn't Vuna or even really Ina he blamed for the darkness that had fallen on Lapvona. He blamed Villiam. How was it logical that the bandits would pillage Lapvona last Easter while the lord sat in his manor with all his riches? Why would God allow anyone to steal from the poor? And now the old milk lady was promising miracles? She was a witch, Grigor thought. Out to trick them deeper into hell. It pained him to imagine Vuna becoming pregnant again. He didn't believe she could carry a child to term. She was too old—already twenty-eight—and too frail. Losing another child would be too much for any of them to bear.

Ina had no regrets about her new life and the work it afforded her. Without milk, her only possible career was as a medicine woman. Her science wasn't faulty: she really did know how to cure maladies with herbs and tinctures. She had a hundred years of experience keeping herself alive. That was worthy of some payment, wasn't it? She walked home through the woods, whistling back and forth to the birds who were gossiping about their approaching migration. She said she'd miss them, but she was only appeasing them. Now that she could see, she had little interest in the birds. They were alarmists, she felt, and she'd grown weak in her abilities to navigate the human world the more she had depended on them. They knew nothing of being an old woman, or a new woman. All they knew were their patterns and instincts. Ina herself wanted new patterns, new instincts. Since she had survived the famine and regained her eyesight, she felt she'd been reborn.

She lifted her feet high on the path now to be sure not to trip over the sticks and rocks and brambles, as they appeared to her twice as large as they really were. The horse eyes bulged from her head and put pressure on her inner cavities. She tried taking cannabis flowers for her headaches, but the buds were too fresh yet to have a strong effect, having only been planted once the rains let up in August. When the pain was too intense, she popped the horse eyes out into a bowl of milk. And of course she took them out each night. She had no need for them while she slept, and her head was grateful for the vacuum of space in the eye sockets. She had saved her old eyes, her original ones, wrapped them in a bit of cloth and hid them on a shelf above the hearth, keepsakes now. When she had first removed them, she had to say goodbye to many of the memories she'd had. But she was not a sentimental woman. Her new eyes didn't know who she had been. And so she was new to herself, at least in her vision. She felt young again. One might expect a young woman to want someone to love and caress, someone to fend for her when she needed fending, to wake her with the horse eyes each morning, to admire her longevity and suck her empty breasts. She had seen Jude on the road a few times. But each time she'd lifted her hand to wave and called his name, he ran away. Anyway, he looked to be in bad shape. There were other men in the world.

How big was the world? Marek was starting to wonder. How far did space extend past what he could see? The window was high enough that he could watch the sun sink down behind the land, its fire burning even while the land had gone cold and dark, he suspected. At night, the stars looked very far away. He would never reach them. He stared out when he tired of staring at his mother. She was boring in her sleep, immune to his poking and prodding. She wouldn't even wince when he pulled her hair.

He had spent every night in Agata's bed since her arrival, waiting for some profound maternal love to return to her ghost, but it never did. Instead, she was dull and speechless. She was unconcerned for Marek. And she was always hungry. Every morning, she finished her plate of breakfast and often ate Marek's, too, before he awoke. Then she went back to sleep. She had traded her dark habit for one of Dibra's dresses, blood red with black stitching. Marek thought it was ugly against the red of her hair and suggested she get a blue dress, but Agata didn't care what Marek thought. The few times he'd tried, in her sleep, to nurse her again, she'd woken up angry and dragged him by the ear out the door of her room and slammed it. Marek thought that was a little motherly of her, finally. To drag him by the ear.

If there was a world past where the sun sets, would they know Marek there? If he went there, would they welcome him? Did they look like the people of Lapvona? Did they have drought and death there, too? Marek wondered about his mother's empty grave, which he had filled with the remains of his father. He did his best to make sense of it all. Why did a ghost need so much food and sleep? She looked and felt real, although weirdly blank in the face. He touched her constantly, her hands, her hair, her arm, thin under the red linen, her legs under the folds of the dress which he disliked, which still smelled of Dibra, whom Villiam never mentioned.

Dibra's room had been turned into storage for Jacob's stuffed animals. It was Lispeth's idea to move them, to make more space for the nun. Lispeth, Petra, and Jenevere had spent a few days carefully wrapping all the kills in muslin and carrying them to Dibra's empty chambers. In some cases the animals had to be removed from their perches on the wall, unnailed or unglued from little varnished twigs and sticks that Jacob had stuck in cracks between the stones. For the most part, the animals remained intact, undisturbed in the hands of the young female servants. The badger, the skunk, the boar, the lynx, the lizards. The birds were handled very delicately so as not to disturb the lay of their feathers. Jacob had been careful to arrange them with glue to cover the wounds from his arrows. Still, a few animals disintegrated in the girls' hands, fur and teeth and cartilage collapsing even upon their approach. The hedgehog, the bats, the marmot, all the lemmings. They preferred to crumble than to be moved away. Agata had watched the migration from her window seat, and Marek had watched her watching. Her eyes moved like a slow animal's. She showed very little on the face beyond blushing, which Marek could not distinguish as the blush of rage or shame or hunger or love or nothing. For him, they appeared the same.

'Will you miss the dead animals?' Marek asked her.

Agata shook her head and flicked her hand at Marek, as if to shoo away a fly. She did not waver in her disgust for Marek, although she was slowly growing accustomed to him. Still, she couldn't stand his inquisitiveness. Everything he asked her was a plea for affection. He didn't care for her, not really. He only wanted to seduce her by seeming to care, so that she would care for him. Children are selfish, she thought. They rob you of life. They thrive as you toil and wither, and then they bury you, their tears never once falling out of regret for what they've stolen. That was how she felt. She was still a bandit at heart: cruelty ran in her blood. Yes, Marek was her son, but he was a bastard, a scar. That's what a child of rape was, in fact—evidence. A pang of pity for Jude rose up in her from time to time. The fool had raised the creature instead of burying it alive. She would have told him, 'This is a bandit's bastard,' if she could have spoken. But Jude must have known. He just didn't care. He had made the decision to keep the baby for himself. A stupid man. But Jude was fond of babes. Oh, he was, he was, Agata remembered. How many times did he squeeze her tiny breasts in his great, hardened hands and whisper how he liked how small she was, that she looked about twelve years old in this light by the fire, and oh, the pleasure of the tight sheath was beyond him. Beyond. Beyond what Agata could tolerate, finally. She'd been raw and insane with shock when Jude had found her in the woods and fallen in love. He could only love a starving child, she thought. No grown woman would touch him. He must have known that. Such stink. She hated Jude. And although she knew Marek was not his, she recognized their similarities—blood wasn't all that mattered, after all. Their stubbornness and their neediness, their longing like a loop of rope around her neck. She'd been happier being a slave at the abbey than she had been at Jude's, a slave to his lust while the creature inside her fed off her body more and more each day, no matter how hard she tried to kill it.

She knew the same was happening now. Another creature had taken hold of her insides, and she was hungry. The hunger was torture to her. It meant she couldn't leave the manor. Before, in her quiet moments at the abbey, she had felt she existed simply as a breath, a witness to light and dark, a weight in the room. With hunger and desire, life troubled her. She couldn't control her hunger any more than she could control her need to breathe. She was a slave now to the baby in her womb. No one had noticed it yet. Beneath Agata's robes, despite the scantiness of her flesh, her face still drawn, drawn further still despite the regular foods—she'd been permitted only wheatmeal and yogurt at the abbey, a fruit now and then—her belly had swollen past her lean silhouette. Marek had figured it was just the taking on of weight, that her body had swollen there because the dress permitted it. He understood nothing about maternity.

'I helped Jacob hunt a lot of those animals,' he said to Agata. She didn't smile. Nothing Marek said made her smile.

Agata had indeed grown fond of Jacob's animals. She admired their faces, the prettiness of their stripes and spots, the funny crookedness of their whiskers. And she had felt a sense of superiority around them, a kind of pride that said, 'I'm alive and you're not.' Trapped in death, each face held an expression of awe—an innocent meeting its maker. Perhaps this was what allowed her the little pity she took on Marek. 'I'm your maker,' she said to him in her mind. He clung to her more and more now that the nights were chilled and the warmth of her body might soothe him. He leaned up against her like a slime, but she wouldn't put her arms around him. She would turn away from his breath and sleep irritably, sometimes elbowing him in the back if she needed more space. Jenevere paid no mind to Marek's nightly presence. Petra and she had an unspoken way of attending to both the nun and the boy simultaneously, getting them washed and ready for bed, lighting their candles, closing the curtains.

Without Marek to serve, Lispeth could have slept all day or taken up a hobby. She could have practiced her singing or dancing. She could have gone for walks in the fresh autumn air. But she would not. She simply sat in Marek's empty room out of spite, waiting for him to come back. She became completely consumed by her longing for something to hate.

There were no tears shed for Dibra. Her disappearance struck everyone silent, no mourning, as neither Jenevere nor the stablehands nor the guards ever spoke a word to anyone about her departure. They didn't even discuss it among themselves. Villiam didn't ask the bandits for details, but he assumed they'd taken care of her as they'd cared for Luka. Unlike Dibra, the bandits liked to make Villiam happy. So forget the woman. She was out of his head as soon as the rains began. 'She cried enough,' Villiam said to Father Barnabas, but had neither the energy nor the interest to finish his sentiment. The priest understood what he meant. Dibra had cried so much, she had exhausted the moisture from the atmosphere. She had been so dreary and morose. It was her, and not Jacob's death, that had steered the story wrong.

'Now,' Villiam began, 'who shall I take next as a wife?'

'The nun—is she still upstairs?' Father Barnabas asked. He was joking.

'Doesn't make a sound. Better than Dibra, then. Shall I marry her?' Villiam was serious.

'Isn't she ugly?' the priest asked. 'I can't remember.'

'Let's have a look and see.'

Father Barnabas went along with the charade, not thinking that Villiam would really take another wife. The lord seemed to be enjoying himself, spending evenings with Klarek, horsing around. But Villiam could not forget the words of his mother: 'A man becomes a man when he marries a woman. Until then, he is just a little brat.'

And so Agata was summoned and examined.

Villiam kept the vetting process very brief. 'Strip. Lie down.' Etcetera. The nun seemed to understand basic instructions and peeled off her red dress without protest. She had no obvious diseases. Her sunburn had peeled and healed nicely. Her face was a pleasant shape, if a bit gaunt. Her hair was red, which Villiam liked, and she didn't speak. Her arms and legs were thin and freckled, which was fine. Better to have something to see rather than plain skin. Villiam didn't like plainness.

Villiam and the priest saw the odd bulging of her pelvis.

'What is that?' Villiam asked. 'Pregnant?'

'I doubt that,' the priest said. 'Are you pregnant?'

Agata shrugged. What could she say? Nothing.

'Lie down on the table,' Barnabas said.

'Yes, you test her out, Father,' Villiam said. Luckily the priest knew little about the female anatomy. When he examined her sheath, it seemed to him that she was intact. He couldn't tell the difference. 'A virgin, I guess,' Barnabas pronounced. 'But pregnant, too?'

Villiam examined her sheath as well, hardly any less ignorant. To him, too, she felt like a virgin. He weighed this in his mind. Such a miracle would arouse great interest and discussion. He would have to send word of this to the council, the king, whoever might be interested in a virgin birth.

'Wasn't Jesus born to a virgin?'

'Well yes, I think so,' Barnabas answered.

'If I marry this nun, I'll be father to the son of God,' Villiam realized. 'That's quite an honor, is it not?'

'I suppose,' Barnabas replied warily.

The two watched Agata's bum as she turned to dress. There was a redness on her cheeks where she had pressed her buttocks against the wooden table so that they could examine her pubis. Villiam didn't dislike the look of her bum, which was dimpled and small, the bum of a teenage boy, more or less. But her hips were wide, and her body was swaybacked and thin, except for the strange roundness of her abdomen. Marek was watching through the crack in the door, fuming with jealousy.

'A man without a wife makes everyone suspicious,' Villiam went on, as though to convince himself. 'A virgin birth is a great boon. It will put Lapvona on the map. The high church will give us money, won't it? Imagine all the pilgrims who will come here to see the child, to be blessed, and all of that. They'll need inns to sleep in, food to eat. The town will grow, and it will all be mine.' Villiam looked as giddy as a little boy.

'Congratulations,' Barnabas said fretfully.

'Should we build a theater?'

'Oh, certainly,' the priest nodded.

'And a circus?'

'I don't see why not.'

'Will I be famous throughout the land?'

'You'll be as famous as Joseph was with Jesus. And the nun will be your Mary.'

'That settles it. I'll marry her,' Villiam said, clapping his hands.

'Excellent,' the priest grimaced. This would all mean more work for Barnabas. He had no idea what to do in such circumstances.

'Bless her, Father,' Villiam told him.

Barnabas blessed Agata as she pulled her dress back on. She hung her head in shame. To the priest, this gesture looked like humility, or real devotion. He was nervous. Surely the nun saw through his act to the man of sin he truly was. If those of the high order came to visit, Barnabas might be questioned. His hypocrisy could be exposed. 'Thank God the nun is mute,' he thought. Still, he would have to spruce up the church. The congregation would need to be reoriented. He barely knew the villagers' names.

'I'll tell Jenevere to make her a nice dress,' Villiam said. 'And to stitch a picture of my face on the belly in golden thread.'

'Should we announce it?' the priest asked.

'A proper wedding in a church, and invite all of Lapvona. I'll give them each a bit of money and they'll come kiss my hand. Won't that be nice?'

'As you wish,' Father Barnabas said.

The two men strolled out into the hall, forgetting Agata, who was still getting dressed in the room. She was strangely calmed by this turn of events. The nuns at the abbey, those who survived the famine, would be sorry they'd treated her so poorly once they heard the news.

Marek, red in the face with rage, slipped inside the room where Agata was rolling on her stockings.

'You're having a baby?' Marek asked Agata, drool and tears sputtering from his lips.

She shrugged.

'If you love that baby more than me,' he said, 'I'll kill myself. Then you'll be sorry.'

Agata shrugged again.

All the flowers Lispeth had to pick were red. Red, the color of blood, of life. Agata's dress would be white and virginal, but the flowers were to express the nobility of Villiam's bloodline, however irrelevant his blood was to the virgin birth.

'Do you think the nun is really pregnant?' Jenevere asked, collecting the flowers in her basket.

'You should know, you're her maid,' replied Petra.

'She has more fat than when she arrived,' Jenevere said, 'and she eats enough for two.'

'She's certainly pregnant,' Lispeth said. 'I've done her wash since she came and she doesn't bleed.'

'You don't bleed either,' Petra said.

'I'm not like other women,' Lispeth said.

'Don't tease her, Petra,' Jenevere said. 'She's still a little girl.'

'We're the same age,' Petra said.

'Don't tease her,' Jenevere said again.

Villiam never wondered who had sired the unborn child. He accepted in his imagination, as he was a man of fancy, that the baby was indeed divinely created and divinely given to him. To Villiam, 'divinity' was a synonym for his own good fortune. He believed that wonderful things came to him because he was wonderful and therefore deserved them. Good that Agata was no great beauty or wit; he would not have to pretend to cherish her in front of company. He would not have to compliment her, as he'd had to with Dibra at first. He wouldn't have to woo her father. He wouldn't have to contend with a jealous brother. Ivan had still not replied to his letter. News of his upcoming nuptials, Villiam worried, might steer Ivan into rage. He could imagine his fury: 'My sister disappears, and now you're God's favorite?' Jealousy was all it was. But Villiam knew he would have to be more careful now that he was marrying the mother of Christ. He couldn't have young guests visit to play games alone in his chambers. He couldn't clown around or make any mistakes lording over Lapvona. He would need to increase security—no more visitors, no more fun. He would have to satisfy his appetite for sex with tansy. It was the only thing to quell lust. Little yellow flowers. They were good for everything. A single blossom down the throat could cure a fever or a flu, and a handful would kill you. Any amount in between could do anything you wished.

Lispeth picked red zinnias, poppies, roses, peonies, and red chrysanthemum, all growing in the indoor flower garden, which was protected from frost by a constantly burning fire. She and the servants were tasked with garlanding the blooms into miles-long strands for the wedding. There was to be a rope of red, like a line of blood, leading from the manor on the hill down to the road and into the village, ending at the apse of the church, where the priest would be robed in red as well. Villiam's attire would be red. The villagers were to wear red, too. The guards had gone around to every home in the village with packets of bath of madder and instructions for all Lapvonians to dye their clothes as many times as necessary to produce a deep crimson. This was Villiam's idea, as he'd had a dream in which everyone wore red at his wedding. He wasn't particularly fond of the color, but he had respect for his dreams and liked to see them actualized.

Although dying their clothes was a chore, the people of Lapvona were happy to participate in the celebration, as they'd been promised a day off from their labor and a zillin each. And word had gotten out that the nun was pregnant. The priest had spread the story through Ina. Along with it was the promise that touching the belly of the virgin would bring health and prosperity, and

Ina advised the female villagers in secret about exactly how to place their hands on the belly. 'Your fingers must be spread like this,' she said, and however they spread them, she corrected them until they were so fussed that they paid her over and over with food and ale to teach them once more.

Grigor was ever suspicious of Ina's lessons, as well as of Villiam's coming nuptials. People were so pleased to dye their garments, 'Oh, our lord is getting married! Isn't this good news?' they squealed. They were idiots. But that was all Grigor knew. His sour face had turned his neighbors against him. They no longer welcomed his herbs or flowers grown past the line between their gardens. He understood. 'I remind you of too much,' he said. 'I've seen it all.' After his fight with Vuna, he said nothing more about Ina, but he watched carefully as the old woman passed, walking so strangely and knocking on the doors of houses, interrupting the people as they supped. What did she want from them? Why did no one but Grigor see that she was mad and vile, or crooked at the very least? She'd been a wet nurse to many of the men she now massaged. Was that not perverse? What would the priest say? And what had she done to her eyes? Grigor could not shake his unease. It was keeping him up at night. He went to confession, finally, in October.

'Forgive me, Father Barnabas.'

'Never mind,' the priest said. 'Begin.'

'I hit my son's wife across the face,' Grigor said.

'And?'

'I suspect there's a witch in Lapvona,' Grigor said. 'Her name is Ina. Calls herself a doctor. Bent on indecency. She's been rubbing the men.'

'Medicinally, I presume.'

'I don't know.'

'You sound tired. And?'

'And I'm angry.'

'At whom?'

Grigor couldn't answer. There was not a soul he was not angry at. He cycled through his options: God, the bandits, William, his family, his neighbors. The list was too long to speak aloud. Grigor was ashamed of that excess, and so he lied.

'I'm angry at myself,' he said after a long pause, 'for not protecting my family.'

'Then bring a gift to the old lady and she will relieve you of your anger. And in so doing, you will relieve yourself of your suspicion. Do it before tomorrow so that you can enjoy the wedding.'

Grigor found the advice clever. If Ina was a witch, she could cure him of his uneasiness. If she was not, he had nothing to worry about. He agreed that he would do as he was told. He thanked the priest for his ear and counsel and left the confessional.

As he walked out of the church, Grigor followed the flowered garland snaking its way from the apse to the door, the already withering blooms tied in knots with what looked to him like human hairs. He found it strange that such flowers could grow in the fall, but again, everything seemed strange to him since his grandchildren had been slain. He didn't like to remember Easter—it felt like years ago, given the famine and upheaval of the drought—but he thought of the day now, how the whole town had been fasting for the holiday, had been weakened by their hunger already, which made them more vulnerable to the bandits. And why had the bandits come just before the spring harvest, and not after? If they wanted to pillage properly, they would have waited until all the crops were picked and ready to be sent to the coast. They could have made off with carts and carts of crops. Had they come simply to torture the villagers? To haunt them? To deter them from hope? What use was it, he wondered? If the bandits were not at all practical, did they act according to the whims of hatred, or was there something even more sinister about them, more intelligent?

Klarek was there at the church, managing the lesser guards who were instructing the villagers in how to position the garland of red flowers. Lispeth had tied them all together with hairs that had fallen from Dibra's head. Many hairs came from her hairbrush. Jenevere untangled them and laid them out carefully on a white sheet as they tied the flowers. Other hairs were peeled off her gowns and coats, her armchairs, wherever she had set her head. The servants missed Dibra. She had been something of a mother to them, had remarked upon their growth and appearance in a way they appreciated. They neither approved nor disapproved of Villiam's marriage to the nun. It meant nothing to them, only a bit of extra work now in preparation for the wedding. The servants' faith excluded marriage. They didn't believe a man should own a woman, nor should a man be responsible for her welfare. They believed that everyone should be free to do as they please. The guards were a bit different, of course. Their duties required that they believe in human authority.

'Old man!' Klarek yelled. Grigor had accidentally crushed a peony under the heel of his worn shoe on his way out of the church. 'You have just crushed a flower in the marital garland!' Klarek liked to take his work very seriously.

Grigor stopped and went back to the flower, squatted to inspect it. Only a few petals were damaged. He plucked the broken petals and handed them to Klarek. 'Forgive an old man.'

'This garland is meant to represent the noble blood line. Every flower embodies a past lord of Lapvona, and his loving blessing on Villiam and his new bride, leading them into Holy Matrimony.'

'There haven't been so many lords in Lapvona.'

'I beg your pardon?'

Grigor looked up and down the garland, assessing the number of flowers strung together to reach the hill and the manor. There were thousands of flowers, he guessed.

'If each flower is a lord, that would mean there were thousands of lords. That's impossible. A man lives fifty years usually. That's fifty thousand years of life, at least.'

'Are you schooling me in science?' Klarek winced. 'That's heathen talk.'

'My father died when I was ten,' Grigor replied.

'And mine at twelve.'

Grigor wiped his brow although there was no sweat on it. 'I'm telling you, Villiam's lineage isn't this long. A few flowers at most. His great-grandfather took the manor over from the Duke of Lapvoon, so the story goes.'

'I don't think you know your history.'

'I know what my father's father's father had to say about it.'

'I don't think you do.'

'Ach,' Grigor said, walking away. 'Whatever.'

'You better dye your clothes soon, old man!' Klarek hollered after him. 'If you don't wear red, you'll be hanged for treason.'

It was odd, Ina thought, that the birds hadn't alerted her of Grigor's arrival, but she herself felt drawn to look through the trees and saw the old man stepping over the new shoots of tansy. She recognized Grigor. She had nursed him many, many years ago, and remembered the little dimple in his bottom lip. He carried with him a small wreath of canniba that he had saved along with his seeds during the drought and rains. It was only on a hunch that Grigor thought Ina might be pleased by the herb; he didn't know she suffered from headaches, only that she was very old. Grigor knocked on the door. She opened it. She saw Grigor's dimple and blushed and smiled.

'Come in,' she said. 'I guess you heard about my fertility treatment?'

'No, no. I have come to confess something.'

Ina stepped back from the doorway to let him enter. Looking around her room, he saw the dried herbs and flowers, a pot steaming on the hearth. The air smelled of frankincense, pine, orange, and fire. Ina sat on her bed and rubbed the place beside her. Grigor did not sit down, but handed her the wreath of canniba.

'I have brought you this gift. It is good for us elderly. It staves off forgetting.'

'Aha.'

'I take it to remember where I've put things,' he said. 'And it helps me sleep.'

'I don't need sleep,' Ina said. 'But I like to smoke it for my headaches.'

'As you like,' Grigor said. The priest had said to give her a gift and she would relieve his anger. But now that he was in her home, Grigor was a bit afraid of Ina's powers. He could not look her in the eyes. They used to be green and small, and as a baby he had wondered up at them as easily as if they were his own mother's. He remembered that now, and so he asked, 'What happened to your eyes?'

'The old ones?' Ina reached for them on the mantel and unwrapped the cloth. 'They're right here.'

Grigor gasped. The eyes were now shriveled and black and smelled of rotten fish.

'I keep them to remember, I suppose,' Ina said. 'Like the canniba. You like remembering things, Grigor?'

'I'm surprised you remember my name.'

'I remember the names of all my babes.'

Grigor's nose had begun to water from the stink of those old eyeballs. Ina sensed his disgust, but she didn't put them away. Instead, she plucked them from the cloth, placed them on a little ceramic plate, and put the plate on the bedside table. She struck a fire to light a tallow candle, whose smoke rose like ribbons in the air and followed her decoratively back to her seat on the bed. Witchy, Grigor thought. She pointed to a chair, a new one she had recently been given in payment for servicing the carpenter and his wife, who was now expecting.

'I came because the priest told me to,' Grigor said, worried he would fall victim to the smoke. It was only candle smoke, but he was afraid.

'Don't be afraid,' Ina said. 'Sit down. Let's have a conversation. I'll say one thing, and you say the next.'

Grigor agreed and waited for Ina to speak.

'Look at me,' she said.

'I'd rather not,' Grigor said.

'Are you disgusted by my beauty?' Ina asked.

'No,' Grigor answered, befuddled. He saw no beauty in Ina, and to be disgusted by beauty was impossible. So he looked at her without really wanting to, to see the beauty she referred to, to test his own disgust, and he felt it, but said again, 'No,' despite the gagging sensation he felt in his mouth and throat at the look of her huge, wet, bulging eyes. The fishy smell of the dead eyes on the bedside table was covered quite well by the smoke of the candle, and he breathed deeply, and then regretted it, thinking that the air might have been laced with something evil.

'Thank you,' said Ina, as though she understood that Grigor had unlashed his disgust for her into a general disgust, which now dissipated through the room like the candle smoke. Grigor was magically calmed. 'I've never had a husband, you know.'

'Yes, I know.'

Grigor looked around the room, resting his eyes finally on a pipe made out of a hollowed bone. He was no expert, but he thought the bone was the same length as a man's forearm, and he was afraid again.

'Shall we smoke the canniba together?' Ina asked. 'So that we remember?'

'Remember what?'

'Whatever you like. Maybe I can help you bring certain memories to mind.'

'Oh, I don't know.'

'I should be the only one to remember?'

'Well no, I remember plenty,' Grigor said, not entirely sure what he meant.

'I bet you this gold ducat that I remember more terrible things than you do.' She pulled the ducat from her armpit. Grigor thought it might be a trick of the light, the slick of her sweat reflecting off her finger. But then she flipped it to him and he caught it in his hand. It was real gold. 'Shall we smoke and have a little game?' she asked again.

Grigor didn't argue. He put the ducat in his pocket and sat back down in the chair, which was surprisingly comfortable.

'How old are you, Grigor?' Ina asked, reaching for her bone pipe.

'Sixty-four.'

'Young enough to remember how long it's been.'

'I'm the oldest man in Lapvona,' Grigor said.

'I bet you remember being born,' Ina said, breaking off a piece of the dried bud and sticking it into the bowl of her pipe. 'Bring me the candle, please,' she said.

Grigor did as she said. He struggled to remember being born, but couldn't.

'I guess we aren't supposed to remember that,' he said. 'No babe wants to hear their ma screaming.'

'I remember when you were born,' Ina said. She took the candle from him and brought the flame to the pipe and sucked. She inhaled deeply, her eyelids unfolding over her eyes. 'Your mother didn't scream a bit,' she said, letting the smoke lump out of her mouth with each word. 'I was there. I was the first one to touch you, even. You don't remember that?'

'I didn't know,' Grigor said. He imagined it for a moment, thinking of a memory he couldn't possibly have had: a vision of his young mother propped up on her elbows with her legs spread on the floor, wincing and blushing, her veil falling from her head, exerting great force as a baby plunked out from between her skirts. He saw a younger Ina pick the baby up and lick the blood from its face. 'Here you are, it's a boy,' she told Grigor's mother, who was going pale, her face sweaty in the sunlight through the window.

'Your ma was a sweet woman,' Ina said, interrupting his reverie. She took another drag from the pipe and paused. 'Never

made a peep. I sewed her up with a horsehair and she was rock-
ing you on the bed by nightfall.'

'I thought I was born in the morning,' was all Grigor could
summon. He felt angry at Ina for so casually telling him of
something so private and pure. But his anger was childish, like
the anger at the colors of a sunset for not being more pleasing.

'Nah,' Ina said. 'You were born in the afternoon. Your pa was
still in the fields. She came to me here,' she patted the bed, 'and
brought her own rags and your big sister. She was pretty, your
mother.'

'I remember,' Grigor said, suddenly emotional. He took the
pipe from Ina. 'I had no idea I was born here.'

'All the babes were born here for a time. I had a way that
made it not hurt. Tansy is good for that.'

Grigor sucked the smoke and held it in his lungs. Ina smiled
and lifted her legs onto the bed, leaned back. 'Thank you,' she
said, nodding at the gray smoke in the air. 'My head hurts since
I got my new eyes.'

'My head and my neck hurt,' said Grigor, exhaling. Ina nodded sympathetically. Grigor set down the pipe and rubbed his
neck.

'Would you like a drink of water?'

Grigor waved his hand to say no. The breeze through the
open door was cold but it felt good to have air circulating the
room. The candle burned steadily on the bedside table where Ina
had left it. From the outside, they would have looked like two
old friends, just sharing an afternoon.

'Where did you get your new eyes?' Grigor asked. He leaned back against the chair, let his mind drift up into the room to receive Ina's answer. He didn't want to seem disgusted by the eyes. He was sincerely curious where she'd gotten them.

'Somebody gave them to me.'

That seemed like answer enough. 'Is it true you lived in a cave when you were young?'

'It is,' Ina said. 'Have you been in a cave before?'

'I found a cave near the creek once, at the foot of the hill to the manor,' Grigor said.

'My cave was further away, past the range, on a different mountain. It was so cold in winter up there, but I kept warm somehow. And so much snow. I had my own waterfall in the summer.'

'That sounds nice.'

'I liked to stand under the water and feel it pressing down on me. I imagine it would feel just as good now. Shall we go?' She chuckled.

'I don't think there's any water in the falls there anymore,' Grigor answered gently. He wasn't angry at Ina anymore. His mind was in her waterfall. He saw her young and naked standing behind a curtain of warped glass, dark hair flowing long to her waist.

'It's too far for me to walk, to be honest,' Ina said. 'But there's water there.'

'Not with the drought. There was no water coming down these mountains.'

'There was,' Ina said.

Grigor tensed a bit in the chair.

'There wasn't,' he said.

'Now, now,' Ina said, and put up her wrinkled palm. 'Pass me the pipe please, Grigor,' she said.

Grigor sat up and passed it. As Ina clutched it, he felt the strong, long nails of her fingers against the butt of his thumb. It was barely a feeling, as his hands were so calloused from a lifetime of work, but it was something. His wife had died years ago. He pulled his hand away.

'If there was water on the mountains, why did we have none?' he asked.

Ina smoked. She realized exactly what Grigor had come for. He wanted his mind changed.

'Villiam kept the water for himself,' she told him.

'Father Barnabas said it was the work of the Devil.'

'Ah, yes, it is.' Ina said.

'But I heard Villiam's wife died from the drought. Like so many others.'

'She did not.'

'How do you know?'

'I cannot say.'

Grigor reached for the pipe and puffed it, his mind turning. 'If there was water up there, and Villiam had it, and the priest knew, then why were we down here starving by the lake?'

'I'm sure Father Barnabas explained it all.' Ina was being coy. She got coy sometimes when she smoked canniba.

'Father Barnabas said that there was a breach of security

down in hell, and that the Devil flew up to Earth, and it made the world hot and dried it all out. And now God has closed heaven's gates to keep him out. If the Devil gets into heaven, I don't know what we'll do.' Grigor stiffened, hearing the preposterousness of the story for the first time.

They were quiet for a while.

'Can I be honest?' Grigor asked. Ina grunted in reply. 'The priest told me to come see you, because I told him you were a witch.'

'Why'd you say that?'

'I don't know. I felt it was my duty.'

'Did he send you here to kill me, Grigor?'

'No, he sent me here to give you a gift, to relieve my anger.'

'Carnage or contribution. That's what priests always say.' She smoked some more and passed the pipe again.

'Do you still feel angry, Grigor?'

'Yes,' he said. 'The priest was wrong.'

'Good,' Ina said. 'Now come let me nurse you. For old time's sake. Do you remember how?'

The wedding procession began at noon. The minstrels began, playing their flutes and drums and lyres. The singer from Krisk had come after all, arriving just that morning. The stableboys had collected him and the best lute player in Tivak along the way, and two drummers from Bordijn. The songs were very good. Then Villiam and the nun stepped out in their wedding clothes. They walked side by side across the drawbridge. As was custom, Agata walked to the left of Villiam; God fashioned Eve out of Adam's left rib. Or was it the right rib? The left, yes, or so the priest thought. He wasn't quite sure. He was tired. Father Barnabas had spent the night with Villiam, playing games and drinking to distract the lord from his anxieties. Villiam had been worried he wouldn't look lordly enough in his costume. 'The people must fear me and love me. I'm like a father to them all. It's a difficult image to project. You wouldn't understand,' Villiam said to Father Barnabas.

'If you want my advice, do nothing. The less you do, the more they will revere you.'

Now Father Barnabas followed the couple on horseback, riding a broken-in tarpan that he had never ridden before. Villiam had chosen the priest as his best man, which meant that he had to carry a sword with the family crest, and it was heavy on his hip as he rode. He was struggling. And he was nervous. He had read the banns the last three Sundays at Mass, each time stressing the magnitude of the approaching nuptials, as if God Himself were taking a wife. 'If anyone knows cause or just impediment why these two persons should not be joined together in Holy Matrimony, then declare it.' Nobody declared anything, of course. First, to declare anything that would inconvenience Villiam was not only frowned upon, it might be punishable by death. It wasn't right to question the lord. It put everybody in jeopardy, and nobody could afford to lose favor. Secondly, nobody knew what had actually happened to Dibra. She was presumed dead once the banns were read. The fact that the priest had not announced her death gave them reason to suspect that Dibra had died as many of the villagers had died—of starvation. The poor woman. Nobility are not immune to famine, they all thought, and they felt sorry for Villiam. He must be heartbroken. There had been whispers of Jacob's disappearance throughout the village last spring, and Marek's. Some of them assumed that, like his father, Marek was a cave dweller now, or had died, or had been eaten.

'Can a savior bring the dead back to life?' someone had asked the priest after Mass last week.

'A savior can do anything. Anything you wish, He will grant. Jesus turned wine into roses, did he not?'

'You said he turned fish into bread.'

'Anything you want. Give Him a gold coin and He'll turn it into a key that opens heaven's gate.'

'Is the Devil still free?'

'Yes,' the priest said gravely. 'We must all be very careful. The gates of heaven are still shut, and the Devil may come back here if he gets restless roaming. We've got to get him back to hell. That's what the savior is for.'

'Get the Devil back to hell, yes,' they all said, nodding, grateful that the savior was on the way. And they loved the nun for this, a holy mother, the deliverer of mercy. Thank God.

For the wedding, the guards had taken posts along the edges of the fields and were directed to execute any person attempting to enter the village. At any wedding, there was a threat that some nefarious party might intervene. But the priest had given specific warnings to Villiam that there were those nearby who would want to sabotage his union, evildoers who knew damn well that the baby in the nun's belly was a savior, and they didn't want anyone to be saved. Villiam played along, directing Klarek to increase security. He felt wise to do so. There was word on the wind that the bandits had heard of the nun's pregnancy, that it was rumored among them that she was of bandit descent. If this were ever confirmed, surely they would storm the manor and take the Christ as their own.

Marek followed the priest's horse on foot, taking the customary place of the groom's parents. The villagers gasped and pointed as he passed. Not only was the boy alive, but his health was much improved. He wore red garments and walked sullenly, coolly, his mind ablur with rage. To him, the marriage was an act of theft. His mother had been returned to him, and now Villiam was stealing her away. He blamed Agata, however. To blame Villiam would have been to break his guilty promise of devotion. Was the death of a son equivalent to a stolen mother? Only God could judge.

It wasn't until they reached the village, with all the Lapvonians in their ghastly red costumes, that the idea came to Marek. He picked a rock up off the ground as the crowds thickened, hid it in his hand, waited for the right moment, then threw it at Agata. The rock hit her in the back, and she tripped and fell, holding her belly, and landed facedown in the dirt. Villiam wasn't paying attention. He simply kept walking and waving and nodding to the crowds.

The priest pulled up on his horse, who neighed, astonishing Villiam, who laughed at what he thought was the priest's incompetence on horseback. And before he could turn to look, a villager had helped Agata up off the ground, an old lady with huge, bulging eyes.

'Welcome back,' she said to the bride.

Agata recognized Ina despite her weird transformation. She was faint and stunned from the blow to her back, but she quickened her step away from the old lady to rejoin Villiam, brushing the dirt off the front of her dress. Ina knew the truth about her. Her name wasn't Agata at all—that was only what Jude had named her, after his mother. Ina knew that Marek was Agata's brother's son, and she knew that her brother had been caught and pilloried and hanged and gutted last Easter, for all of the town to see. The birds had told her everything. Agata didn't know that her brother had come looking for her last spring. All she knew was that she could never go home, and that Ina knew that. Agata was a prisoner wherever she went—at Jude's, at the abbey, and now at the manor. All of this had passed between the two women in their small moment. Now the priest's horse settled and clopped after Agata through the crowd.

Klarek ran ahead, dragging Marek with him, past a man standing slightly apart from the crowd. His clothes were rags, brown and black and caked with shit and mud. His face was so dirty, nobody but Marek could have recognized him. Marek moved in astonishment, as though he'd seen a ghost. Or perhaps the man that looked like his father was an emanation of his own conscience. That must be it, Marek thought: I have lost my mind. But Jude had looked exactly like a dead thing that had come back to life and unburied itself. Could it be? His father, risen from the dead, too? If Jude had returned to interfere with the wedding, he ought to be throwing rocks himself.

'Never mind, never mind!' the priest shouted back from his high horse.

Klarek pulled Marek back into the procession.

The ceremony was over as soon as it began, and Villiam was happy now as the villagers sang him songs of praise as he made his way back through the church, doling out zillins. Agata was a bit too slow down the aisle, so Villiam walked up ahead, flanked now by Klarek and the priest. The church steps were treacherous in the tight, leather shoes made especially for the nun for this occasion. The villagers had all touched the shoes at the shoemaker's, had wondered over the measurements of her foot as though the numbers had some sacred meaning. 'Did you really touch her foot?' they asked the shoemaker. 'Yes, yes.' 'And was it very beautiful?' 'Looked like any foot, a lady's foot.' 'A lady's foot, ah,' the women said. The men wanted to know whether her toes were long or short, as long toes indicated great beauty. 'I saw her face,' the shoemaker told them all. 'She looks like any nun from the abbey.' This disappointed them. But Agata looked beautiful now, aglow with her pregnancy, and her eyes squinted with irritation and awe at the commotion around her. Her red hair poked out from under her veil. The village women caressed her arms and shoulders as she passed. 'Should we touch her belly?' one asked. Ina gave her assent. And then they were all upon her, kneeling at her feet, arms sneaking around her from behind, hands flat against the bulge as if they could suck the divinity out through the fabric of her dress. Agata surrendered. The men simply removed their tattered red hats as she passed and held them over their pubises, to shield the baby from any power that might offend it.

Villiam's legs hurt from all the walking. He had walked so long—from home to the church and back—only once before in his whole life, and the memory of that humiliation had returned halfway back up the hill, when he could no longer lift his feet and needed to be carried. When it happened on his first wedding day, his father had laughed and chided Dibra. 'He'll die quick, so make him spawn soon. You're no lazy woman, are you?' His mother looked ashamed. Today, when he tired, Villiam threw a fit and sat down on the road. It had been quite a shock to go from the cheering and singing of the village to the relative quiet of the walk back to the manor. It was too boring. Klarek tried to help him up. 'I don't want anyone but my own blood touching me,' Villiam said petulantly. And he felt a bit of pity for himself then as he recognized in that instant that there was nobody left on Earth in his lineage but himself. Except, wait—Marek stood before him and knelt down so that Villiam could ride on his shoulders—didn't that lamb herder say they were cousins?

Villiam steadied himself and lifted his tired leg over Marek's shoulder. Light as a feather. 'Get ready, my boy,' Villiam huffed as he straddled Marek by the neck, clutching the thick red hair in his fists to balance as he swung his other leg over. 'Now get up, slowly,' he said. Marek did as he was told. It was not unlike carrying the water buckets, he thought. He stood, trying to move smoothly so as not to topple Villiam, and succeeded despite the lord's yelps of fear that the boy wasn't strong enough to carry him. But in fact, Marek had grown strong enough that he could carry Villiam quite easily, his only stumble occurring when he turned back to see if Agata was watching. He wanted to show her that he was useful and important, someone she would need to carry her through her own hardship one day, he thought. And then he was sorry for throwing the rock. Agata looked tired and distant and sad, as though her life were a term of deployment, and she had reached surrender. She had seen that Marek had turned to her to show off his strength, but she hadn't tilted her eyes at all, no. Just to spite him. And she was pleased when Villiam snickered at Marek to keep his head straight and pulled at his ears like a man riding a donkey.

Eventually, Villiam grew tired of Marek's shuffling gait, and decided to ride with the priest on horseback to the manor while the rest of the procession walked. He was glad the wedding was over. His new shoes had gotten scuffed on the church steps when he'd tripped a bit.

'Did anybody see me trip on the steps of the church?' he asked Father Barnabas.

'Nobody noticed. They were all too stunned by your lordliness.'

Villiam had made a spectacle of his vows, reciting them by heart, his voice so loud that Agata bristled and turned her head away from the words. 'To have and to hold, in bed and at the table, whether she be fair or ugly, for better or worse, in sickness and in health, for as long as we both shall live.'

Agata made no vows, as was customary for the bride.

'I think we both performed well,' Villiam said to the priest.

'Everyone was very impressed with us,' Barnabas replied.

Villiam spent the rest of the ride with his arms wrapped around Father Barnabas's middle. He imagined Dibra would be jealous now, knowing what good fortune awaited him. She had never been grateful or tender with him, only distracted and annoyed. And her affair with Luka was embarrassing. What kind of woman wants a man who cares for horses? Villiam watched the land pass—each jolt of the horse hurt his bones, and he gripped the priest a little tighter. Dibra had been so protective of Jacob, as though she didn't want Villiam to even know the boy. But now he had a second chance at fatherhood. Maybe he would enjoy it this time. He would teach the baby to be funny. And he would make sure the boy would take his side in any argument. It would be easy to mold the babe to his liking, Agata was so mute and passive. Was she even a real girl? he wondered. He'd barely given her any thought. She'd stood so still during the service. Her hand emitted absolutely nothing when he placed the ring on its finger. Her lips were dry, almost imperceptible when he'd kissed them. She was nothing, she did nothing. But Villiam trusted the priest that the child would be a blessing. He rested his head against the priest's shoulder, cool with sweat. He breathed in deeply. It never occurred to him that the priest was crumbling under the pressure. Barnabas had never had any faith in the Second Coming, but now faced with the possibility, he worried that a messiah would outsmart him as soon as it was old enough to speak.

Villiam lifted his head up and spoke softly into the priest's ear.

'I love you, Father,' he said. It wasn't quite love that Villiam felt, but an enduring trust and need for constant affirmation that was as good as love.

'And I love you,' the priest said back.

Grigor had missed the wedding procession. He had stayed the whole previous day and night with Ina. They had eaten eggs and wheatmeal for their supper, and then eggs again for breakfast. Ina had snored like a chirping bird as she slept. Grigor had woken up a few times in the darkness to listen, amazed. In the morning, he preferred to do her the favor of clearing the brush outside the cabin, sweeping inside, and fixing a few loose boards on the door while she went off to the church. Any anger and suspicion he'd once had for Ina had now transferred to the priest and Villiam. He didn't want to show his face and let his fury be seen in the village. Anyway, it had been too late for him to dye his clothes. The villagers would have shunned him. 'Old man can't be bothered.' Alone at Ina's, he felt light and empty, detached from the great weight of confusion he had carried there the day before.

After mending the door, Grigor beat Ina's mattress and the small worn rug, brought water from the well, chopped wood and stacked the pieces outside, dug up a dozen wild potatoes and put them on the fire now to roast. He was eager to hear what Ina had seen at the wedding, what of the nun, any gossip. But he was more eager just to be with Ina again, to feel the space that she created with her mind. The world felt bigger in her presence. Perhaps it had something to do with her eyes. Grigor wanted to see them again. Maybe he had been wrong to think they were grotesque. He loved her irrespective of her beauty anyway. Ina had taken him in and touched his mind with hers. She did not address him like a man, but a neutral soul, and Grigor liked that, finally relieved of what he had felt had been useless for decades— the need to prove his manhood, to be something other than himself. He could change now, like he wanted to change. He felt there was more to learn from Ina, and he was afraid to return to his son's home, where he wasn't really wanted anyway. Vuna and Jon were not free. Their idea of life was to work the land and worship, and to have another child who could work the land and worship when they were gone. Their only anxiety was in what the land would produce for them. Didn't they know that the land was God itself, the sun and moon and rain, that it was all God? The life in their seeds of wheat, the manure from the cow, that was God. The priest had nothing to do with it. Grigor could see that now. Ina had cleared his vision. He poked at the potatoes in the fire, threw a fistful of rosemary at the singeing skins. They filled the cabin with a delicious aroma.

There were six perfect crab apples on the table. Grigor had climbed the tree and picked them from the tallest branches. Now he polished them and set them in a line. It was beautiful to see how each apple was different. He sat and rested his head in his hands and stared down at the apples. They seemed to smile at him. How easy it was to see their beauty. He would need to try again with Ina.

# WINTER

By Yuletide, a gray hair had sprouted on Villiam's pubis. It gave him great alarm. Suddenly he was aging. The idea threw him into a dark depression. At the same time, he felt he ought to start acting a bit more mature—the father of the son of God was a role that demanded some gravitas. Word had spread throughout the entire kingdom about the virgin mother, his wife. Letters of congratulations had arrived, each including an expectation that Villiam represent his fiefdom with perfect righteousness, as every citizen, from Arat to Yxtria, would soon make a pilgrimage to Lapvona to see the baby. This put a great strain on Villiam's sense of self. He became more self-conscious. His self-confidence waned. He knew he ought to be more self-reliant, but he had been too spoiled his whole life to learn any dignity. He had to try to do things on his own. While in the past he would have asked the priest to pluck out the gray pube, Villiam had to do it himself now, contorting his body to find its root in the gatelike crevasse of his crotch. The self-intimacy did not delight him. He didn't even show Clod the pube. He was too ashamed—he put it in his mouth and swallowed it. The looming exposure, having to host all the vassals and lords and every measly priest and villager from near and far, he feared, would only cause more gray pubes to appear. Soon he would look old and decrepit. Was he being punished for something? He studied himself constantly in the mirror, looking for more signs of the reaper. Any little twitch or wrinkle and Villiam went into a panic. But he had to hide his feelings. No, he couldn't indulge in his fear around the others. Rather, he was supposed to inspire strength. Holiness. This caused him great anxiety. He threw all the servants into a frenzy, directing them to fix every little crack or worn edge in the manor. Everything would have to gleam. No longer could he request ridiculous feasts and marathons of childish entertainment simply because he was bored or lonely or hungry. There were more serious matters afoot. He hired Ina to keep watch over the nun, to be her servant and her midwife. And he would need a new horseman, someone he could trust. He had learned his lesson with Luka.

'I need an unattractive man to run the stable,' he told Barnabas.

'Your cousin Jude would do well,' the priest had said.

Villiam couldn't refuse. He even felt a bit of pride in giving employment to someone he was related to, as if he were acting out of loyalty to his ancestors. He told this to the priest, who laughed at him.

'Employing your cousin to shovel horse shit is nothing to boast about.'

Villiam didn't pout or pounce in response, but rather took the ridicule to heart and let his pride pass. He thanked Barnabas for his counsel and called for Klarek to go find the man and bring him up here. 'This is not out of loyalty,' Villiam told Klarek. 'I would never boast to that.'

Villiam's self-awareness grew alongside budding self-doubt and, worst of all, self-loathing. For the first time in his life, he was not in love with himself. He had no libido left, and even his appetite for food had started to touch its limit. In early December, Villiam replaced Clod with Lispeth as his personal servant because her company was stiff and removed. Villiam thought she would have a good effect on his self-seriousness. She did not indulge him or draw his picture. That silliness was over. She didn't laugh or clap or even really listen anytime he complained of woe or pains or worry. He felt he needed this kind of stern support.

'Why do I feel unhappy?' he asked Lispeth.

She shrugged her shoulders.

'Don't you have any wisdom?'

'No.'

Villiam missed Clod. That he knew. And perhaps this was why Marek began to have even more appeal to him: Marek's capacity was limited to servile flattery. The boy's sense of self-worth was far worse than Villiam's could ever become. So the lord used the boy as a kind of prop, a measuring stick. In Marek's company, the lord felt more lordly. They began to spend more time together.

Marek, by turn, resorted to even more pathetic servility to occupy the space of horror that opened further and further within his heart the bigger Agata's belly grew. He had a growing paranoia that God was punishing him. He went over his life story again and again, but he reached no enlightening conclusion about its moral. First his mother rose from the dead, but not for his sake, apparently. Then his father rose, too. Marek's young mind could not make sense of it. Since Ina had come, keeping everyone away from Agata, and since Jude ignored him, completely obsessed now with the horses, there was only Villiam. No one else could distract him from the mysteries of his own life. He tried to look at Villiam kindly, not to think the worst of him. Hiding all indications of disgust or resentment took some exertion of will at first, but then it was natural, and he felt better. The exercise forced him to smile like an idiot at Villiam's lame attempts at good-natured comedy, to agree with all he said.

'Marek takes after me, don't you think?' Villiam asked the priest one day.

'I don't see how that's possible,' Father Barnabas replied.

Lately, everything the priest said inspired a minor existential crisis in Villiam. Just the slightest provocation and Villiam was tense and seething. But the lord kept quiet. He worried, needlessly, that the priest would report any signs of weakness to the vassals and high priests. Then they might come after him, boot him out, find him unworthy of the sacred role he would soon play. If he played it well, he might become a saint, he thought. Like Joseph. He'd better act like one, he knew, but it was so boring. It was terribly depressing.

Villiam's depression didn't have a profound effect on the goings-on at the manor. It was simply a charge that followed him around now, a kind of desperation. The servants noticed the change, but they were too consumed by their duties to really care. Along with depression, Villiam had been growing increasingly suspicious that there was a force outside the limits of Lapvona that wanted to destroy him. He had Father Barnabas arrange for a shipment of wine and spirits for Christmas from the south, where the priest's good standing would ensure that the drink would be untainted. Villiam was even suspicious that the wine already stored in the cellar had been tainted somehow. He instructed the servants to bury it all in a far corner of the estate, where the priest promised nothing would leech into the ground and poison the dirt. Even so, Villiam was worried. His waning appetite was probably due to his fear that the earth now held something toxic.

Villiam had moved his chair at the dining table to the center, next to Marek's. The priest had moved his place setting down to the other end. Viewed from above, it looked like the remnants of a chess game, king and knight lined up side by side, and a rook in the corner. The game was almost over. Ina, although she'd moved into the manor to monitor the pregnancy, didn't eat with the others at the table; she was considered, like Jude, one of the servants. And she and Agata were in strict quarantine in Agata's room. Not even the female servants were allowed in. One stray germ and the Second Coming wouldn't come. It was too dangerous. Food and water and herbs were left by the door.

Inside the room, Agata was not even allowed out of bed. Given how Agata had wanted Marek destroyed, and how he'd turned out in the end, Ina didn't trust her to care for the unborn child. Ina took full charge. 'Do as I say, or this time the baby will surely kill you.' Agata didn't mind the incarceration or the pillows propped under her back or the ropes around her wrists and ankles tying her to the posts of the bed. When she was awake, she was made to eat the stewed livers of chickens to strengthen her blood. Ina fed them to her with a spoon, blowing on the brown stuff and testing each bite with her own tongue. The tonic she gave Agata made her sleepy all the time. Winter herbs were especially potent. Agata felt no pain in her womb, not a kick or a single cramp or pressure. Ina sat with her ear to her belly constantly, whispering to the baby inside, sometimes going up with her hand to caress its face or let it curl its tiny fingers around her thumb. As long as Agata took what Ina gave her, she felt nothing. Less and less.

Grigor came to the manor once a week to deliver the herbs Ina needed. Often he stopped by the stables to say hello to Jude in an effort to get to know him. He had seen Jude whenever he'd brought his babes to market and herded them up onto the cart, crying in the dust like a man bidding adieu to his wife and children. Grigor had heard gossip that his boy had died.

'I know what it's like to lose a child,' Grigor told Jude. 'I lost my grandchildren to the bandits.'

Jude told Grigor the truth of his situation—that he had traded Marek for Jacob when his son had killed Villiam's, that Agata was the bastard's real mother, but the Christ babe was his. Grigor wasn't sure what to believe, but he saw the poor man's heartache, and that was enough to earn his sympathy. He admired Jude's solitary lifestyle at the stable, how he'd refused to conform himself to the ways of Lapvona, and now the ways of the manor.

'Work harder this year and the Devil will scare,' Father Barnabas still said. On top of farming and smelting and baking and building, now the villagers were also restoring the old church. Every available hand was expected to rebuild, repaint, sand, and polish the place, while Barnabas barely even showed his face. It was all crooked. Grigor could tell that Jude knew it, too.

'Why should I be a slave to fear if Jesus has already saved me?' Grigor asked.

'Everyone is ashamed. So they pretend they're perfect. But everybody sins. Only God is perfect,' Jude said.

'That's what I keep telling my children,' Grigor said.

'People don't like it when the truth is easy,' Jude said. 'Let them think what they want.'

'I will try that. Thank you, Jude.'

Grigor's son, Jon, and his daughter-in-law, Vuna, assumed that the old man's mind was fading due to age and the damage of the summer starvation. They could see that he had changed since the drought. Grigor was grumpier. He couldn't get settled back in the house after he'd spent so much time with Ina. He felt odd when he went out into the village, knowing what he now knew; that he was saved and had been saved, and only his doubt had kept him from ever being truly happy. But now he had a chance. He could walk around with love in his heart, fearlessly. He tried, during the days, to feel it. He tried feeling it standing in the sun in the village square. He tried it visiting the neighbors. He tried it talking to his daughter-in-law about Ina's herbs. Grigor wasn't sure he was doing it right. Society felt awkward now. It took everything Grigor had not to scream sometimes. When he looked at Jon, he saw someone tired and worn beyond his years. It seemed lunatic to be eating a crust of bread and sipping a cup of broth and to give thanks for just that. Thanks for nothing? The world was full of bounty. Just look up at the manor and you could see Paradise. Why had nobody realized it before? His boy was so grim and serious. He worked too much.

Grigor said, 'Work or don't work. It doesn't matter.'

'How will we eat if we don't work?' Jon asked. 'Who will provide for us?'

'Oh, someone.'

'You don't know what you're saying,' Jon said.

'I finally heard the truth,' Grigor told him. He couldn't explain when he'd heard it, or from whom, but he'd heard it in his heart, without words, a deep knowing, and nothing could hurt him or frighten him now. It was so simple that the reasoning of it tended to slip through his mind as soon as he touched it, like a rabbit in the woods. Once you breathe, it's gone. He tried to explain this to Jon and Vuna, but he was not good with words.

'God rewards hard work,' Jon said. 'If I don't serve God, how will He know I'm any good?'

'How will we pay the monthly tax?' Vuna asked.

Grigor shrugged. 'I don't know. Don't worry.' Speaking with them was useless. It didn't matter. And they seemed to resent his new attitude. He was acting lazy around the house. He spent more and more time away, wandering in the woods and resting in Ina's empty cabin. He liked it there. He liked to dust and keep her place tidy. When Jenevere had come to pick tansy and canniba per Ina's request, and she saw Grigor there, he had offered to pick the herbs himself—she told him which ones—and deliver them to the manor. The task made Jenevere's work easier and made Grigor very happy. He had missed being in touch with what grew from the dirt. The herbs were all wild. Picking them was not like harvesting the crops of his farm, but like a discovery of nature's magic. He hunted through the forest and picked them carefully, wrapping each bud or branch in its own clean cloth, like jewels. His heart felt cool and calm as he picked the herbs, as though even just the discovery of them had healing properties.

The horses had all been well trained by Luka, and the stableboys were attentive and did whatever Jude asked. He had an intuitive knowledge of how to care for animals, and he was gentle and generous with each horse, taking the time to get to know them, their differences, and ride them and pet them and speak to them and lie across their backs and hold them around their necks and tickle their ears. They liked him. He fed them handfuls of barley and wheat from his hands and kissed their noses. Now Jude dressed not like a beggar but like Luka. He wore Luka's old chore coat and hat and gloves and fit his hands into the worn leather wraps on the ropes and the wood fence of the corral when he took the horses out to run. He slept in a horse stall, shared the thick hay with Dibra's blind horse. The blind horse had no name, and it did not run with the other horses. Jude worried it might hurt itself if it stumbled or ran up against a steed or into the fence. It seemed the other horses didn't like the blind one, like a wounded soldier who had seen too much and reminded them of their own possible fate. So Jude took the blind one out alone at dawn, leading it by hand and walking beside it, no tether or harness, not even a rope around its neck. He envied the eyeless horse in a way, that it required and received so much careful attention, like a babe, and that it was blind to the disturbed looks on the other horses' faces. Creatures were cruel. It reminded Jude of how the villagers had regarded Marek—a freak. But Jude had sympathy for the horse. It was not a freak by nature, but as a result of betrayal and abandonment. He felt they had that in common.

Jude and Marek were like enemies now, each keeping his own secret belief about the other. To Marek, Jude was a ghost, a revenant of guilt. And so was Agata. To Jude, the boy was a blight, a curse, something that had come to Earth to punish him for a sin he couldn't recall. Hadn't he been a good man? Hadn't he prayed enough? Hadn't he lashed himself correctly? It never occurred to Jude that the capture and detention of Agata as an adolescent was anything but his rightful duty as a man. He was a man and she was a girl. How could it have been wrong to have claimed her as his? He'd saved her, after all, wandering the woods with blood still oozing out of her mouth. If he hadn't, she would have died, been eaten by wolves or frozen to death. He had not caught sight of her since the wedding, and although he understood that she belonged to Villiam now, he preferred to think of her as not there, but dead again. Otherwise it was too painful. In his heart, he knew the babe was his. A cruel joke this was—finally a child of his own seed and he couldn't claim it; it already belonged to the lord and God. No. Jude couldn't even think of it. He pushed Agata from his mind. The pregnant nun Villiam had married only resembled a girl he once knew, and she herself was a nobody. His memory of her was only a fixing of his mind upon a dream on a lonely night. He told himself that he knew nothing about her, cared nothing. She was ugly now, anyway. She'd looked so old in her wedding dress—a grown woman. He liked the look of Lispeth better, enough that any nights he felt lonely for his own hand, it was Lispeth's face that he envisioned, her body stripped of its heavy servant's uniform, writhing sensually under him in the hay. He saw her whenever she rushed outside to throw rubbish in the field or fetch eggs from the henhouse. Her figure from afar had a certainty to it, as though she understood more than she could think in words.

That was a good girl, he thought, a pretty face and a mind that doesn't know its own strength. He would marry her, perhaps, if he could one day command her attention.

Christmas in Lapvona had a strange, ominous tilt to it that winter. The birth of the last Christ was so many hundreds of years ago, and there was some trepidation around celebrating while Villiam's new wife was pregnant with the next one. This concern over tradition wasn't any trouble at the manor—nobody there had any loyalty to Jesus Christ—but there was apprehension about the holiday in the village, as though it would be the last. Jesus would soon be displaced by the new baby, and nobody knew what might happen next. It felt strange to the villagers to put down their tools and stay home for the while, to amuse themselves with games and songs while the future was so unclear. And the wreaths of holly that had been delivered to each house per Villiam's orders had thorns that pricked the ladies' fingers as they hung them on their front doors. With blood on their hands, they rolled out the dough and pressed cookies into the shape of the Cross.

Marek had thought the baby would come soon—the lambs had only taken four months. He was nervous that the birth would push him out of favor with Villiam. He imagined that he'd become unwelcome, a pest, while everyone rejoiced in the presence of the Messiah. Petra assured him that there were still months yet to pass before Agata's baby would be born. 'Ina is sure the baby will come in April,' she said.

'What will I do then?' Marek asked.

'You'll be a man soon,' was all Petra could think to answer.

The idea of growing up horrified Marek. Where would he go, and what would he do there? He prayed for an answer that night, but his dreams weren't helpful. First he saw only the darkness of the room in his sleep, the space open and wide like the night sky before a cliff. Then his dreams descended on Lapvona, where he saw his old self shuffling along the roads, picking berries and looking in on people in their cottages. Dogs lurched out from their penned yards to sniff him, ducked away when he tried to pet their heads. He knocked on the door of Ina's cabin, but she wouldn't answer. Birds shat on his head and shoulders as he walked away, tripping on gravestones he'd never noticed before, there in the woods. His dreams were so lonely. Several times he awoke sweating, with the feeling that he was trapped, his arms and legs and head stuck in the stockade still sticky with blood from the Easter bandit, but he was only tangled in his blankets. He threw them off and stretched his back by twisting from side to side. In the mornings he had a burning ache in his muscles, as though they were growing even further in the wrong direction. Was he dreaming the wrong things? He couldn't ask Ina for medicine. Each time he knocked on Agata's door, Ina screeched like a vulture and told him to go away. He woke up on Christmas Eve in such pain that he asked Petra for a bottle of strong wine to soothe him. She complied and expressed her pity for him that he felt so bad on the holiday.

Unlike Lispeth, Petra didn't hate Marek. She was an easygoing girl with no ambition. Lispeth was still prickly and mean. When Marek and Villiam played chess or danced together, she always set down Marek's food and drink carelessly, spilling things, just to let him know she hated him as much as ever. But Villiam's attention overpowered Lispeth's disdain. Marek felt lucky for that. The wine did help him to relax. And he was curious what would happen on Christmas, relieved that the baby was still months away.

For the entire day, he remained in a drunken stupor.

As he had done every Christmas past, the priest had directed the servant girls to create a crèche in the stable, this time in the hay of the stall that had been empty since Luka's disappearance. Marek had never seen a crèche before and was anxious to go look. It gave him a reason to spy on Jude. Marek hoped Jude would see him with Villiam, feel enraged with jealousy, and do something to embarrass himself. He imagined that a ghost would do something insane when it got angry, such as run into a wall or melt into a puddle. To Marek's disappointment, Jude was out with the horses when Lispeth brought Villiam and Marek to inspect the crèche in the afternoon.

'This is where the manger is, and here is the Jesus doll,'

Lispeth said, pointing to a pile of hay covered with a soiled horse blanket. Wrapped inside was a wooden doll that Clod had carved and painted. It was not much to look at.

'Who will play Joseph and Mary?' Villiam asked, trying to control his disappointment.

'We thought you and your lady would want to do that,' Lispeth said. She was being cruel. She knew Agata couldn't leave her bed.

'You play Mary, Lispeth. My lady can't be bothered.'

Lispeth's head jerked in revulsion at the idea. 'You and your guests can come see it after the feast,' was all she said.

On Christmas Eve and Day, two different families from the village were selected to join Villiam for celebratory feasts. The selection of each family was purportedly alphabetical, according to names on the census, but there were rumors among the villagers that the priest chose the most pious and venerable citizens each year. So, qualities of the first family picked would be analyzed, and the villagers placed bets on who would likely get picked next. If the first family was strong willed and confident, the next would be, too. But there was no real reasoning behind the selections. Klarek simply knocked on the door of a house he'd never knocked on before, and announced to them in the morning that they were expected at the manor that afternoon. On Christmas Eve, Klarek had woken late, dreading the day, and had taken a horse down to the village. He knocked on the first door by the farms, just past Jude's old pasture. Inside was a young couple, a northern man, his wife, who was descended from old Lapvona, and their two young children, half dressed. The place stank of burning potatoes. The man was bashful and apologetic for the mess, but invited Klarek inside, bowing and smiling, unsure of what to do.

'No need,' Klarek said, already getting back up on his horse. 'Come up to the manor as soon as you are dressed. It's your lucky day.'

Once the news reached the villagers, they would say that the choice of family was made based on mixed breeding. There were dozens of families of different backgrounds in Lapvona. But these lucky ones lived too far from the center of the village to run out and spread their joy. Anyway, they were too busy digging through their rags for something decent to wear, rubbing the mud and chicken shit off their shoes. By chance, some neighbors passed by and looked through the windows, saw them putting on their red clothes, and the rumor spread.

Villiam had never cared for the Christmas visitors. They always seemed too stupefied by the circumstances to be entertaining. But this year was different. Villiam was different. He was feeling insecure, and he wanted the visiting families to give a good report to the villagers. Gossip was important now. So on the walk back from the stables to see the crèche, Villiam told Marek that they must both be on their best behavior. Marek burped and staggered. Villiam didn't notice.

'If you see me scowling at dinner, Marek,' Villiam said, 'pound on the table with your fist, and I'll laugh.'

Marek agreed.

The rest of the day passed stiffly, the servant girls scurrying and cooking, Marek and Villiam lying on the floor in the light through the window of the sunroom.

'Who is the baby's father?' Marek asked, sipping from another bottle. 'Is there one?'

'I am the baby's father.'

Marek lay back. He felt the warmth from the sun on his face, and felt his back relax a bit against the hard stone floor. 'Do you think my bones are right?' he asked Villiam.

'Please, don't ask me about bones. Tonight, we will only talk about normal things.'

Marek nodded. He had no idea what that meant. The wine had made him a bit softer in his mind, but no wiser.

So when the feast was served and all were gathered around the table—Lord, Marek, Father, and the visitors—Villiam tried his best to express his enthusiasm for the holiday. Everyone looked to be in the right spirit. The family wore their red clothes, dyed for the wedding, a bit faded by now but still vivid. Villiam considered it a sweet gesture. The northern man was typical—tall and bright-eyed and blond. His dark-haired wife was very small and nervous, reaching up to her dripping nose to wipe it now and then with a rag she pulled from her sleeve.

'Isn't it a blessing? It is, it is,' Villiam nodded. 'We are blessed to have you. As you are blessed to have us. Father, will you tell us all the story of Christmas? You always tell it in the most holy way.'

Villiam had always enjoyed the priest's summary of the Nativity. It had been one of the few stories Barnabas had actually remembered from the seminary: 'On Christmas Eve, Christ's parents went to Bethlehem to be counted in the census. But they had no money to pay for a proper bed, so they took refuge in a horse stable, and that's where Jesus was born.'

'Well told,' Villiam had said in the past. The priest's commentary had focused mostly on the discomfort Mary must have felt, how the hay must have pricked at her back and bum as she lay there splayed open for all the livestock to see.

'The son of God born in a pigpen, or what have you. Hilarious,' Villiam had chuckled. No such foolery would be made tonight. Villiam sat up straight, smiling stiffly and holding his hands in prayer as he waited for Barnabas to recite the story. Marek yawned, and Villiam wanted to scold him, but the family was watching. 'Father,' Villiam said again. 'If you would, I do believe the spirit of Christmas is upon us. Ahem.'

But now Father Barnabas was flustered. He couldn't remember any details of the story, and the more he tried, the more flustered he became. Finally he cleared his throat: 'The two of them traveled to Bethlehem, of course, and we all know what happened there,' he said, lifting his cup. 'To Christ.'

'Hear hear,' Villiam said and smacked his lips.

The priest was being boring on purpose, Villiam thought, simply to rub him the wrong way. How depressing. He tried not to frown. He looked from face to face around the table. The village children had tawny hair and smooth olive skin, light hazel eyes. One girl and one boy. Instead of following the priest's lame toast with some irreverent quip as he would in the past, Villiam asked the boy's name.

'Emil,' the little boy said, his mouth a soft pink thing. Villiam nodded, comforted by his beauty.

'Eat well,' the priest said. 'And give news of the feast to all in the village.'

He scowled at Father Barnabas for his laziness. Marek immediately pounded his fist on the table as requested, and Villiam startled but didn't laugh. He was now sufficiently distracted by the little boy to be quieted.

'Marek, did you want to say something?' Barnabas asked.

'No, Father. Only to bless you and this food, amen.'

'Amen,' said the visitors.

'Yes, amen,' said Villiam.

The young couple sat shyly and waited for Villiam to begin to eat. They watched with lowered faces as he took a leg of goose from the silver platter and set it on his plate. He licked his finger. But Villiam was not interested in the food. Rather, he focused on the softness of little Emil's mouth as he chewed. The young mother didn't lift her eyes beyond her plate. She seemed very obsessed with her dripping nose. The daughter, however, ate as hungrily as her father, who thanked Villiam profusely for inviting them to take part in the occasion. 'We've heard stories of the place, but to see it with our own eyes, nobody would believe us, how fine it all is. I didn't believe it. I wouldn't believe it. I had to see it to believe it.'

'You're too kind, young sir,' Villiam said. 'It is all a testament to God's glory, not mine.' He looked at the priest to say something further, but Barnabas was picking the bones out of his fish stew. He'd been ornery and distracted lately. Perhaps the priest suffered from envy—Villiam would soon be father to the son of God; Barnabas would never attain such glory.

'Do you remember me?' Marek suddenly asked the man from the village. He had grown bolder the more he had drunk. 'I used to live in the pasture with all the lambs. I remember you. There was thistle growing in your front yard, wasn't there?'

The man wiped his hands on his shirtfront and regarded Marek, whose face was waxy in the candlelight. He bristled a bit to see the lopsidedness of the boy's eyes. He had heard of the trouble with the lamb herder, the slaughter of the ram. Nobody had ever mentioned Marek by name. But the man did remember the boy, bent and creepy. He'd seen him regularly scurrying like a cat down the road, looking for someone to pity him. He'd thought there was something wrong with the boy, that he was dumb and ought to be sent up to the monastery where he could be cared for, out of sight. He recalled remarking to his wife, 'Don't let that boy into the house. He'll only waste your time with his grief.' The man was afraid of strange people. Anyone deaf or crippled or ugly, he felt, was cursed. This was the attitude of most northerners. His wife, of course, being a native, understood that lameness or strangeness was a mark of grace. If one suffered purgatory on Earth rather than after death, heaven was easier to access. She, too, had seen Marek scrambling up and down trees, kicking rocks and picking flowers, shuffling down the road. She wasn't afraid of him. She thought he was lucky to live so freely. But then he'd disappeared. Husband and wife had assumed that the boy had died during the famine like so many others. But there he was, fattened, with shorn hair.

'Yes, I think I remember you now,' the man said politely.

'Do you remember my father, the lamb herder?'

'Quiet,' the priest interjected. 'It's not a party for reminiscences. We are here to feast for Christ.'

Marek looked at Villiam, who scowled again. Marek pounded the table. Villiam laughed falsely.

'My boy, Marek, has a fondness for wine, it seems,' Villiam said.

'Your boy?' the woman asked.

'Mm. And for the pastures. He likes the outdoors, don't you?'

Marek wilted. Of course Marek liked the outdoors, but what did Villiam know about it?

'Sure I do,' he said.

'And Emil,' Villiam said, clearing his throat. Emil sat up. 'Do you like the outdoors?'

Emil looked toward his parents, who nodded encouragingly for him to answer. They were not entirely perplexed by the lord's claim to Marek: men of power often enjoyed the company of boys, and there were great gifts to be gleaned from a lord's affections.

'Tell the lord if you like the outdoors,' the mother said quietly.

'Yes,' the little boy said.

'How wonderful!' Villiam cried. 'A boy who likes the outdoors. And where is your favorite place outside?'

'The lake,' the boy said, a little more confidently.

'And do you swim like a little fish?'

Emil didn't respond. He was remembering the summer and the horror of his hunger. Marek didn't look at the little boy. He didn't want to feel jealous or guilty. Emil took a bite of venison and chewed it slowly. Villiam watched his lips, anxious for his reply.

'Tell him,' the mother said.

'No,' Emil said. 'I can't swim.'

'Then we must teach you,' Villiam said. 'After dinner, come and have a bath with me. I'll show you how to float. My bathtub is so big, it can fit two grown men.'

At this point, Marek gave up on helping Villiam control his darker urges. He himself had never been invited to swim.

'Can I swim, too?' Marek asked. 'Why can't I swim?'

Villiam turned red and banged his own fist on the table, then chuckled and forced a smile. 'Nobody's asking you, that's why,' he said through clenched teeth.

The mother spoke up, blushing a bit. 'Our boy might be dirty,' she said. 'He'd ruin the lord's nice bathwater. He may splash you by accident, or he may drown.'

'We camped beside the lake during the drought,' the father said. 'The children weren't allowed in the water.'

'Maybe they could sing you a song instead,' the mother offered.

'That's quite all right. I don't like it when children sing,' Villiam said in reply.

'What nonsense!' the priest cried out, as though he had been waiting to explode. 'You love songs. Your whole life you've forced us to sing you songs all day long.'

'I don't like songs anymore, Father,' Villiam said. 'The coming birth of my Christ Child has changed me. I like swimming more than singing now.'

Barnabas kept his mouth shut. Marek pouted and drank more wine. He may once have been the lamb herder's son, but now he was as spoiled and petulant as a young lord. The visitors collectively ignored him, out of kindness.

'We would have liked to sing in the choir,' the northern man said, looking a bit drawn and stupid. 'But Elba died. She had been our leader, she knew all the songs.'

Villiam looked at Barnabas. He had never even known that the church had had a choir.

'Elba? Was she a good singer?'

The priest filled his mouth with stew. Who was Elba? He didn't care. He didn't want to speak of any church activities. He was mostly concerned with the look of the church now. The congregation had, in fact, taken to renovating the church with sincere devotion. It glistened and sparkled. Barnabas was running out of complaints: he knew he was procrastinating. He'd need to prepare a speech, something truly intelligent for when the vassals arrived in April, to prove his worth as an apostle, he supposed, whatever an apostle was.

'Let's not talk,' he said once he had swallowed. 'God wants us to be quiet. Maybe you are right, Villiam, that silence is holy.'

'Did I say that?'

'You did. Take note, all of you. The lord is wise.'

So they finished their meal in silence. Afterward, they left for the stables to see the crèche. Villiam insisted on carrying the torch, as though it required his great strength and authority. As they passed through the hall and out into the darkness of the wintry night, the air shifted into something soft and strangely delightful—a coming snow was lifting the chill from the air, pulling it upward. It was not a wind as much as a magnetic force, and to Marek it felt like an ominous sign from the heavens. He hung back in the group and watched the dark shapes of the family trailing behind Villiam. The priest had elected not to go, saying that he wanted to be alone to pray, which was a lie. He simply couldn't stand to be in Villiam's company any longer out of fear that the man would point to him and demand that he extol the meaning of the crèche and its components. And it was true: Villiam wanted a narrator for the scene. 'Do you like make-believe?' he asked Emil, reaching for the little boy's hand in the dark.

'No,' Emil replied.

Villiam's torch cast a red glow on the snowy ground. The young couple, the little girl in her father's arms, stepped around the periphery of the glow, as though they didn't want to get too close. Marek followed as they traversed the footbridge and took the path down to the stables.

Inside, the stableboys were ready in their robes. Marek held the torch as Villiam put on his Joseph costume—a drab brown cloak. He teetered a bit under the weight of it, unsteady on his long thin legs. Villiam had drunk wine out of thirst but eaten very little, and the wine had gone to his head, making him feel funny but not good-humored. He was drunk, he realized. He took the torch back from Marek, who was drunk, too.

'Where is our Mary?' Villiam asked, moving the torch around sloppily, looking for Lispeth. He hadn't noticed that the girl had not joined them for the promenade. 'Lispeth!' he called out into the dark. He tried to form the word more accurately with his lips and tongue, pronouncing the two syllables distinctly so nobody would detect his inebriation: 'Lissss! Peth!' She didn't come.

Marek peered around the stable, looking for Jude in the darkness. Past Christmases in the pasture had been spent fasting. The holy days were reserved for silence and introspection. Jude and Marek didn't know the story of the census, or that Christmas marked the birth of Jesus. Jude had thought that the reason Jesus was so revered was that He had been so brutally punished by soldiers on Christmas. This was what inspired him: his passion was brought on by torment. So between the two of them, Jude and Marek, they had made quiet Christmas offerings of self-abuse, cruel words spoken carefully in their minds: 'I am bad. I am shameful. I am a waste of life. I have done no good.' And then they abused one another: a punch in the gut and on the jaw, vicious words of contempt and disapproval. It was the one time each year Marek struck his father, an intimacy that he now missed.

'Lispeth! Goddamnit!' Villiam called again, lifting his chin and yelling into the rafters of the stables. Lispeth still didn't come. The stableboys scratched their heads. Villiam held the torch out to illuminate the Jesus doll.

'Marek, you be Mary,' he said.

'Me?'

'Go on. Don't get fussy.'

Marek didn't want to be Mary. He froze. It was, perhaps, the first time in his life that his judgment was good. To play a pregnant woman was a perversion he simply could not entertain. 'Where's my mother?' he asked.

Villiam opened his mouth, ready to deliver some grand speech, but he was interrupted.

'I'll be your Mary.' It was a male voice that spoke from the dark corner of the stable, muffled under the pawing of the horses against their sleeping hay.

'Who said that?' For a moment Villiam pictured Luka in the corner, back from hell or wherever he'd gone. 'Who goes there?'

Jude didn't answer aloud, but it seemed he spun the air at that moment, and a wind swirled through the stable, lifting a flame from Villiam's torch and spilling fire onto the pile of hay at his feet. Within an instant, the crèche was burning. The little Jesus doll crackled in the flames.

'Goddamnit!' Villiam cried again, dropping the torch and running out. 'Lissss! Peth!'

Much of the stable burned, but none of the animals were hurt. All the servants and visitors exhausted themselves spilling the buckets of water that Jude and the stableboys loaded back and forth from the reservoir on the horses. Marek and Villiam watched through the windows of the house for a while. Thank God Villiam was unharmed. But he was worried that the visitors—who were still putting out the fire—would go down to Lapvona and report that he had burned the crèche on purpose. He wasn't sure what had happened.

'Do you think they'll tell?' Villiam wondered aloud.

'Probably,' Marek answered. 'People like to gossip.'

'Will they say I was sloppy with the torch?'

'I don't know.'

'Then what good are you?' Villiam snapped. 'I thought you knew these people.'

'If you ask me, it was the horseman who did it.'

'The horseman started the fire?' Villiam rubbed his pale chin. 'Yes, yes. I think you're right. My cousin. He is a rather rough type, no? I'll go tell them.' Villiam turned to go out again. 'Should I put the horseman in the stockade, Marek? Would that make the story more true?'

'They might kill him then,' Marek said. He wasn't opposed to that idea. His father had died once before. Maybe this death would teach him to be kind.

'No, you're right,' Villiam said on his way out. 'That would only make more of a fuss.'

Marek watched through the window as the lord approached the young couple, straining with the buckets toward the fire. Villiam barely noticed the heat and smoke. The northern man had burned his hand and wrapped it in his wife's veil. 'God trusts your honor not to gossip,' Villiam shouted over the crackling flames. 'The poor horseman didn't mean to spark this inferno. Let's leave it at that, all right?'

The villagers coughed and wiped the cold sweat from their faces and promised they would only say that they'd had a beautiful Christmas Eve at the manor, and that they would cherish the memory as long as they lived.

Of course, it would be impossible not to gossip, as everyone was awaiting a report, and the young family were not liars but good honest Christians.

In the morning, Lispeth cleared the table of the feast, which had been left overnight to feed the ghosts, as was tradition. She saw that someone had eaten the bread and the cakes, but the pheasant had been untouched and was stiff and coagulated on its platter. She poked at it in disgust, then carried it into the kitchen. Her eyes were sore after the long night and she wet them with a few tears as she tilted the platters of food into the slop buckets. Then she carried the buckets out to the pigs. She could tell by the look of the pigs that they were angry. They turned their asses toward the slop. Lispeth was apologetic. The largest of them, a pretty sow with black ears, had been slaughtered and was now roasting on a spit in the kitchen, in celebration of Christmas. Clod had been put in charge of that.

'Happy Christmas,' Marek said to Lispeth later as she passed by the door to the great room on her way to wake Villiam.

She said nothing, just kept walking up the stairs. There was no good in speaking to the boy. Even opening her mouth toward him made her feel she had done too much. His face looked to her even more twisted and ugly than before, its flesh like the cold fat jiggling off the pheasant she had just thrown to the pigs. Lispeth felt in her heart that he was not long for the manor. She couldn't picture him living into the future. Something would happen to free her of his face—the persistent reminder of Jacob's absence. She ought to kill Marek herself. She'd thought about it many times.

She knocked twice on Villiam's door and went in and opened the curtains. It was past noon, and the next guests would be arriving soon. Christmas lunch was the most work-intensive meal of the holiday. The girls would have to set the table with the usual implements, bring out the courses one by one. That was normal. But on this day, the tablecloth would have to be changed after each course, and the bowls for handwashing would have to be cleaned and refilled. All of this to do, and when it was over, the servants would go down to the cellar to eat their cabbage and silently sing their prayers. Lispeth was hungry. At least she could rest on that virtue.

'Get up,' she now said to Villiam as she pulled the blanket off his body. He wore a white nightshirt to sleep, and he had been sweating under the heavy wool covers. Lispeth could see the dark triangle of his pubis through the wet cloth. He turned and pressed his bones into the down mattress.

'Go away,' he said.

'It's Christmas, my lord,' she said.

'Come wake me when the food is on the table.'

Grigor and his family were already on their way up the hill by then. They had been stunned that morning when Klarek had knocked on their door. Grigor was suspicious of the invitation but said nothing as Jon and Vuna scurried to ready themselves for the festivities. They had only scraps left from Vuna's holiday cooking a few days earlier, and the food hadn't been any good to begin with. They were all hungry, and it was a long walk up to the manor.

Nobody in the village had heard from the family selected for the feast the night before. In fact, Klarek had directed the young couple and their children to wait until morning and take a back route down into the village so that they would not meet Grigor, Jon, and Vuna on the road on their way up. The soot on the children's clothes and the bedragglement of them all would surely give cause for alarm. He gave the northern man a gold ducat.

Jon was nervous about the visit. He was afraid of saying the wrong thing and embarrassing himself, or looking unfit. He had suffered a bruised thumb from swinging his hammer a few days earlier, and it pounded and throbbed still as he walked. He complained of it to his wife.

'You're only nervous,' she said.

'Hold your hand up, the blood will drain down,' Grigor told him.

'You're the one who's nervous,' Jon said to Vuna. The two of them had been irritable and angry for weeks now. They blamed each other for their bad moods, but really it was an effect of energy put upon them by Grigor. He was the one who made them irritable and angry. He was like a raven, judgmental and repetitive, staring down from the rafters and asserting over and over again that the world they lived in was a sham. 'But it doesn't bother me. I'm free,' he proclaimed. His freedom was grating on them all. Finally, they had told him to keep his freedom to himself, and he had agreed.

'I am nervous,' Vuna confessed. She had good reason to be.

She was pregnant—she could feel the thing inside her, like a gnarled fist twisting in her womb—but she hadn't told Jon yet. She wanted to wait until she was sure. She had miscarried before, and Jon had blamed her. A week of silence and snubbing, his cold back turned to her in the bed, no warmth or comfort, only shame. He had sneered at the blood in the water when she did the washing, tears and snot dripping down the poor girl's face. This time, she hoped, the babe was more certain. Keeping the secret made her feel powerful and ornery, a feeling she didn't often allow herself. 'I'm nervous because you hurried me out the door!' she said to Jon. 'And now my cap is crooked.'

'What do you care about your cap? You're a married woman. And you barely have any hair.'

'It's Christmas,' Vuna hissed. 'Everyone wants to look their best on Christmas.'

Grigor held his tongue. He and his wife had bickered, too, of course, but they'd had an easier time of life. They'd had only one son on the first try. Jon's mother had been smart and hearty. Vuna was more delicate, quick to blush and fume and cry, but not weak, no. She had a wisdom that nobody could recognize; the deaths of her children hadn't torn the innocence from her heart, but had calloused her against her own rage. She knew that fighting was pointless. As a woman, she would always lose. It was not her place to stage a battle, but to back away to preserve what life she had left to live. Grigor felt sorry for her. In his eyes, her passion had been depleted. But he pitied his son more, as Jon had no clue how ruinous his rage was to his own spirit. Grigor could see him aging day by day, the creases in his brow deepening like burrows, or like tracks from the plow. Good that Jon's mother died before the grandchildren were slain. She would have been bitter until the end, would have talked ceaselessly about the injustice, turned hard and rancorous. Nobody would have been capable of putting up with her fury. Grigor's angst was nothing in comparison. There was no right way to deal with grief, of course. When God gives you more than you can tolerate, you turn to instinct. And instinct is a force beyond anyone's control.

Grigor didn't miss his wife, he realized as they walked up the road toward the manor. If she were there now, she'd be leading the way, telling them all what to do when they arrived. 'Let me do the talking,' she'd say. She'd have had no patience for Grigor's new outlook. And she would have disapproved of his relationship with Ina. She'd have kept me trapped, Grigor thought.

'Is that what you're wearing?' his wife would have scoffed.

Grigor wore his old brown coat, which was tattered at the cuffs and collar and stained with black mud along the hem, and the same pants and tunic he'd worn for decades. He felt this was appropriate—why should he pretend to be richer than he was? Jon and Vuna wore their red garments under their coats. They walked on into the bright light. The snow was no longer falling, but the wind picked up the glitter of the top layer of white and swirled it around in the light shivering through the naked trees.

The swirling snow instantly dissolved in the sunlight. Vuna and Jon walked up ahead, Jon going first. Something was amiss between them, Grigor thought, realizing that he, too, was nervous. He quickened his pace to catch up. He didn't want to walk in the bright light alone.

'We haven't brought a gift,' Jon said, grinding his teeth.

'We pay our taxes. That's gift enough,' Grigor said.

'We had no time,' Vuna said.

'You could have wrapped up a cake,' Jon said.

'What cake? I made no cake.'

'You could have.'

'When could I have made a cake, Jon? Did you know we would be invited?'

'Of course I didn't.'

'Then don't blame me.'

'Nobody's blaming you, Vuna. But you might have made a cake. That's all I'm saying.'

'Shush,' Vuna said. They kept walking.

'Ina will be there,' Grigor said after a while.

'That witch?' Jon sneered. He was still sore about the cake, even though he knew it was ridiculous.

'Don't say that,' Grigor said. 'Ina must be the reason we have been invited to this feast. She is a friend to me. You're hungry, aren't you?'

'I'm not hungry,' said Vuna.

'Then maybe you should go home,' Jon said crossly.

'Don't be cruel,' Grigor said to Jon. He turned to Vuna.

'You'll be hungry when you smell the food, don't worry.' She said nothing. 'Maybe Ina can fix you something to calm your nerves.'

'Merry Christmas,' Villiam said as he trudged into the great room. He took his seat at the head of the table. He was disappointed by the look of the guests, who were in turn disappointed by the absence of the nun and Ina. Grigor, especially, had hoped they would have a chance to see one another. Villiam sensed their displeasure. Later he would have to complain to Klarek that he ought to have invited more cheerful visitors. These were haggard and ugly. The girl's cap was crooked, and she looked bald underneath, and the boy's face was grouchy. The old man reminded him of his own father, spiteful and suspicious, and so Villiam forgot to say a prayer, and reached for his wine to refresh himself.

The priest, completely distracted, was already slurping his soup. He'd had a rough night's sleep. His head hurt. The approaching miracle of the new Christ had been gnawing at his nerves, so much so that he had begun to hear things. First, strange growling noises that he thought came from the barracks—dogs or goats. He wasn't very smart about animals. But recently, as the holidays began, he'd been awakened each night by what he was sure was the barking of dogs. Their voices echoed from afar, sometimes yipping and reffing, other times howling long notes in harmonies that twisted painfully in his ears. He'd slept through most of the fire last night, but had woken to huge black clouds of smoke hanging in the air. They seemed to extend infinitely toward the horizon, like a road in the sky. The barking of dogs was louder than it had ever been, so loud that Barnabas couldn't hear the crackling of the fire or the calls of the stableboys as they conveyed the buckets of water down from the reservoir. He only heard the snarling reffs and calls, which scared him, so he drank more spirit of elder. He kept a bottle by the bed for such troubled nights. He drifted off for a moment, covering his ears with his pillows, only to be awoken by a deafening howl that seemed to be calling for Barnabas specifically. There was something familiar to its tenor. It got louder and louder, as though the howling dog were riding up the road of smoke in the sky. Barnabas couldn't stand it. Eventually he gave up on sleep and lay there listening, surrendering to the bellows and pondering the meaning of such dogs, recalling as best he could the teachings of the church. One story—he barely remembered it— had to do with hunting dogs, he thought, and ghouls on horses chasing souls into hell. He wondered if he'd been right all this time about the Devil roaming free. If God had locked heaven's gate to keep the Devil out, the wicked one might lead a wild hunt and take whomever he could with him back to hell. 'This must be the Devil's cavalry,' Barnabas thought. Now they were coming for him. He had risen from bed and opened his window to the cold night to get a better listen. There he saw, lit by the stars, the wild hunt, a thunderous crowd of animals trampling across the smoke in the sky, heading straight toward him.

Barnabas ran back to bed and clutched his pillow and his cross, as though its power suddenly meant something to him. After that he didn't sleep at all. He barely moved until the sun broke into dawn and the echoes of hooves and howling had retreated, and he could hear his own heart beating again. 'I've gone insane,' he thought.

In the morning, he wandered down to the great room before the guests arrived and found a gift on the side table, a bottle wrapped in red cloth. He asked Petra where it had come from. One of the guards had delivered it for Villiam that morning, she'd said. It was a bottle of wine from Ivan, Dibra's brother. Father Barnabas stashed it in the cellar, afraid of its power, certain that it was poisoned. He didn't tell Villiam about it, nor did he hide it very well. He simply placed it on a stool in the corner of the cellar, sniffed the sulfurous air, then scrambled up the stairs, afraid to be alone down there. He'd sat in the great room in a stupor, grateful for the footsteps and mundane chatter of the servants as they set the table and swept the floor.

'This is my son, Marek,' Villiam said now to the visitors, nodding to the boy.

'Hello,' Grigor said. Jon and Vuna smiled.

Marek sat with his head in his hand, already spooning the thin soup up and spilling it back into the bowl to cool it. Marek, too, was hung over and tired from poor sleep. He didn't acknowledge the guests.

'Let's eat,' Villiam said. He snapped for Lispeth to refill his cup with wine.

'Our Father,' Grigor said, determined to make good on this day of God's gift of His son to the world. So he prayed while the priest slurped and Villiam gulped his wine. Jon and Vuna bowed their heads but kept their eyes open, glancing at each other, their eyes widening as though to say, 'What is wrong with these people? Is it not right to pray before you eat?' Grigor was unperturbed. He had been prepared for any weirdness. Finally, he reached the end of his prayer and Father Barnabas reached the end of his soup.

'Amen,' Grigor said.

'Amen,' said Jon and Vuna, and crossed themselves and lifted their heads.

'Amen,' said Marek and dropped his spoon. His soup tasted gamey. There were chunks of mutton at the bottom.

The priest waited for his empty bowl to be cleared away, staring down at the bits of herbs and carrot stuck to the bottom. While the rest slurped their soup now, he was debating with himself about what to do about the gift from Ivan. With that wine, he knew, he could kill whomever he pleased. He could do the Devil's work. Perhaps that was what his vision of the cavalry was meant to tell him: 'Kill. Be a hunter. Join us.' Maybe he should, he thought. Better that than to be endlessly harassed. He'd never really believed in such things before—spirits, messages, anything beyond the trite reality of the world around him—but his sleeplessness had indeed made him susceptible. For the first time, he entertained the possibility that there was some deep meaning to life. Was he destined to be a killer? He looked around the table to test whether he was tempted. Of course, Villiam's scowl was what caught his eye first. The priest considered this, sitting back in his chair while the servants now removed the bowls and replaced the dark linen tablecloth with a blue silk one. Or he could kill himself, he thought, yawning. Or no one. Perhaps that was the best choice, to do nothing.

Next came a stew of wild leeks and fennel. Barnabas gazed at Vuna as he ate. Her cap was still crooked but her veil cast a shadow along her face that haunted her cheeks with wonder. Would he kill her? No, no. She was too easy. He would rather kiss her than kill her, if he had to. Had he kissed too many girls when he was a boy? Was that the problem? Was God torturing him in retribution? Was God capable of that? He could remember each girl he'd kissed back in Prepat: the black-haired girl with the harelip; the brown-haired girl with freckles in her dimples; another brown-haired girl with battered eyes. Even at the age of four or five, she'd looked as if she'd seen the fires of hell already. What had happened to those little girls he'd kissed and pinched? Had they hated him forever? Had they told their husbands, years later, 'There was an awful boy who kissed me once, and they sent him up to the monastery?' Did their husbands get jealous? Did those girls get beaten for his stolen kisses? He felt sorry for himself that he couldn't see their faces now. He looked back up for a moment at Villiam, who was prattling on about something—'Leeches are good for virility, unless you leech too much'—and watched his mouth move. Had Barnabas really dedicated himself to that spoiled rat? Was that the great tragedy of his life—had he traded in a life of kissing whomever he pleased to guard the rotten soul of a man who couldn't clean the shit from his own asshole? He could have done better than that, the priest reckoned. Maybe that was the message he was meant to receive.

And then the servant girls took the bowls away again—the priest hadn't even touched his, but no matter. They changed the tablecloth now to a mustard yellow linen and brought out herring and a tureen of eel soup and a platter of oysters and crab. The village guests looked horrified. They'd never seen such creatures of the sea, and truthfully they were not commonly served at the manor. Since the drought, the trade rate for seafood had gone quite high.

Grigor took a crab for himself and bit into it, shattering its exoskeleton between his teeth. He hadn't realized that it was a dead animal. He thought it was a root vegetable, or maybe a strange bread. He spent the rest of the course surreptitiously picking the blades of broken shell out of his gums, which distracted him from the conversation, which was not a conversation but a monologue given by Villiam. He talked simply to keep himself from falling asleep, he was so tired, following any stray thought that entered his mind no matter how dull or ridiculous. 'I try to lead a simple life,' he was saying. 'Health, wealth, and wisdom. No time for horseplay. Never. We really don't like anything trifling, do we, hmm?' Nobody was listening. He took a break from blathering and speared an entire eel, flayed it clean off its spine and sucked down the flesh.

Jon and Vuna were hesitant about the food. They didn't want

to appear rude, so they each had a few bites of the fish. Marek ate nothing. Grigor watched him, knowing full well that he was Jude's boy. There was something menacing in his face, Grigor thought. And the red hair was troubling.

'They say an eel on Christmas is good tidings,' Villiam said.

Soon, legs of beef and capon, duck, plover, lark, and crane swirled around the table. Then the sow, and a peacock, roasted in its feathers, with a bowl of special gravy to pour on top. Villiam went after everything. Father Barnabas ate whatever was in front of him. The food distracted him from his thoughts. He dropped his napkin and stooped to pick it up. The rush of blood to his brain darkened his vision for a moment. As he lifted his head, he saw Jon and Vuna holding hands under the table, and it saddened him. He had never held anybody's hand. Was there time yet? he wondered. If he ran out now, could he find love before the cavalry found him? Could he defy their order to kill and find himself some fair lady to sin with instead? Either way, Barnabas knew, he wouldn't last long. The ghouls wouldn't even get down off their horses, he knew. They'd pull their swords out and cut off his head and keep on. They wouldn't bother to hang him. The Devil had no respect. That stung Barnabas. At least the villagers treated him with honor, didn't they?

'Your names?' the priest asked the guests. He should have known their names. 'Forgive an old man. I've had a headache,' he said.

Grigor turned a bit red. He was baffled that the priest didn't recognize him.

'I am Grigor,' he said. 'This is my son, Jon, and his wife, Vuna.'

'You come to Mass regularly?'

'Every Sunday,' Jon said, thinking this would win him some credit.

'Except on the Sundays you're not there,' Grigor said to Barnabas. Jon threw him a hard look.

'What happens when he's not there?' Villiam asked.

'When you're not there,' Jon said, 'we still worship. We try to remember the things you said last time, and we pray.'

'Good boy,' Barnabas said and went back to his food, satisfied momentarily that he was at least adored a little.

'How is your wife?' Grigor asked Villiam shakily. 'Is Ina caring well for her?'

'Ina, yes,' Villiam answered. 'The child of God is coming along just fine, I hear, but we don't hear much, which is good, as you know. When there is nothing to say, there is nothing to worry about.' He took a leg of heron and nodded and sucked at the slimy flesh. He was bored. The priest looked pale and drunk. Marek was useless. The visitors were provincial and banal. Villiam wasn't used to being the one to entertain. Usually, on Christmas, the male servants would perform a mystery play, a reenactment of the shepherds coming to see Jesus. That always provided some good humor, and Villiam would critique them afterward, and they'd do the reenactment again and again, funnier and funnier, until the thing devolved into a play of Villiam's own creation and had nothing to do with the story of Christmas at all. But that kind of entertainment was no longer appropriate. Villiam would have liked to brush off the strange sense of foreboding and dread in the air with a good joke. He looked over at Clod, who stood with his back against the wall.

'Clod,' Villiam said. 'Join us. Let's play a few rounds of the King Who Does Not Lie.' It was a game of truthfulness. As 'king of the feast,' Villiam would ask any guest a question. If the guest answered truthfully, he or she could ask a question of the 'king' in return. It was custom to drink ale during the game. The lower-class drink was supposed to make people more honest.

The tablecloth was quickly changed and ale was served, along with a spread of desserts—custards, cakes, nuts, and candied fruits. Villiam was tired but hopeful now that there was some diversion. He sipped his ale delicately and grinned. He liked the flavor of ale. It tasted like his own sweat, like something rotten and private, a relief to him, finally, this flavor so uncouth. It had been exhausting bearing the burden of being such an upright man since his wedding. Perhaps he could let down his guard now a bit, he thought, looking around the table. There were no children to take offense. Only an old man and these two young stiffs. Who would believe them if they went back down to the village and complained that the lord had told a few unsavory jokes? He deserved to let loose a little, he decided. It was Christmas, after all.

'All right,' he began, rubbing his hands together to invigorate himself. 'Who wants to go first?'

Nobody raised a hand.

'I'm not playing,' Father Barnabas said as Petra poured his ale. 'I think I'll go upstairs to pray,' he lied and pushed his chair from the table.

Villiam didn't stop the priest as he bid adieu to the guests and wobbled out of the great room. Maybe he would pray indeed. Or maybe he would throw himself from his window. Or maybe, Father Barnabas thought, passing Lispeth in the hall, he would spend his last day on Earth lying with a girl—just once before the Devil dragged him away—and discover the flesh that he had always coveted but never grabbed. Lispeth seemed available. She was walking beside him, carrying a soiled tablecloth.

'Lispeth,' Father Barnabas said. 'Would you come upstairs and lie with me?'

'No,' she replied.

'God would be pleased if you could. There really isn't any risk.'

'No,' Lispeth said again. 'I would rather die than lie with you.'

'Ah, what a nice girl you are,' the priest said, patting her on the back. 'I was only testing your will. Have a blessed night celebrating in the cellar. I brought a very good bottle of wine down there. Please drink it. And may God keep you. Good night.' He disappeared up the stairs.

Lispeth put aside the priest's strangeness and continued with her labor. In the great room, the game was getting started.

'Clod, you first,' Villiam said.

Clod sat up straighter. He also had a cup of ale, and he sipped it calmly, waiting for the question.

'Have you ever licked your left finger?' Villiam asked, his face a mask of seriousness. He lifted his cup of ale and waited for Clod to reply. Clod's face went blank as he searched his mind for an answer. He held up his left finger and licked it. He had never done so before, the left hand being the hand one used for washing. Villiam couldn't hold in his laughter after that, so finally he exploded with a loud guffaw and his nose erupted with froth. Everyone watched him wipe his face and cough, still laughing. Then he turned around and yelled, 'Petra! More ale!' and looked back at Clod for his answer.

'Yes,' Clod said, his head jittering slightly.

'Oh that's good! Oh that's hilarious! You of all people! Disgusting,' Villiam said. 'And very honest. That makes you the king now.'

Clod, ever the sport, turned to Jon and asked him the same question, knowing that the imitation would flatter Villiam. 'Have you ever licked your left finger, sir?'

Villiam laughed and laughed. Jon shook his head, turning red.

'No,' Jon said.

Grigor stood and protested. 'I don't think this is very Christian,' was all he could think to say.

'You ask a question next. You do it, you do it,' Villiam said, pointing to Jon and tearing up with laughter. 'Ask your wife a question.' Villiam turned to Vuna. 'What was your name again?'

Vuna hid her face behind her veil, afraid to answer. Jon was mum.

'I think we'll be on our way. Jon?' Grigor said, buttoning his coat.

'Ask me! Ask me anything!' Villiam cried, aroused by Grigor's discomposure. 'And sit down, old fellow. Our game has just begun.'

Grigor sat, strangely humbled by the lord's chastisement. Villiam sipped his ale and gestured for Jon to get on with it.

'What was your mother's name?' Jon asked, hoping to quiet things down.

Villiam's face fell. 'Is that really the question?'

Jon looked down, not understanding how he had failed.

'We should go,' Grigor whispered to Jon and began to stand again. Villiam stopped him.

'Do you have a question, sir?'

'No,' Grigor said. He didn't know how to make his exit appropriately. He didn't want any trouble.

'Is there nothing about me you want to know?'

'There is not,' Grigor said.

'You can ask me anything you want.'

'No, thank you,' Grigor said.

'Why not? You don't find me interesting?'

Grigor looked around. Everything he could see—the great room, the finery, the food, the lord's spectacular Christmas costume, none of it inspired him. It was not God's fortune, but the bounty of a thief: Villiam hadn't worked for his blessings. The villagers had. That was the great tragedy of Christmas as Grigor now saw it. Not one word of gratitude. Instead, there was this stupid game.

'I pray your death is quick,' he said quietly.

Villiam smiled. He took this as a compliment. 'That's very nice of you, but it's not a question. Don't be a loser—ask me anything. Winner gets a gold ducat.'

Grigor still had the gold Ina had given him when they had first met in her cabin in the fall. He'd been carrying it around in his pocket all this time for good luck.

'How is it that you are so rich, and the rest of us so poor?' Grigor asked.

'It's because of breeding, plain and simple,' Villiam answered. 'That was too easy. Ask me something personal. Something about me, your lord. Aren't there things people wonder about? Now is your time to ask.'

'Did you steal the water this summer? Did you cause the drought?'

Villiam smiled, then coughed. He looked around the room, from face to face. Jon and Vuna and even Marek seemed to be interested in his response. But he couldn't possibly answer. Whatever he said, he would sabotage himself. He didn't like to lose.

'If you have nothing to ask,' Villiam replied, 'then I guess the game is over. Pity.' He gulped the rest of his ale. 'Ah well. I thought all the nice food and drink would make you merry. But I guess you'll be going home now to your little village, where all the interesting people are. I suppose you'll go and tell them all, "The lord is a great bore." So be it. I've done my best.'

Grigor tugged at Jon's sleeve, and the young man got up. Vuna followed, curtsying and straightening her cap. They all shuffled away, their footsteps like mice scurrying across a mantel.

Marek finally lifted his head. 'You ought to be kissing his feet, not spitting in his soup,' he said.

'Nobody is spitting in his soup,' Jon said, trembling.

Lispeth, who had been listening from the doorway with a new jug of ale, let out a titter. She had been spitting in Villiam's soup for years.

'We should be on our way,' Vuna said, pushing Jon toward the door. 'Night falls early this time of year.'

'Please give my best to Ina,' Grigor said to Lispeth on his way out.

Marek and Villiam watched them leave, the lord so stunned by their rudeness that he kept picking up his cup, forgetting to sip it, then putting it down again.

'Can you believe that, Marek? The indecency? The ingratitude?'

'Peasants,' Marek said. 'They think pride is a virtue. They haven't learned yet that it is a vice.'

'Wise words, my boy,' said Villiam. But he was still upset. He was huffing and puffing, red in the face, confused. Not since his own father had anyone rejected him so bluntly. He looked like he might cry. Lispeth walked in and refilled Villiam's cup of ale. Her hand on his shoulder seemed to subdue him.

'You're tired,' she said.

'I'm not tired, Lispeth.'

'You look tired.'

'I do?'

'Come up to bed and I'll bring you a special bottle of wine. The priest told me it is very good.'

'Only if you join me in a cup. It's Christmas after all, and I'm all alone now.'

'What about me?' Marek asked.

'Get your own servant,' was all Villiam said.

'Go on upstairs,' Lispeth said. 'I'll go fetch the wine.'

Once they had cleared the drawbridge and were far enough away from the house to breathe a bit easier, Jon and Vuna started arguing, each blaming the other for what had gone wrong at the manor.

'Why didn't you say anything?' Jon asked Vuna.

'What was I going to say?'

'Something nice. Girls are supposed to be nice.'

'Why should I have to be nice? Nobody is nice to me,' Vuna whined. 'You're the one who said the wrong thing, Jon. I wish I'd stayed home.'

'I wish you'd stayed home, too. I can't be expected to manage the old man and the lord at the same time. And you blame me for the trouble. Now I'll have to hear you complain about what a terrible Christmas you've had, while you're the one who ruined it with your bad mood. Don't I deserve to have a good time ever?'

'I wasn't stopping you! I didn't spoil your time!'

'You did,' Jon said.

'I didn't do anything!'

'I know what you were thinking. "Jon is so stupid, there he is making a fool of himself."'

They had stopped on the road to look back up at the manor. Perhaps it was because of the tiny baby twisting inside and sparking her heart that Vuna was suddenly sorry that she had been grumpy that day and saw that Jon was not truly against her, but suffering from a grave insecurity. It was hard for a man to drink from another man's cup. Vuna hadn't understood that Jon was so proud.

'I'm sorry,' she said. She looked at him and he looked back at her, and they looked at each other and softened. And as Jon was the kind of young man to spring back into love at the slightest invitation, he rubbed his eyes and sighed, then lunged for Vuna and kissed her. Their mouths opened immediately, suddenly desperate to exchange the warmth that they'd been denying each other while fighting. 'Forget it, forget it,' their kisses said. They didn't need to complicate their lives with analysis, although they were prone to do so because they were more intelligent than average. And Jon had seen Grigor and his mother do it—constantly explain things to one another. 'But I think this is true.' 'And I think that.' He was more comfortable bickering. For Vuna, arguing was torture. Which was why Jon loved her so much: she was innocent. And her features were so strange, her eyelids a shade of gray that made her brown-green eyes look like mirrors. They parted lips and looked up to see if Grigor had seen them kissing. But the road was clear. They kept on down the hill toward the village, hand in hand now.

They were both pathetic. Blind, Grigor thought. He walked slowly, letting the frigid air chill his bones. It was colder now that the sun had sunk. At least he had spoken up, he thought, however badly it had turned out. The lord was incapable of truth, of course. He should have predicted that. He imagined giving a speech to a crowd in the village square, his face lit by the yellow light of torches, his heart thrumming in his throat. 'He steals our food! He steals our money! We should demand he return his wealth to us—we built this village, not him! And he stole our water. Down with Villiam, I say!' They'd all cheer and hoist Grigor up into the air. 'Let's storm the manor! Let us be the bandits this time!' he'd cry.

That was only a fantasy. Nobody would listen, of course. It was pointless to think of taking up arms, going up to make demands. Nobody could ever get past the first line of guards anyway. Those northern guards were so skilled with their arrows, they would pluck each man off one by one if they marched up the road. And what did Grigor really want from Villiam? An apology? All lords were corrupt. If he wanted to live freely, he would have to live like Ina lived, in a hovel. Poverty had its limitations, but if you had nothing, there was nothing to be stolen.

He moseyed down the hill across the snow. Jon and Vuna were now out of sight. Once they were home, everyone would be coming around to ask about the feast.

'What should we tell them?' Vuna asked Jon as they turned the corner toward the woods.

'We'll tell them we all sat around naked,' Jon said and laughed.

Vuna liked to see Jon laugh. He reached for her again and kissed her, slipping a hand under her coat to feel the small of her back. Vuna pulled away, afraid that he would feel the swelling of her belly. Jon took this as yet another retraction of love. He put his hands in his pockets, his face falling serious yet again.

'Let's tell them the truth,' Jon said.

'Tell them what?'

'That Villiam is a scoundrel,' Jon said. 'He's a heathen. Who could make a joke like that on Christmas? Licking my finger?'

Vuna shrugged. 'I don't want to make anybody angry.'

'They should be angry at him, not at us.'

'The neighbors will say that your father has poisoned our minds against the lord. We'll be the heathens then.'

'Don't be a coward,' Jon said.

'I'm only thinking of our future,' Vuna said.

'This is the trouble with women,' Jon replied, his heart curdling against hers. 'They would rather lie and pretend all is well and let the men tell the truth and pay the price for it.'

'That's not true!' Vuna cried.

'It's true,' Jon said.

Of course, Jon himself had no intention of telling anyone of the strangeness of their Christmas visit to the manor. He would never put himself in a position to be ridiculed. He was too proud. It was easier to lean on Vuna's fear than to admit his own.

'Fine,' he said after a long silence. 'We'll tell them it was a nice time.'

'Don't be angry at me,' Vuna said.

Jon was quiet.

When Grigor, Jon, and Vuna got back to the village, they found all the houses empty. The whole village was meeting in the square in the disappearing light. Apparently, the young couple who had visited the manor the day before had told the story of the fire in the manger, and all the villagers had taken great interest in the drama. They wanted to know what burned, how the fire started, how big the flames were, how far it spread, and how the fire got put out.

'There was a big lake up there full of water,' Emil said.

A more discerning group of people might have questioned this. But nobody questioned anything. There was no mob, no uprising. 'Poor Villiam. He must have felt so sad to watch his crèche burn,' was all they said. 'Did you see the nun?'

The young couple shook their heads.

'Did you see the fire?' the villagers asked Jon and Vuna when they reached the center of the crowd.

'We didn't,' Jon said.

'Did you see the nun?'

'We saw the lord and his son,' Vuna said.

'And the priest,' Jon said.

'Tell us what you ate,' the villagers wanted to know.

So after a description of the fine food, how the servants changed the tablecloths between courses, the regal cloak the lord wore, the warm fire, and the strong ale, the villagers sang a few Christmas carols, then went home and thanked God that they had survived another holiday. They prayed for the lord and his wife and the unborn baby.

Perhaps it is most miraculous when God exacts justice even when no human lifts a finger. Or perhaps it is simply fate. Everything seems reasonable in hindsight. Right or wrong, you will think what you need to think so that you can get by. So find some reason here:

By midnight, Villiam had drunk half the bottle of wine, Ivan's gift of poison, and was now dead on the floor of his bedroom next to Lispeth, who had died from only a drop on her tongue, so fragile was she, and so willing to leave this stupid life behind.

The priest had wandered into Villiam's chambers, hoping to find some comfort in the lord's arrogance, only to discover him dead, his mouth blackened with wine, his hands stretched out toward Lispeth, who lay silently on the floor like a doll. I must be imagining things, he thought. Barnabas went back to his room and locked the door, determined to go to bed and wake up to a bright new day, the horror of his hallucination wiped clean by sleep. But there was banging on his door. Mad with fear, he believed it was the Devil himself pounding his fist, his vicious dogs panting right outside. So Barnabas hanged himself with his bedsheet thrown over the rafter. Better to take his own life than have it taken, he reasoned.

It was not the Devil, of course, but a draft from the hall that shook the door. Marek had told Petra to leave a window open while he slept. A warm wind was coming in from the south, and it carried with it the strange, wistful scent of violets.

# SPRING

From the hallway, Marek could hear it crying. Like a crow cawing, arrogant and spoiled. A regular, gnawing complaint of need echoed through the door. Silence perturbed Marek, too, as he imagined the baby's cries had been quieted by Agata's breast in its mouth. And then there was the horror of Ina's cooing, the singing, the laughter at the wee one in her arms, he presumed. Marek remembered the last time he'd nursed, a year ago now, in Ina's small cabin in the woods, her nipple hardening in the back of his throat. That felt like a lifetime ago. Now he could demand that anyone nurse him. He could go down to Lapvona and point at any woman with an ample bosom and assign her to be his wet nurse for life, if he wanted. Maybe one day he would, he thought, if he grew desperate enough. If only his own mother would be willing, they might actually have a happy little family now at the manor. But the baby would be a distraction, always. Especially one that had been proclaimed the Christ. But who was there to verify that? The priest was long gone by now.

In a year, Marek had gone from lowly lamb herder's son to the lord of Lapvona. He hadn't asked for the title, but there was nobody left to hand it to. He tried his best to make himself feel at home. He took over Villiam's chambers and outfitted himself with all the clothes from his closet. He had hoped that fine clothes and nice food would distract him from his woe, but of course they only gave him more anxiety, as wealth and power always do. Ivan sent a staff to account for the land and earnings and to manage the manor. Marek had nothing to do, they said. 'Just be happy that Ivan has this all taken care of.'

Despite Marek's lordship, Jude still refused to be a father to him. He refused, too, Marek's offer of a room in the house, preferring to keep his bed with the eyeless horse even though Ivan's men now managed the stable. Jude had nothing to do. Marek even had Petra go down to buy some lamb babes from a farmer in the village. They had brownish gray tufted hair and black faces, ears, and feet. Marek brought them to Jude on silk ropes tied around their small necks and handed him the reins.

'You can start again,' Marek said hopefully. 'And you can keep as many babes as you like. Forever.'

'Babes don't stay babes,' Jude said back. 'Anyway, these are not the right kind.' He let them go, refused to even pet them.

'Will nothing make you happy?' Marek asked.

Jude shrugged and walked off. Marek let the babes go free, trusting that Ivan's men would know what to do with them. He gave up. He had everything and nothing. His father couldn't even look him in the eye.

'Sometimes something new can remind you of something you lost,' Petra said later, trying to comfort him.

'How do you know? What new thing have you ever got?' Marek asked. He liked to bully Petra because she took all his accusations very literally.

'Let me think. I had a new apron once. And when I think about it now, the new apron did make me sad, because the old one had fit me so well for so long. But then it caught fire and the left part got burnt, so I had to replace it. I miss that old apron,' she said mawkishly.

'The nun,' Marek asked Petra. 'Is she happy?'

'I don't know,' she said. 'I haven't seen her since the wedding.'

'Take a guess.'

'Hmm.' Petra had to think about it. She rubbed her hands together and stared at the wall, as though conjuring some kind of mystic knowledge. Marek leaned back in his bed. He had developed an obsessive habit of picking at his cuticles. He peeled tiny strips of his skin up from the nails, chewed them up and spat them out on the bedspread.

'Every new mother must be happy,' Petra said after some time had gone by and Marek had given up on her answer.

'She's not a new mother. She's been a mother as long as I've been alive,' Marek argued.

Petra winced at her misstep. 'You are right. She must be so proud to have you as her son, the lord of Lapvona. Just like Villiam, God rest his soul.'

He didn't like to be reminded of Villiam. He had been so

stunned by his sudden ascension to lord that he'd had no idea
how to give instructions for Villiam's burial—the one responsi-
bility Ivan's men would take no part in. Marek was paralyzed.
'Where should we dig?' the stableboys asked him. 'I don't know
yet,' Marek answered. 'Leave him where he is, I guess.' And then
an Indian summer came and Villiam's body bloated severely. His
neck was thick and white and laced with yellow seeping into the
white collar of his shirt, which had strangled his bloated throat.
His eyes were swollen—they looked just like Ina's horse eyes—
and his lips had split, revealing his long, gray teeth, like something Clod had carved out of wood. Lispeth, on the other hand,
had been buried right away by the servants. Klarek and Clod
dug her grave in a clearing in the forest, where all the past servants' bodies were laid to rest.

Finally, Marek assigned the task of burying Villiam to Jude.
It seemed just punishment for his father's coldness. Marek
watched him digging from afar, forbidding anyone from stepping in to help him. In the end, the grave was very shallow, only
a few inches deep. It was something to see, at least, Marek
thought. The body didn't disappear up to heaven—by burying
him so poorly, Jude deprived him of his chance to ascend. So
Villiam simply lay there under a thin blanket of dirt, slowly
picked apart by magpies and rats and squirrels and mink, all the
sweet little animals, God's gentlest creatures.

'And what about Jude, Petra?' Marek asked, still picking his
cuticles. 'Do you think he is proud of me?'

Petra knew better than to answer.

'Would you like a little song and dance?' she asked.

'Sure.'

Her dance was simply a curtsy and sway and another curtsy and sway back. She sang nicely, Marek thought. When he'd had enough, he patted the bed beside him and said, 'Stop and sit for a moment.'

Petra complied.

'What is it, my lord?'

'Do you think I'm ugly?'

'Oh no,' Petra said. 'You have nice red hair, and your knees have such a nice shape to them.' She traced his knee with her finger to demonstrate. Marek pushed her hand away. 'My lord, what have you done with your fingers?' She grabbed his hand and held his fingers close to her face to inspect the bloodied cuticles.

'It's nothing. I do it to myself. It distracts me from time.'

'I should put something on these wounds,' she said and went to fetch her salve.

Grigor moved into Ina's old cabin and did the best he could to figure out what grew wild in the woods. He brought morels and wild asparagus to market. Dandelion buds and ramps, ground-nuts and pokeweed that he found by the stream. Juneberries, hickory nuts, barberries, burdock root. Chickweed, pigweed, and acorns he found in a grove of trees further out past where he'd ever gone. He loved to forage. He felt wisdom in his eyes, directing him to scan the ground and follow the birds in the air to where food grew like manna from the trees and bushes. He traded the wild things for favors to help Jon and Vuna prepare for the baby. It was still months away, but he already loved the wee thing inside Vuna's belly. He had big dreams for the child, to teach it the truth. He wanted to ask Ina if she would be the child's godmother.

So one day, Grigor came to the manor to bring Ina a wreath of canniba along with the herbs he picked. Petra went down to greet him and to pay him with a bit of wool from the lambs. Marek watched from the window as the two talked in the yard outside the kitchen.

'Vuna could knit some socks for her baby with this wool,' Petra said.

'Thank you,' Grigor said smiling, and then he asked what he asked upon every visit. 'Could I see Ina today?'

'She will say no like she always does,' Petra answered.

'But today I've brought her some canniba. Maybe we could smoke some together, Ina and me.'

From the window, Marek watched Petra disappear back through the kitchen door. He heard her steps through the manor, up the stairs toward Agata's room. She knocked. Marek went into the hall to listen.

'Ina, Grigor is here. Do you want to see him?'

'No,' Ina said through the door. 'I'm just putting the baby down for a nap.'

'He has canniba today, and he has asked every time if he could see you,' Petra said. 'Should I tell him to go away?'

After a few moments, Ina went out into the hallway, much to Petra's surprise. Nobody had seen Ina in a long time. The old woman looked younger than she used to. The comfort of the manor had done her good. Her hair was now thick and brown, hidden under a white veil and swept cleanly away from her forehead, which was pale and smooth. Her wrinkles seemed to have filled with joy, restoring her to a vibrancy that, in her previous decrepit state, no one could have imagined. Her bulging eyes seemed to have shrunk into their sockets, or perhaps her face had widened and rounded out so that they didn't appear too large anymore. And her body had broadened, tightened against the clothes she'd taken from Dibra's closet. From down the hall, Marek stared in awe at her changed appearance and at her smooth stride—had she grown taller?—as she hurried down the stairs. Petra followed her.

Marek saw his chance to sneak into the room for a private conversation with his mother. He had prepared what he would say. 'I'm lord of Lapvona now, and I demand that you be a mother to me.' His lower lip already trembled as he lifted his hand to knock on the door. To his amazement, the door swung open, revealing the sunlit room, the cradle by the open window, and Agata lying behind a gauzy curtain that hung down from the canopy bed.

'Mother?' he called.

She seemed to be asleep.

Marek crept slowly across the stone floor, careful to step on his toes so that his fancy heels didn't strike the ground and make a noise and wake the babe. The light from the window streamed powerfully into the bassinet. He wanted to see if the child was the son of God indeed. Did it resemble Marek at all? As he approached, he felt a heaviness in his limbs, as though the life were draining out of his body. The baby was doing it to him, he thought. When he finally got close enough to look at it, the babe was curled up in a ball, its face hidden by a little bonnet. He reached toward it and gripped its tiny, soft shoulder to flip it on its back. He had never touched a baby before and wasn't sure if he should be afraid of it, if it might wake suddenly and bite his hand like a sleeping dog. But it didn't bite him. It merely opened its eyes, which were large and brown, and looked up at him and smiled a toothless, baby smile. Marek felt his heart drop. Having never known love before, he couldn't recognize the feeling. Something was terribly wrong, he felt.

'Mother?' he called again.

Agata was silent. Marek went to her bed and lifted the curtain of gauze. A strong perfume struck his face. The bed was covered with tansy, piles of flowers in different states of decay.

'Mother,' he said again, and reached for her shoulder under the flowers. He swiped at the drying blooms and shook her. But she would not wake. He cleared the tansy from her face. It was hollow and gray, her eyes black holes. A maggot crawled out of her bony nose. Marek let go of the gauze. If she'd never died before, perhaps he would have been sad that she was no longer living. But instead, what dismayed him was her rotting corpse. God had not come to take her to heaven. The Devil had left her to rot.

He picked the baby up and hid it in the inside of his jacket. It nestled in the space above his jutting belly, held securely against Marek's chest by his tight spring jacket. Then he went out, creeping along the halls. He saw Petra coming up the stairs.

'I think I'll go for a walk,' Marek said as she passed.

'Do you want me to follow you like last time?'

'No, Petra. I want to visit Villiam's grave and pray for his soul.'

'Oh, all right.' Marek knew Petra would not want to come near Villiam's grave. It stank and teemed with flies.

He walked out and was surprised that nobody stopped him, nobody cared to know where he was going. He clutched at the wee thing in his jacket, peeking down to see its face—so pure, its fine red hair like a ray of light across its crown and eyebrows. He followed the sun down the hill toward his old pasture, and then up the mountain, where he hadn't been since he'd thrown the rock at Jacob. If this baby was the savior, Marek thought, maybe he could pray to it and turn back time.

Without the church bells, the days had a wistful magic to them in the village. Lapvonians stopped waking up before dawn to pray and slept until the roosters crowed, and then even still, some of them liked to sleep later into the morning, rising only when their bodies had rested enough and their bones were getting sore against their beds. They rose and stretched and looked at the sun to align themselves, and then they ate and drank and went out to greet their happy new blond-headed neighbors. There were no bells to signal when it was time to rest or return home for lunch from the fields. People came and went as they pleased. Grigor explained this to Ina as they smoked in the sunshine by the garden. Ina squinted and covered her eyes with her hand.

'You can't believe the difference in my sleep,' he said, 'now that I know what time is to me, and not what it meant to the church.'

'That's good, Grigor,' Ina said, inhaling. Grigor had brought a pipe he had carved from a branch of rosewood.

'You can keep the pipe,' he said.

'Thank you. I like it. I know the birds who live in this rosewood tree. Are they back now that spring is here?'

'Yes, they're back.'

'Are they singing?'

'Yes.'

'That's good.'

'Ina,' Grigor began. He didn't know how to speak to her now that her appearance had changed so drastically. To Grigor, it did seem that the Christ Child had turned back the hands of time. How was it possible? He figured it would be best to speak directly. 'You seem very different, Ina,' he said.

'I am different,' she said. 'I'm a mother now.' Grigor could see her eyes fill with tears. 'I finally have a babe of my own,' she said.

Grigor felt a nerve of fear throb in his jaw. What of the mother? He couldn't ask. He sucked the smoke and let it pass and tried to be reasonable.

'I thought the church was rotten,' he said. 'But you say there is a real Christ?'

'Forget that church.'

'I try to. You know that Ivan's men tore it down.'

Ina didn't care. She wiped her tears away and sat back against the stone wall of the manor, her hands resting across her full belly. Bees and dragonflies and butterflies seemed to dance for her in the garden, buzzing in a harmonious song of spring. Grigor saw that there was wet at her nipples. Her bosoms were swollen.

'I do all the milk and I hold the Christ and sing to it. I do all of it,' she said.

'My, my,' said Grigor. 'You must be so happy.' And he saw that it was true. He wanted to speak with Ina more about how Ivan's men had dismantled the church stone by stone, how they'd used the stones to build a large well in the village square, with a fountain. He had been hoping to declare his own happiness to Ina, to tell her that he had discovered real freedom of spirit. He wanted to tell her that he felt like a new man. But he realized as she sat beside him that his hope to declare it all was actually a way to stave off the emptiness left by what was now gone. Lapvona was a lonely place. There was no church, and there was no

God to speak of. Nobody prayed. Everyone just talked about themselves and each other. If it weren't for Grigor mentioning it, they would have forgotten about the Christ Child. Nobody believed it was a true messiah, as nobody believed in the meaning of a messiah anymore. Grigor had not given up completely. There was something sacred still. He recognized now that the sacred thing had been Ina herself.

'I love you,' he said to Ina, handing her back the pipe.

She looked at him with a soft expression that he couldn't understand. 'I would nurse you again,' Ina said back to him, 'but all my milk is for Christ now.'

She took Grigor's hand and delivered into it some divine power. Grigor could feel it leach through his skin and into his flesh and bones. It traveled up through his wrist and arm, his shoulder, crept across his chest, and stopped at his heart. He suddenly felt very hot. He took a deep breath.

'What are you doing to me, Ina?' he asked.

'Open up your heart,' she said.

'I'm afraid it's broken.'

'If I was knocking at your door, would you open it?'

'I would, of course.'

'Even if the door was broken.'

'I would try.'

Grigor's whole arm was pulsating now. His heart beat powerfully in his chest. Ina took him by the other hand, too. He could not fight. She overpowered him, and the force of God entered his body like a rash spreading across his skin, and he felt his heart surge, then stop. He waited for it to start again. He looked at Ina in the eye.

'If you don't let God into your heart, you'll die,' Ina said. 'That's what kills people. Not time or disease. Now, open up.'

'Are you trying to kill me?' he asked. She gripped his hands tighter.

'Do you want me to?' she asked.

'No,' Grigor answered without thinking.

Ina smiled. His heart beat again, slowly and steadily. Ina kissed his cheek. It was done now. He blushed. Ina tucked the rosewood pipe between her breasts and stood.

'Come see the child,' she said.

She helped Grigor up and kissed him again. They walked hand in hand into the manor through the kitchen door.

Marek was nearly at the top of the mountain. He was surprised by his own strength and endurance. While the baby had at first sapped him of energy, it seemed now to drive him powerfully to reach the top of the cliff. He held it against his heart and scanned the ground, as though looking for his old footprints, but he found none. Then, in the branches of a forsythia bush, he saw Jacob's old bow, and further still, at the top of the cliff, Jacob himself. It was not his ghost or his grave, but his skeleton. The bones were pure white, lying in a pile. The skull was missing. Marek assumed it had rolled off the cliff, or a vulture had wrenched it off and dropped it somewhere to enjoy it in private. Jude had left the body there as a sacrifice, Marek assumed. He must have felt it would please God.

The baby turned inside Marek's jacket. He looked down at its face and held it tightly. It was true that the baby was something very valuable. Anyone would be completely hypnotized by its beauty. It was so perfect and small. It would be easy to throw it. Marek unbuttoned his jacket and pulled the baby out into the sunshine. It smiled and reached its hands toward its brother's face.

'Don't worry,' Marek said. 'Death is not the end. You shall rise. What are the birds but angels? You will never have to walk among the monsters. It's much better up there. You'll see, you'll see. You will be so happy and free, you'll sing.'


THE END